I0672142

COLD CASE: FBI

The Curse of the Bayous

By William Dusty

Timminy Press, LLC
Springfield, MA USA
www.timminypress.com

The characters in this book are fictional and a product of the author's imagination. Some of the crimes committed in the Cold Case: FBI series may have been derived from actual cases on file with law enforcement authorities in the United States and are a matter of public knowledge and record.

Other books by William Dusty

The Cold Case: FBI series
The Salem Witch

The Stellar Conflict series
Friends and Enemies
The Quiet World
Predator in Our Midst
The Girl with the Strange Green Eyes
Sebastian's Prize

ISBN-13: 978-0-692-05536-6
Published by Timminy Press
Springfield, Massachusetts USA | 2018
www.timminypress.com

Shutterstock images by Elisanth, Volodymyr Tverdokhlib, Andreas Gradin, Eric Isselee.

Table of Contents

*"She who casts her gaze upon the
sea shall be your liberator."*

– The Invisibles

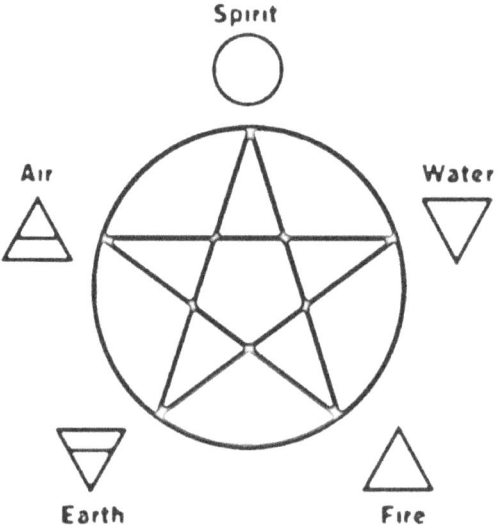

-1-

The Edge of Heaven

I grows up in the small town of Choctaw, Louisiana, in the southern bayous that I calls home. Back when I bein' young, I had dreams, just like any little girl had, of findin' me's a good, honest man, and us makin' a family of our very own. Life in them days was hard real hard—for all us kids. But I's made my own way pretty well. And then, after I's left school in the ninth grade, I worked in places doin' theys cleanin' and watchin' theys babies and all, and makin' just enough money to be helpin' my momma and poppy get along.

I done spent a lot of years livin' at home, doin' chores and helpin' take care of ours house, before I finally did meet my man, Marcus, and we got ourselves married. After a little whiles livin' in a one-roomer, we found our own place up by way of the L'Ours Bayou, next to Bobby Tildon's shack off in the woods there, and we's had a good life together for a little while goin' on.

Thens, after about another a year or so, I gots to carryin' our first child.

1

Now Marcus, he wasn't all so keen on us havin' a baby so soon—him sayin' we's had our bills and all to tend to, first. But for me, it's what I always wanted to help make my's life whole and complete, just like I always hoped for.

And Lord! When my boy Julien did finally comes into this world, I was about the happiest woman anyone ever's seen! He been my light and my joy, I swear to Heaven! My precious angel, he was, in a hard life we's had that didn't give us all much else in this world.

Marcus, now, he took up the drink as we got to strugglin' with things. And things got real bad for us—me 'specially. And so thens after we done parted our ways, I feels like I's all alone in my life—'ceptin' for my parents back in Choctaw, and, of course, my beautiful baby boy.

My little Julien was my whole world.

I made sure my baby went to daycare's and preschool, where'n they taught him how to tie his shoes and eat proper. And I worked myself two jobs—one in the mornin' and then another's into the night—takin' care of us.

It was hard livin', for sure, but done be worth it well enough for my Julien.

Meanwhiles, for a lot of years goin' on we been hearin' about them peoples gone missin' here abouts. Happenin' all over, they says, and no one knowin' why it is. They's took to callin' it the Curse of the Bayous which done take 'em all's away. Fate is what somes did say it was. Others sayin' it be the Voodoo Lord himself, Bondye, havin' his way with thems. I never paid it no mind myself, thoughs, since I had my own life to get on with and my little boy to take care of.

It was the spring and summer of 2010 when my momma and poppy done passed away. They's both been old, and after my momma passed on first, that April, my poppy, he's just not have the heart to live anymore. That's what we's all said, anyway. He went to God later on that summer.

One year went by from then, I remember. It was summertime and the flowers was all 'a blossomed, pretty in the morning air, when I got my visit from Sheriff Mickens, who'd come up from Thibodaux. He had a old, tired look on his face, and I knew he was 'a bringin' sorry news to me.

God! I cried awful when he told me! I's cried like I never cried before or ever since! My boy—my precious baby boy—gone missin' in the bayous!

They's all looked around for days and weeks come after, but they's never could find my little Julien. They says the curse—that Curse of the Bayous that been takin' all them others away—done took my baby, too!

For three years, now, I been walkin' this earth without my baby boy. My heart and my soul, they done left me a long time ago. I prayed to the Lord for a long whiles, askin' Him why he's took my baby aways. I ain't knowin', though, if he ever hearin' me. And every night, still, I look up at the stars, and I know my little Julien, he be lookin' down on me. He be there, just a' smilin' bright, and waitin' for me's to join him up in Heaven.

He been'a waitin' too long.

Momma's comin' to youz, now, my precious baby. She done made her peace on this earth and she's a comin' to be with her little baby boy. And I holds you in my arms, like I always did before. And just like I always knows it, we be together, the two of us, forever in Heaven.

"Ms. Hawkins?"

Regina Hawkins grasped onto the bridge railing, her eyes fixed on the dark, swirling waters of the river far below her. She looked off to her right, there to see a young white woman with long, dark red hair, dressed sharply in a dark pantsuit, standing nearby her in the dimly-lit early morning air. She had come as if from nowhere.

"Yes?"

The woman pulled out a billfold from her jacket pocket and flipped it open to display her identification.

"I'm Special Agent Joanna Weirdlee , Ms. Hawkins, with the FBI."

Regina looked at her curiously, wondering if she were merely a dream. For the woman's voice, it seemed, was like a spirit's own, come to life...

"We're here to investigate the disappearance of your son."

-2-

At the Bayou L'Ours

THIBODAUX, LOUISIANA
September, 2014

"Was a bad day, all ways 'round."

Lafourche Parish Sheriff Randy Mickens sat behind his desk in his glass-walled office. FBI Special Agents Samuel Nicks and Danny Fielding, both seated before him, had come to see him about a missing child investigation gone cold. The case had caught the eye of Assistant Director Marvin Ledds, and so he sent his top investigator, Nicks, to look into it.

"Once we got through talkin' to folks at the park," the sheriff explained in a thick Louisiana drawl, "I had my men goin' door-to-door in the area, askin' if anyone had seen the boy anywhere abouts."

The sheriff, a paunchy, well-tanned man in his mid-forties, looked resigned as he recited his department's efforts to locate the missing son of Regina Hawkins. The boy had been playing in a local park where his dad had taken him on that fateful, springtime Saturday afternoon.

"We took dogs out, searchin' the nearby neighborhoods. Then later in the week we dragged the river all along the Bayou Boeuf." He shook his head. "Tough goin', there. Impossible in some places."

Nicks glanced at his partner, then nodded to the sheriff. "I'd imagine so. These bayous deep, are they?"

"Not really," Mickens replied. "It's not about their depth. It's the tangle, the roots, branches, all the weeds. Plus, on top of that, we got the wildlife."

Fielding raised an eyebrow. "Crocs, ya mean?"

Mickens corrected him. "'Gators."

"That a big problem for you, Sheriff?" Nicks asked.

"No, I wouldn't say," Mickens replied. "Just gotta be aware of 'em, is all. And snakes, too."

"You think it's possible the boy could have been attacked by an alligator, Sheriff?" asked Fielding, his own Southern accent coming on.

Mickens nodded. "Sure. Anything's possible. The bayous are big, and 'gators all over. The boy was only, uh, what, four years old at the time? Not much learnin' in him. He coulda wandered off and got himself into trouble like that. That's one of our angles, anyway."

"The report that I read said his father was with him that day?" Nicks asked.

"Yeah," Mickens confirmed. "He's our *other* angle."

"He surely wouldn'ta hurt his own son," Fielding said with some alarm.

Mickens frowned. "Mr. Hawkins is not what one would call a devoted father, Special Agent. Anyway, we don't think he'd intentionally hurt the little kid, either. But he wasn't watchin' the boy that day, that's for sure. Instead, he's off socializing with some friends of his in another part of the park, not paying attention."

"Lost track of him," said Nicks.

"Yeah," said Mickens. "That's his story."

Fielding looked at Nicks, resigned. "Not sure there's much to this, partner. Looks like that poor kid got himself killed by nature, either ways around."

Nicks looked back at him thoughtfully, then turned to the sheriff. "Is it that easy to get into the swamps around here—the bayous?"

Mickens shrugged. "Sure. If you had a mind to. I mean, there's some fences and trees and thick bush and all that. But other places are open, just like anywhere—especially around the dock areas. And we got plenty of those in these parts. People live right on the water here."

Outside of the sheriff's office, Special Agent Weirdlee arrived at the front entrance of the large station room, accompanied by a black woman appearing to be in her late twenties.

Mickens spotted the black woman. "There's Miss Hawkins, now."

The two FBI agents turned, looking behind them.

"That's our partner, with her," said Nicks.

A police officer directed the two women to the sheriff's office. As they got to the office doorway, Regina Hawkins looked at the sheriff and then to the two strangers seated before him. "It's true?" she asked them all anxiously, "youz lookin' for my boy?"

Mickens put up a hand. He said to her in an easy tone, "Miss Hawkins, please. You know we never stopped lookin' for your son." He looked off to the officer standing behind her. "Jerry, get us a couple more chairs for the ladies, here."

The officer gave a nod. "Sure thing, Sheriff." And off he went.

With introductions made all around, the new arrivals took up the chairs that had been fetched for them. Both women sat to the right of the visiting men.

"Miss Hawkins," Mickens began, gesturing to Nicks and Fielding, "these men, here, are with the FBI. They come down to look into your son's disappearance."

"It's the Curse," Hawkins said under her breath. "I knows that's what it was."

"The curse?" Nicks asked the sheriff.

Mickens raised an eyebrow. "That's what some of the locals hereabouts been blamin' for all the missin' persons in the past twenty, thirty years."

"It is," Hawkins said to Nicks. "It's gots to be."

Nicks cleared his throat. He glanced over at Weirdlee, aware of his fellow agent's own occult background. For her part, Weirdlee simply looked down at her lap as the conversation continued.

"Well," Nicks said, "I suppose we could start by getting a look at the park where the boy disappeared from. Then maybe talk to some of the people who were there that day."

"We got their names on file," Mickens said. "I'll have my criminal investigations commander, Captain Phillips, drive ya'll out to the park. It's up northways a bit, out by the Bayou L'Ours in Kraemer."

"I lives up that a-ways, too," Hawkins added.

Nicks glanced at her, then looked back to the sheriff. "We'll need a list of anyone else Ms. Hawkins or the boy may have known at the time of his disappearance."

Mickens flashed his eyes and sighed. "Well...tall order, there."

"I give you all I gots," Hawkins said to Nicks. "But I knows where my baby is, sir. I knows theys took him away from me."

"*They*, Mrs. Hawkins?"

Hawkins replied in a soft, frail voice. "The angels, sir. The angels took my boy away. He up in Heaven now, waitin' on me."

"I'll talk to the folks over at the preschool the boy went to," Mickens offered. "And, uh, there's a daycare nearby the school, as well. Foster's Daycare."

"I's had to put him there," Hawkins said. "I been workin' two jobs—so's to support my boy, you know. It's hard."

Nicks sympathized with her. "Sure, Ms. Hawkins. I understand."

Weirdlee put a hand on Hawkins' own, reassuring her. "It's okay."

Nicks said to the sheriff, "What about the father?"

Hawkins scowled at the mention of her ex-husband. "He no good!" she cried out. "That man's no good!"

Mickens put up a hand to calm her. "Take it easy, Mrs. Hawkins. It's all right." Then he answered the special agent's question. "That guy's a real piece of work, sir. He was more worried about gettin' blamed for the boy's disappearance than he was about findin' out what happened to him. Real loser."

"He 'a drinkin' man," Hawkins added. "He took to the drink, and it's all he care about, now."

"He live with you, Ms. Hawkins?" Nicks asked.

"*No...*" Hawkins fumed. "He *out*."

Mickens clarified the situation. "They're estranged a few years, now, special agent. Divorced. Miss Hawkins had a restrainin' order against him at first. That expired a few months before the boy went missin'."

Hawkins stared off. "He was askin' me to let him be. Let him visit his boy. Make things right."

"He made an effort?" Weirdlee asked her.

Hawkins shook her head. She said with a scowl, "*Lies*. He justa gettin' sweet on me—maybe get off 'a his child support or somethin'. He never cared about Julien at all. Never did."

Nicks looked at her thoughtfully before pulling his attention back over to the sheriff. "I suppose we can head out there now."

"Sure thing," Mickens said with a nod. "Lemme ring the captain."

As the sheriff called up his detectives commander, Nicks looked over at Special Agent Weirdlee.

"Can you drive Ms. Hawkins home," he asked her, "then hook up with us at the park afterward?"

Weirdlee nodded. "Sure, Sam."

Nicks smiled at her, noting her preference for first names. "Thanks."

* * * *

The drive up north to the Bayou L'Ours area was uneventful, yet informative to Nicks, just the same. As the FBI agents followed behind detective Captain Phillips' unmarked cruiser, the senior agent had opted to let Fielding drive their rented black 2010 Ford Taurus so that he himself could admire the view during their journey.

The region they drove along, he saw, bore little resemblance to what he'd imagined the area would look like. He'd only been to Louisiana a couple of times previously—once to visit the state capital, Baton Rouge, and another time just a couple of years ago on a visit to New Orleans. Still, Nicks had always pictured thick, lush forests and swampy bayous covering every square inch of the land in these parts of the state—which basically lay as one big river delta at the mouth of the Mississippi River. Perhaps at one time, he imagined, all of it was. But hundreds of years of human development had since tamed much of the land where most people nowadays lived. The areas the agents drove by on that day, he saw, had wide open spaces, with fields and trimmed lawns and paved streets with shops and businesses lining them—just like any place you might find anywhere in rural America. He did know from satellite maps, though, that once they arrived in the less settled regions of the bayous, the cleared lands were pretty much reduced to mere slivers of properties that lay huddled around roads that cut through the thick, wild forests there.

Still, he was beginning to change his mind about the likelihood of a kid wandering off into a swamp, unawares.

The lawmen drove north along Route 20 for a time before taking a right and travelling east on Route 307. The road took them past the Jean Webre and Grand Bayous, off to their south, and on up to the Bayou L'Ours area—a thinly settled rural stretch of land that lay just south of the Bayou Boeuf, which itself led to the open waters of the shallow Lac des Allemands lake.

Their destination, Kraemer Park—a small, sparsely-treed field—came up on their right, just before the L'Ours river crossing. They pulled off into the gravel parking lot there and everyone left their cars. Captain Phillips, himself joined by another plainclothes police officer, led the party to the south side of the little park, which, at its edge, fell away to a steep embankment bordering the L'Ours as it snaked around and continued on its meandering, upstream course, leading southwest into the deepening wilderness.

"This is about where the boy might have gone in," the captain said to the others. "But, really, it could have been anywhere along here," he gestured, pointing all along the eastern edge of the park fronting the nearby river.

Nicks saw that the embankment trailed off northward, with thick vegetation covering it further along. He noticed, too, that all along the top of the embankment a narrow dirt path followed a thin line of trees bordering the park.

"Where's this path, here, lead to?" he asked.

"Oh, that goes back up to the road," Phillips said.

Nicks looked off to the rest of the park. It was a Sunday morning, and a few of the locals were wandering about the place, playing with kids or walking their dogs. Most of the trees there, he noted, were scattered about the southern area of the property, with a thin line of trees bordering both the western and eastern sides.

"You guys said the father was here with the boy?" he asked.

Phillips nodded. "Yeah, there was a bunch of people here that day, actually. They were havin' some kinda annual outing—a fundraiser for the local boys and girls club." He turned and pointed off to the open area of the park. "There was lots of tents and such set up along either side here," he said, gesturing to the left and right. "They had craft booths, snack trucks, shit like that. It was hotter than hell that day, too."

"You remember how hot it was?" Fielding asked.

Phillips gave him a sober look. "It was the middle of summer. After the boy came up missin', we spent the rest of day hereabouts, and then off down by the river bank, there. We checked downstream a ways, and upstream, too. It was hotter than hell. Never forget it."

"What makes you so sure the boy was back here?" Nicks asked.

"'Cuz," said Phillips, "he was playin' around with some other kids for a little while, and they was all back here."

Fielding asked, "And none of them saw where the boy went off to?"

"We questioned 'em all," Phillips said. "They all said their 'I dunnos', or said he was still here when they left, themselves."

Nicks listened in, but he'd also turned his attention back to the dirt path. He studied it in silence, and then looked off again to the open part of the park.

"So," he said, "you said there were tents out here?"

"Yeah," said Phillips. He pointed off to the left and right again as he described the scene. "There was a row of tents and booths over yonder, and another row here on this side. The food trucks were all set off by the lot, there."

Nicks brought up his hands and pointed them at each other. "The tents were facing each other, toward the center of the park?"

Phillips looked out at the park, trying to recall. "Yessir. I reckon so."

Nicks turned again to the dirt path. "So, the backs of the tents on this side were facing the path, here."

"Yyyeah..." Phillips figured. "I reckon so."

"That important?" Fielding asked his partner.

"Well," Nicks replied, "there's a lot of obstacles that could have blocked the view to the path, here—the tents, the trees and all. It's possible the boy could have walked all the way back to the road and no one may have noticed."

"But somebody woulda seen him on the road," said Phillips.

Nicks eyed the path as it led off north, towards Route 307. "Or picked him up."

"Shit..." Fielding swore.

"Now, that's possible," said Phillips. "And it's something we considered, too. If that boy was abducted, then whoever took him could have murdered him and dumped him anywhere."

Phillips' partner, who'd been standing nearby, cast his eyes to the river. "The curse," he muttered.

"What's that?" asked Nicks.

"Oh," the officer said. "I was just sayin', maybe it was that curse goin' around—the Curse of the Bayous."

Fielding snickered. "You don't actually believe in that stuff, do ya?"

Phillips put up a hand. "Now, hold on a minute. We're just callin' it what the locals call it, is all. Did the sheriff tell ya'll about the bodies we found?"

"The *what?*" Nicks exclaimed.

"Bodies?" Fielding echoed.

"I guess not," said Phillips. He glanced around to ensure no one else was within earshot before continuing. "We done found three bodies from all the ones gone missing in the past twenty years. Two males, one female. All of 'em suffered identical injuries."

"Death related injuries?" Nicks asked.

Phillips raised an eyebrow. "Had their hands and feet severed."

Fielding winced. "Ouch."

Nicks rolled his eyes. "I guess that's probably death related."

Phillips nodded. "Another thing: They all had what looks like the letter H cut into the foreheads of their skulls."

"H?" Fielding repeated.

"Yeah. Which is leadin' us to thinkin' it's some kind of cult thing goin' on."

"I'd say that's a pretty good guess," Nicks said. He looked off again to the dirt path. "Are any kids a part of your missing persons list, Captain?"

"In the parish? Yeah, there's a couple besides the Hawkins boy."

"So…" pondered Fielding, "ya thinkin' maybe this curse thing ya'll got goin' on could be a serial killin' spree of some kind?"

"That's exactly it," said Phillips. "We've been consulting with local religious leaders from all around here. We're focusing on a couple of offshoots of the voodoo sects in these parts."

"Shit," Fielding swore ruefully. "Voodoo."

14

Phillips shook his head. "It's not what ya think. Most of the voodoo in these parts is peaceable enough. In fact, there's a mambo woman who's been a big help to us on this."

"Mambo woman?" Fielding asked.

"A voodoo priestess—Haitian. Her name's Marie Corbet," Phillips said, using the *aire* French accent at the end her name. "She got off the boat from the island about fifteen-twenty years ago. Got a good reputation hereabouts. She says it's possible there's a sect out here— an offshoot of the main voodoo religion—goin' around doin' this shit."

"There many offshoots around here, Captain?" Nicks asked.

"Dozens," he answered. "Shit, maybe hundreds. Problem for us is, voodoo is a big tourist draw in these parts, too, and we've got a heck of a time separating the entertainment part of it from the serious side."

"Yeah..." Nicks conceded.

"Now, there is one other woman who you might want to talk to," Phillips said. "She's sort of a kook, though."

That got the attention of both Nicks and Fielding.

"Her name's Zarah Devillier. Lotta years ago, she used to be a pretty well known voodoo queen around here. She got herself mixed up in the drug scene, though, a ways back, and she's kind of a head case these days. Packs a bunch of mud on her face and dances around campfires— that sort of thing."

"Sounds like a job for Agent Weirdlee," Fielding quipped.

"Who?" asked Phillips.

Fielding chuckled. "She's *our* resident kook."

"Fielding," Nicks groaned.

"Sorry."

Nicks asked Phillips, "Does the woman live around here?"

Phillips pointed off to the south. "She lives in the swamps, out by the Grand Bayou river junction. It's about a two mile boat ride—no roads. She lives out there with her three sons. One of the boys has a car that he parks at the docks over by the L'Ours—an old beat up Volkswagen. He's their taxi when they need to get around."

Nicks gave a thoughtful nod.

Then, still curious about the narrow dirt path leading north along the eastern side of the park, he said to the others, "I think I'll take a walk out to the road, here."

He started off toward the path.

* * * *

Special Agent Weirdlee dropped off Regina Hawkins at the woman's mobile home, located on a dirt road just off Route 307. The agent drove a green, 2011 Jeep Grand Cherokee on this assignment, and was presently heading west on 307 to meet up with her colleagues at Kraemer Park, just a short drive away. Travelling along the road, she slowed down then as she came upon a small group of people on the left curb, nearby the entrance to a river dock that serviced the Bayou L'Ours. Three young, light-skinned black men with dreadlocked hair and dressed in raggedy clothes shouted angrily and shook their fists at passing cars, while a fourth person, an elderly woman with long, stringy gray hair and dressed in a gray smock-like dress, had her arms extended to either side, palms facing skyward. She gazed straight ahead, as if entranced.

As Weirdlee passed by the group, eyeing them curiously, the old woman suddenly took note of her. She locked her eyes onto the FBI agent, and she grinned at her knowingly. She laughed then, in a lazy fashion, as she pointed at Weirdlee with a bent, wrinkled finger.

"Wiiitch..." she muttered.

Weirdlee leered back at her, puzzled by her attention.

"Wiiitch!" the old woman declared louder, appearing quite pleased with her discovery as the young men around her, all the while, kept up their shouting and fist pumping.

Weirdlee looked up into her rearview mirror as she drove on by them, keeping her eyes focused on the old woman there. An unsettling feeling crept over her.

The woman, Weirdlee sensed in her mind, had the Gift in her.

The old woman smiled menacingly at the passing vehicle, and then laughed again.

"Wiiitch...!" she repeated between snickering chuckles. "*Wiiitch!*"

Weirdlee kept driving ahead.

After a short distance, the agent came upon a bridge spanning the Bayou L'Ours. Returning her attention to her business, she drove over the bridge and in no time at all arrived at the park, turning left into its gravel parking lot.

Her colleagues, standing nearby the road, had spotted her arrival, and, after she left her car, Nicks waved her over to them. She started out.

Phillips raised an admiring eyebrow as the pretty agent, dressed sharply in her dark pantsuit, approached them.

"Jesus," he said to Nicks and Fielding, "you folks got a lot of those over at the Bureau, do ya?"

Fielding chuckled at that. "Trust me. She's one-of-a-kind."

"Let's behave, guys," Nicks said.

Weirdlee came up to them. "Gentlemen."

"Is Ms. Hawkins okay, Special Agent?" Nicks asked her.

She nodded. "Yeah. She's all settled down, now." Then she glanced about the park. "What's up, here?"

"Oh," Nicks replied, "we're just checking out the lay of the land." He pointed off to the dirt path behind them. "This path, here, leads all the way to the back side of the park."

"We're thinkin', maybe Miss Hawkins' boy mighta come up this way and got up to the road, here," Fielding added, pointing at the main road.

Weirdlee nodded thoughtfully as she glanced down the path. "I see," she mulled. Then she looked back at the road, and then off to the parking lot. "And you think he might have gotten into somebody's car up here?"

Phillips detected a noticeable accent to Weirdlee's voice—either Bostonian or from Maine, he thought—as she'd softened the "r" in her "car" and "here."

"I was just tellin' your partners," he said to her, "everyone that was here that day kinda knew each other. If anyone saw that boy up here, they'da said somethin' to him, or come and got him."

"We got us some people we can talk to," said Fielding. "Including a couple 'a voodoo women."

Weirdlee flashed her eyebrows at him. "*Woo.*"

Nicks said to her, "Fielding and I will go have a talk with the father, if you can handle the two he mentioned."

She shrugged. "Sure."

"Marie Corbet is the name of the mambo woman," said Phillips. "I can give you her home address and the address of where she works at. She's a hairdresser in South Vacherie. The other woman, Miss Devillier, will be a little harder to get to."

"Why's that?" Weirdlee asked.

"Lives in the swamps," said Fielding.

Phillips nodded. "That, plus she doesn't have what you'd call an on-site job. She kinda gets around all over, panhandling and such. Tells fortunes to the tourists, too. You can't mistake her, though, once you see her. Old woman with natty gray hair, old clothes—usually black. Her sons tag along with her a lot, and they do their chanting routine together. The two elder boys got full time jobs during the week, but the youngest is, uh, mentally disabled, so he's always around."

Weirdlee pursed her lips. "Hmm," she mused. "Actually, I think I saw her already."

"Oh yeah?" said Phillips.

She pointed off toward the L'Ours. "Back over the bridge, there. She and three younger guys were shouting at cars passing by."

"That would be her sons," Phillips said. "We've had to haul 'em in on occasion, too, for stoppin' cars and disturbin' the peace."

"Nice," said Fielding. "Maybe me or Special Agent Nicks should go along with ya, Agent Weirdlee."

She frowned at him. "Don't worry, Daniel. I can handle people."

Phillips added, "They never hurt no one before. Just a general nuisance, is all."

"Just the same," said Nicks, "talk to her in a public area if you can, Agent Weirdlee."

Weirdlee rolled her eyes. "Okay, dad."

Nicks frowned at the remark. He didn't want to be overprotective of his female colleague, but at the same time, there was a degree of danger in visiting places alone.

"They've found some bodies, Agent Weirdlee—three of them," he told her. "And they're all from the state's missing persons record."

"Oh really?" Weirdlee replied, taken by the news.

"Yeah," Nicks went on. "So that adds a new dimension to our investigation. The three were possibly victims of some kind of ritual killings."

Weirdlee looked at Phillips. "Ritual? Are you sure?"

Phillips nodded. "Yeah. The bodies were mutilated that kinda way."

"Okay," Nicks said. "Let's get started." He looked at Fielding. "I want to go back into town and talk to the sheriff before we start interviewing people."

"Right," Fielding said with a nod.

Nicks snapped his fingers. "Oh—we'll need to find a place to stay around here, first, I guess, too."

Weirdlee put up a hand. "Already done. We've got rooms at the Swampy Inn, down the road a ways in a place called, umm, Chackbay."

Fielding smirked. "The Swampy Inn? That sounds homey."

"It's clean," Weirdlee said.

"It'll do," said Nicks. "Let's roll."

The group headed back to their cars.

~ | ~

-3-

Which is Witch

"I been the first born out of six children, and the only one gifted with the powers that God gives me. I am the seer of fortunes and the keeper of nature's secrets. And I will tell you yours fortune, here today."

Zarah Devillier sat in front of a small, collapsible table, tending to a young woman who'd stopped by for a quick reading. The two sat inside of a flimsy, foldaway type of aluminum and nylon canopy that Zarah had set off to the side of a crowded parking lot in the town of South Vacherie. There, a small street fair was ongoing, and the old woman had paid her vending fee to be there. Standing nearby the booth, as they always did on the weekends, were her three sons, eagerly clapping and coaxing passersby to have their fortunes told.

The twenty-something, blonde-haired woman sat before Zarah, curiously anticipating her reading. A crystal ball was set at the center of the little table, ready for Zarah's use.

"I hope it's all good things," the woman said with an innocent smile and an airy southern accent.

Zarah grinned back. "One never knows what the *loa* will reveal."

With that, Zarah cast her hands around the crystal ball, making like she was focusing all of its energies. She hummed as she leered into its orb.

This, just like her phony tale of upbringing, was all for show, actually. The truth was, Zarah already knew unsuspecting woman's future, of a sort.

"Tell me your name, child..." she murmured to her.

"Jill Truscott," the woman replied eagerly.

Zarah peeked at the girl from out of her periphery while still staring intensely at the crystal ball. Truscott was a short woman, easily handled, no more than twenty-four years old. She wore tight-fitting jean shorts with a white t-shirt, and had white sneakers on her feet.

The slut, thought Zarah. Tell her what she needs to know.

Long ago—back in the distant days before her gradual, ignominious fall—Zarah Devillier had once been a promising spiritualist. She'd helped many people in her time, and was considered to be, for a white woman, exceptional in her abilities and knowledge of the voodoo faith. "New Orleans voodoo" is what they called it, this version she followed, which included many Catholic symbols and saints in its rites. It was a departure from her family's true dark past, too—a past of ruin and murder that Zarah herself had very nearly escaped as an orphaned child.

Fate, however, had already determined there would be no such evasion.

Soon after joining a small sect of believers, Zarah climbed her way to the top of the hierarchy, and in just a few short years, she'd managed to expand the sect's roll of followers by several hundreds, spread throughout the southern bayous of Louisiana. Her success brought with it, as well, an eagerness to expand her own spiritual abilities, which she felt she'd only just begun to realize. And so it was that she turned to narcotics to help her "see" the spirit world, and to better communicate with the *loa* themselves. As she plunged ever deeper into addiction then, she soon lost interest in the day-to-day running of the group she'd helped to grow. She retreated into her mind until, after just a few transformational years, it came to be that all she ever saw in her life were visions and shadows, and everything she sensed or comprehended she felt certain to be some manner of mythic, sacred sign, portending the course of some dark future for those so revealed in her dreams.

"Bewares!" she told everyone around her. "The devil lurks nears us all! And he will take your soul!"

The group, by then dysfunctional with its leadership so compromised, eventually dissolved itself, and its followers drifted off to other sects and religious dominations. And so it came to be that sometime thereafter, Zarah herself—now left on her own—descended into a demented, delusional state. She saw evil and heretics everywhere in her mind. She saw lost, wayward souls—the homeless, runaways, and street vagrants—all in need of her guidance, so to be justly delivered to their predestined fates. And always, as well, her deeds fell under the watchful eyes of the *Ghede* spirits she worshipped so devoutly.

Murder.

Death.

Justice for all!

It was some years after this dark period in her life took hold of her that a young man showed up who would change Zarah's life forever. She'd gone broke on her own, and so would spent much of her days wandering about the streets of New Orleans, herself homeless and begging. There this man first spied her, and, after a few visits and chats, he decided this delusional woman had a purpose, after all. Unknowing at first of her murderous path in life, he saw instead only the power that she wielded—that genuine magickal ability that so separated her from all the other phony fortunetellers who abounded in the region. All she needed, he decided, was a helping hand to get her back on her feet again. A provider of things, as it were.

And so it was that he provided for her. He provided her with the drugs she needed. Any alcohol she desired. And in return for these things, he pried from the wretched Zarah Devillier all of the knowledge she had of the magickal ways of the Higher Craft. Thrice he impregnated her, and, to keep him out of debt, she lied for him to keep his identity unknown. So deluded had Zarah's mind become, in fact, that soon she came to envision this man as not merely a lover, but rather the master of her entire life. She had come to worship him, quite literally, as a spirit in the flesh!

This man's name was Paul Basil. When first he met Zarah Devillier, he was little more than a street-savvy drug dealer with an untapped knack for spiritual divination. He'd had some voodoo training behind him, but he'd never been able to capture the power he so longed to wield. That is, until he met Zarah. The former voodoo queen's abilities were genuine enough, he saw, and so he would have her tutor him until such time as he was able to command a righteous name for himself all on his own.

Throughout the 1990s then, his magickal abilities grew. The easy money lay in the tourist trade, and so he hatched a routine for himself as an entertainer working the nightclubs until eventually he would headline shows in New Orleans and its outlying towns, where tourists arriving from all over would flock to see his captivating voodoo magick, practiced right there before their very eyes! And he called himself Marcel Unate'—*Voodoo King of the Bayous!*

But for him, all the while, the abilities he'd acquired from his slave, Zarah, were still not enough. He saw

24

himself by this time as merely an entertainer of fools—a cheap parlor magician whose true abilities lay hidden and unused. The magick of voodoo, he knew, however, held many other ways in which one could attain power, both light and dark. Yet only in darkness, he decided, would he find a much less demanding path to fulfillment.

One need only dedicate himself to its end.

"Youz a free spirited girl," Zarah told Jill Truscott. "Livin' up the young life like you is."

Truscott smiled. "Yeah," she agreed. "That's me."

The old priestess leaned closer to her crystal ball, peering into its reflections. She didn't actually need the ball to divine the passing of events in her mind. It was, for her, more of a stage prop, there just to help sway the weak minds she encountered. And Truscott, she determined early on, had a very weak mind, indeed. She was a gullible, stupid girl, easily tricked by placing thoughts of doubt and persuasion into her young, naive head.

Zarah's powers were quite diminished from what they'd once been in her youth—distorted and broken by years of drug and alcohol abuse—but she could still see the echoes of the future. Flashes and hints of things to come. And so, in her twisted mind, a shadowy vision of the girl came into sight. She was staggering in the swamps, her clothing torn, face beaten, and weeping madly. And Zarah's master, Paul Basil, was there, too, controlling her. Holding her firmly in his powerful grasp.

The old woman laughed aloud.

"What do you see?" Truscott asked her.

Zarah stopped laughing, and she leered at the girl. "Your future, girl. Both the good and the bad."

"Bad?" Truscott asked. "What kind of bad?"

The old woman smiled coyly. "Oh, you know the kind I be speakin' of, girl. You young people and your trysts. Your

parties and your drugs. I sees you cavorting with all sorts
of dangerous peoples. Troublemakers. You be gettin'
yourself carried away, girl."

"Are you for real?" the girl asked in disbelief. "Am I
gonna die or something?"

Zarah's smile softened. "No..." she said. "I do not see
that right away in your future." She returned her gaze to
the crystal ball. "But you will have hardship in your life,
girl. Unwarranted. Unnecessary. Your young years will not
be the pleasant ones you hoped for." She slowly raised her
eyes to look at Truscott. "It needn't be this way, though,
girl. You can change your destiny, if you choose."

"I can?" Truscott asked anxiously. "How can I do that?"

"Trust in the *loa*, girl—the spirits. Talk to them. They
will guide you."

Truscott shook her head. "But, I don't—"

"There are those who can help you, child," Zarah told
her. "They can speak to the *loa* for you, and counsel you.
Steer you away from harm."

Truscott mulled her troubles in her mind.

Zarah let her stew for a moment. Then, she produced a
card from a small pocket in the folds of her raggedy dress.
"Here," she said to the girl. She placed the card on the
table before her. "Talk to this man. Go to him. He is a
powerful priest, and can speak to the spirits for youz."

The girl frowned, eyeing the card. "I'm just a student
here. I'm going back to Missouri next week."

Zarah lost her smile. She looked at the girl coolly, and
forced her own corrupted power of persuasion upon the
young woman. "Go to him, child," she said. "You must go
to him, or else surrender your fate to the will of the spirits
with thems minds unswayed."

The girl swallowed anxiously. She picked up the card
and looked at it. It read:

Marcel Unate'
Voodoo King of the Bayous

The picture on the card showed the priest himself—a dark-skinned man with piercing black eyes. A phone number was also printed on the bottom left corner.

"I'll think about it," Truscott said with uncertainty.

"You do that, girl," said Zarah. "You think about it very well."

Truscott got up from her chair then, and she said goodbye to Zarah Devillier.

The tainted former voodoo queen just tossed the girl a wave in return.

After the young woman left, Zarah returned her gaze to her stage prop crystal ball. She laughed once again, sensing how things would go. The girl would visit with Basil, she knew. The girl would surrender to him. They always did.

A chill shot through the old woman just then. She stopped her laughing and took in a quick breath.

There was, she sensed, some turmoil coming to her in the future. In her mind, a shadowy vision of the witch she'd seen earlier in the day came to her. The woman wore a dark cloak, its hood drawn back about her shoulders. Strung about her neck, too, was a finely engraved silver pentacle necklace. She'd come to the bayous, Zarah perceived, from the north.

From Salem.

"I'll get you, too," Zarah whispered to herself, nodding reassuringly.

"I'll get you for Marcel."

* * * *

South Vacherie, similar to the rest of southern Louisiana, was largely made up of homes and businesses that lined either side of various intersecting main roads, with tracts of farmland and thick forests of wilderness in turn surrounding those.

Special Agent Weirdlee arrived at Marie Corbet's home after calling first to make sure she was home. As it was close to noontime on Sunday, she was—and she answered her door still dressed in her robe and nightgown.

"Come in," the woman offered Weirdlee, bringing her inside of her small, single-story home and escorting her into the kitchen. There, she invited Weirdlee to sit at a small, round dining table while she made tea for them.

Weirdlee had examined the home discretely while heading into the kitchen. A couple of ceremonial Haitian vodou masks—clearly cheap fakes—hung from a living room wall, each set to either side of a window. Dollar store trinkets, candles, and assorted tableware were set about on an end table they passed by in the hallway. Coming into the kitchen then, the agent noted the place lacked even the slightest hint of Haitian cultural decor. She might just as well have been in any typical American kitchen of the South.

Corbet herself kept her thick black hair pinned up. Her dark, black skin was smooth and unblemished, and she carried herself in a relaxed fashion. She wore no jewelry that Weirdlee could see. In fact, the Haitian woman appeared to have Americanized her lifestyle to a surprising degree, overall. A notion Weirdlee thought odd for such a well-known mambo woman.

Corbet set a cup of green tea before Weirdlee, then fetched the teapot and a cup for herself. After pouring her own tea and setting the pot on the table, she joined Weirdlee.

"So, what can I do for the FBI today?" she asked, taking a seat opposite her guest.

"A pleasant home you have here," Weirdlee said to her.

Corbet smiled. "It's modest. But it's all I need." She noticed, too, Weirdlee's New England accent. "You from Maine, dear?"

Weirdlee eyed her plainly. "No, not actually. I'm from Salem, Massachusetts."

That was a miss on Corbet's part that Weirdlee thought quite odd, especially seeing that it was also entirely unnecessary.

"I thought so," Corbet said, pretending she'd come close enough.

The agent sipped her tea before starting.

"I understand the police talked to you about the missing Hawkins boy—Julien Hawkins?"

Corbet recalled, "Yes, they did. The boy from the Bayou L'Ours area, right?"

"Yes," Weirdlee said, nodding. "I think that's the place. I haven't familiarized myself with the area, yet, though."

"You won't, either. Not in a week or so's time, anyway."

Weirdlee raised an eyebrow. "Is that how long we'll be here?"

Corbet sipped from her tea. "Probably."

Weirdlee went back and forth from examining her tea to looking at Corbet as she continued.

"Some of the locals are saying the boy may have been the victim of a curse, or perhaps have been targeted by a serial killer."

Corbet looked back at Weirdlee thoughtfully. "Serial killer?" she mused. "Now there's a thought." She took another sip of her tea. "And you believe which to be the most likely?"

Weirdlee considered the question. The whole time she sat there, as well, she searched for some kind of spiritual presence in the room, using her own tea's watery reflections to aid her. She detected nothing, however, so far.

29

"Why not both?" she replied to Corbet.

The mambo woman tilted her head. "True, I guess."

"You know," Weirdlee went on, "I've found that, most times, the evil that men and women do tends to have a mundane, earthly motivation."

"That's true, too," said Corbet. "I told the police in Thibodaux that the boy had been abducted. Still, they suspected he might have also fallen into the bayous, without foul play."

Weirdlee looked purposefully at Corbet. "Can you see the boy now?"

Corbet sighed. "I sensed his fate a couple of years ago. I felt his presence in my mind." She shook her head ruefully. "I see nothing, now. The boy, I'm afraid, is gone."

"But..." Weirdlee surmised, "you don't know for sure."

Corbet frowned at her guest. "You FBI folks will do what you do. You'll do your searches, you'll ask your questions. But the boy will still be gone." She sipped from her tea again. "When I try to see him—and I have tried for these past few years—I see nothing but black waters, and weeds floating in the currents."

Weirdlee brought a finger to her tea and swirled it around, then took the cup in both hands and sipped from it.

She said to Corbet, "We'll also be talking to an old woman. A Miss, uh, Devell-ier?"

Corbet laughed. "Zarah Devillier?"

"Yes." Weirdlee nodded. "That's her."

"Zarah is insane. You'll get nothing from that madwoman."

Weirdlee pursed her lips and leered thoughtfully at Corbet. "Hmm." Then she sat back in her seat and asked her, "Isn't she a local, though, from where the boy disappeared?"

"Yes," Corbet scoffed. "And if you ask me, she would be just the kind of person who might actually abduct the boy, herself."

Weirdlee challenged her. "Did she?"

Corbet stared back at her, mulling things in her mind. She said to Weirdlee, "Do you believe in the ways of magick?"

Weirdlee hesitated. This was something the mambo woman should have already discerned on her own. She reached under her blouse then and pulled out a necklace. Corbet saw the finely made silver pentacle dangling from its chain.

"I see," she said to the agent, raising an eyebrow. "You practice the Craft, do you?"

"I do, actually," Weirdlee replied.

"That's strange for an FBI agent. I would think such beliefs would disqualify you."

Weirdlee gave her a curious look as she replaced her necklace under her blouse. "Oh really? Why would that be?"

"Well..." Corbet sighed. She sat up straight in her chair. "Not sure how they view things up north, but down here most people are wary of such beliefs. I know I get my own fair share of odd looks when people learn of my faith. And yours is even less welcome here."

"Yes, well," Weirdlee said, sipping the last of her tea, "my boss is pretty open minded about such things."

"More tea?" Corbet asked her.

"No thank you."

Weirdlee got back to the boy then.

"So, I think maybe this woman, Zarah, might be useful in our investigation, regardless. Anyone, really, who can help us learn the fate of the boy would be."

"She'll be nothing but trouble for you," Corbet insisted. "Beware, if you meet up with her."

"Actually," said Weirdlee, "I was planning on going to her house this evening."

"*No!*" Corbet recoiled. "You must not go to her home! She lives in the swamps. There is danger there."

Weirdlee snapped her eyes to her, taken aback by her reaction. "I tried seeing her earlier today, but she'd already left where I last saw her. I do have to meet her somewhere, and she doesn't seem to stay in any one place for very long."

"If you go to her home, you will be in *her* territory. *Her* lair. You know about her sons, don't you?"

"Yes." Weirdlee nodded. "But I was told by the police that they're all fairly harmless."

"They are as demented as their mother," Corbet said. "And they are hungry."

Weirdlee lifted an eyebrow. "Hungry?"

Corbet leaned forward in her chair, eyeing Weirdlee coolly. "You are a beautiful woman, my dear. You should not go where hungry men prowl." She sat back in her seat again. "There is only one way to get to the Devillier home, anyway, and that is by boat ride, up the river to the Grand Bayou junction."

"I'll rent one, then."

Corbet laughed. "You do not rent boats in that area, dear. They only do guided tours, for the tourists."

"They'll rent one to the FBI," Weirdlee assured her.

"On your own?" Corbet asked.

Weirdlee smiled back at her. "I do some of my best work on my own."

Corbet smirked at her. "Then you are a fool. And you will be raped if you are not watchful."

Weirdlee dropped her smile. She patted her belt underneath her pantsuit jacket, where her holstered Glock lay fastened. "I'll have more than just my faith going along with me for the ride."

Corbet shook her head slowly, evaluating her visitor.

"It's your life," she said to her. She leaned forward again. "But I see you in a desperate way in the very near future, my dear. You will not be the strong woman you are here today."

Weirdlee eyed her seriously, in turn. "We shall see."

The FBI agent got up from her chair then.

"Are you sure there's nothing else," she said, "nothing further you can tell us about the fate of the boy, Ms. Corbet?"

Corbet kept her eyes on Weirdlee, but remained seated, herself. "No. He is with the angels, as far as I can see."

Weirdlee gave a nod. "Thank you, then. I'll see myself out."

Corbet smiled. "What is it you witches say? Merry part?"

Weirdlee gave her a half-hearted smile and left.

Outside, the agent got into her rented Grand Cherokee and started it up. She took in a deep breath and then slowly exhaled. She would need, she decided, to head up to New Orleans and talk to a couple more mambo women there—if she could find them. She knew she needed more local knowledge and advice before confronting Zarah Devillier. The old woman, Weirdlee sensed, was truly gifted, and even with her voodoo powers much diminished through the years, there was still a degree of danger in meeting with her alone—that much Marie Corbet had been right about.

And so what of Ms. Corbet herself?

The woman, Weirdlee decided, had nothing to offer to the investigation.

I see nothing but black waters, and weeds floating in the currents.

This would be the same landscape, Weirdlee surmised, that anyone might come across practically anywhere in that part of the state. Corbet, she surmised, was a cold reader. And Weirdlee noted, too, that the woman had no idea that her visitor was a practicing witch until Weirdlee herself had mentioned it. A true woman of ability would have known when a sister was in the room.

Weirdlee put her Jeep in gear and drove off, heading east to New Orleans.

Marie Corbet, regionally renowned and respected mambo woman from Haiti, was a fraud.

~ | ~

-4-

Pieces in a Puzzle

"Sheriff, why didn't you tell us about the bodies you found?"

Nicks and Fielding stood in the office of Sheriff Mickens, with Nicks fuming about their not being fully informed.

"Now hold on," the sheriff said, sitting behind his desk. "I was gonna tell ya'll everything—includin' that we'd found some bodies. But the Hawkins woman came in, and I wasn't about to start talkin' about corpses with her in the room."

"You could've asked her to step outside," Nicks said.

Mickens raised an eyebrow. "Really, Special Agent?"

"Yeah. Why not?"

"We've got plenty of time to go over the investigation," Mickens said. "The woman was in the room, her son's gone missin'—probably dead. I ain't kickin' her out so's I can tell you two about some dead bodies. My captain told you well enough, didn't he?"

"That's not the point, Sheriff," Nicks insisted. "We had our partner, Agent Weirdlee, drive Ms. Hawkins home. She was out of the loop entirely until she met back up with us. And we're talking about mutilated bodies, too, right? That's not a small detail."

Mickens sighed. "Look, I'm sorry, ya'll. All right? It doesn't change anythin', though, so let's get past it, can we?"

Nicks put his hands on his hips. "Is there anything else you didn't have time to tell us, Sheriff, that we really outta to know?"

Clearly annoyed by the agent's continued hostility, Mickens pointed off to two chairs set nearby his desk. "Why don't the both of ya's have a seat, here, and we can go over the whole thing, square one."

Nicks grudgingly took a chair. Fielding, for his part, wasn't nearly as upset about the situation. He casually grabbed his own chair and pulled it up close to the sheriff's desk before plopping himself down in it.

"Now," Mickens said, clasping his hands together, "let's talk about the bodies we found, first. Captain Phillips told you about their condition."

"Yeah," said Nicks.

"Hands and feet chopped off," Fielding said, using a hand to mimic chopping.

Mickens eyeballed Fielding. "Uh... Yeah." He cleared his throat. "We, uh, found 'em all in different places—some fishermen and tour guides found 'em, actually, while cruisin' the water."

"In different parts of the state or just different areas around here?" Nicks asked.

"Different areas hereabouts is what I meant. From the outskirts of New Orleans, on down to Houma."

"What about that 'H' thing the captain told us about?" Fielding asked.

"Ya mean he 'H's cut into their skulls?" Mickens asked.

"Yeah."

Mickens rapped his knuckles on his desk. "Gotta have some kind of symbolic meaning—ritualistic, maybe. We're not sure. Heck, it's not like whoever is doin' this is leavin' us notes explaining why."

"Hate," offered Nicks. "Heathen. Heretic. Maybe Heaven?"

Mickens nodded. "Could be anything."

"Is there any similarity between the victims, Sheriff?" Nicks asked. "Anything they have in common, like a religion, or where they worked?"

Mickens slid over a file folder he had on his desk. "I figured you'd ask," he said, opening it up. "We did a complete analysis on the victims, as a group. Here's the rundown..." He read from the file: "Jordan Washington, fifty-four years old, black, did warehouse work in New Orleans, and lived in Delacroix. He was a Baptist, accordin' to his family. Went missin' twelve years ago. Kathleen Rogers, forty-two years old, white, lived up in Baton Rouge, and was down here visitin' when she disappeared six years ago. Worked as an insurance agent. She was a Methodist. And then we got Joseph Fairbanks—young kid, twenty-two years old, white. College student livin' in New Orleans. No religion. He did originally come from Raceland, though. Brought up there. He disappeared...seventeen years ago."

Mickens closed the folder, then plopped his hands on it. "All three had their hands and feet severed. All three had a capital 'H' carved into their foreheads—least, that's what it looks like."

"Was the woman sexually assaulted?" asked Fielding.

Mickens shrugged. "Hard to tell from the remains. There was definitely an indication of sexual intercourse, though—she had traces of semen in her. But whether it was consensual or not, or even prior to her death, we don't know for sure."

"Sheriff," Nicks said, "did you happen to find any of the severed hands or feet?"

"Well, yeah, actually. That's another little tidbit to the story."

Nicks frowned at him. "Oh, really?"

Mickens reclined in his chair. "Each of the victims had their hands and feet wrapped in burlap bags. The bags were tied to the bodies with a rope."

"Jeezuz." Fielding cringed.

"It's religious," said Nicks with resigned certainty. "Or a cult."

"More than likely, I guess," Mickens admitted.

"How long ago were the bodies found, Sheriff?" Nicks asked.

"The young kid's remains were found about seven years ago. The woman's four years ago, and Mister Washington's just last year."

Nicks turned to Fielding. "Call up Agent Weirdlee. Find out where she is."

"Right," said Fielding. He pulled his smartphone from his belt.

As Fielding contacted Weirdlee, Nicks said to Mickens, "I think we're ready to pay a visit to the boy's father, now. And we'll want to interview the staff at the boy's preschool, too, this week."

"And the daycare," Mickens added. "That's just down the street from the school."

"Good." Nicks nodded.

* * * *

Regina Hawkins' ex-husband, Marcus, lived in the city of Houma, about fifteen miles south of Thibodaux. After first stopping for lunch, the agents drove down there to interview him.

Hawkins lived in a small, one-bedroom apartment located above a convenience store. The agents arrived at his door, accessed via a stairway from the back of the building.

Nicks gave the door a rap.

"Who is it?" came a reply from a man inside.

"FBI," said Nicks. "We're here to speak with Marcus Hawkins."

A pause followed as the man tried to comprehend what he'd just heard. You don't often get a visit from the FBI.

"*Wwhat?*"

"FBI," Nicks repeated. He pulled out his ID, preparing to show it. "We're investigating the disappearance of Mr. Hawkins' son."

"Hold on a minute," said the man.

The agents heard some stumbling around inside before padded footsteps approached the door. The doorknob clicked, turned, and the door opened. On the other side, a bare-chested black man wearing jeans and white socks greeted the two agents.

"Yeah?" the man asked, glancing at the two men and appearing somewhat disoriented. "Whatchu want?"

The wafting scent of marijuana drifted past the doorway.

Nicks showed him his ID. Fielding flipped his own out and did the same.

"I'm Special Agent Nicks, and this is my partner, Agent Fielding," Nicks said. "Are you Marcus Hawkins?"

"Yeah." Hawkins nodded. "That's me."

Nicks noted that Hawkins, his short hair matted in places, appeared to have just gotten out of bed. "We're not interrupting anything are we, Mr. Hawkins?"

"What?" Hawkins said, snarling back at him. "No. I ain't doin' nothin'."

"Good," said Nicks. "May we come in?"

Hawkins glanced back behind him nervously. He turned back to Nicks. "Whatchu want, man? We can do it right here."

Nicks gave him a nod. "Okay." He tucked his ID back into his suit's inside breast pocket, then retrieved a small notepad from the same. "Mister Hawkins," he began, "first, I want to say we're very sorry about your son. We'll do whatever we can to locate him."

Hawkins replied with a lazy shrug, "Yeah, whatever, man."

Nicks went on. "You were with your boy the day he disappeared, correct?"

Hawkins bobbed his head. "I was at the park with him, yeah. I lost track of him for a little bit, though. He was playin' with some of his friends."

"And you were off playin' with some of your friends, is that right?" Fielding asked.

Hawkins leered at him. "I was over by the beer tent, man. So were a lot of other dads, too. What the fuck you want us to do all day, play around with the kiddies?"

Nicks answered his question. "Yeah, actually."

Hawkins snarled. "Is that what ya'll came here for? To bitch me out?"

"No," Nicks said. "We're sorry about your missing son, Mister Hawkins. We're just trying to find out what might have happened to him."

Hawkins shook his head. "Man...we have been through this before. My boy is dead. That's all I know. He done wandered off and got himself killed."

"You seem pretty sure of that," said Fielding.

"Well, what the fuck else happened?" Hawkins replied. "We was right by the river, there. No one seen him goin' nowhere."

"There's another possibility," said Nicks. "He could have gotten picked up."

"Yeah." Hawkins nodded. "The cops said that, too. But who the fuck's gonna take a poor kid outta the bayous and, what, hold him for ransom? We ain't ever had no money."

"There's other reasons kids are abducted," Nicks said.

Hawkins looked directly at him. "Yeah, well, no one took Julien. He's at the bottom of the bayous. Fish food."

Nicks couldn't believe what he just heard. He eyed Hawkins sternly. "Is that what you told your ex-wife, too?"

Hawkins scoffed. "Regina? That dumb bitch? All she ever did was pray to God and say her Hail Marys. Never got us nothin' for it."

"Maybe you coulda supported her a little. Been there for her," said Fielding with an air of contempt. The young FBI agent was a father himself, and Hawkins' attitude was pissing him off.

Hawkins leered at him. "Go fuck yourself. I don't need no lecturin' from you."

"All right," Nicks intervened. "Is there anything you remember about that day, sir, that may give us an idea of where your boy might have been just before he went missing?"

Hawkins shook his head. "Nope. I saw he was off in the corner of the park, there, with a bunch of other kids. That's why I figured he was okay. Hell, the daycare people was there that day, too, doin' their shit with 'em."

"Their shit?" Nicks asked.

"You know—games and shit," Hawkins said. "They had a couple of booths there, too, for 'em. Face paintin', colorin' books—that kinda shit."

"No strangers around that day?" Fielding asked.

Hawkins shrugged. "Not that I remember. How the fuck would I know?"

"You folks ever have a babysitter or anyone else watching your son, Mr. Hawkins?" Nicks asked. "A friend or a relative?"

"Yeah, I guess so. There's a neighborhood girl who used to babysit on the weekends if Regina had to work and the daycare was closed."

"The daycare's open on Saturdays?" Nicks asked.

"About a half day, I guess. They closed on Sundays, though."

"Can you tell us the name of the babysitter?" Fielding asked.

Hawkins rolled his eyes, thinking. "Sara…something, is all I know. Don't know her last name. Regina would know it, though."

"Okay." Nicks nodded.

The back and forth continued for another ten minutes, with Nicks asking about how often any friends or family visited, how well they all got along with Julien, and did the boy ever stay at other peoples' houses, either overnight or longer. The answer to the latter was never. Regina always had her boy home with her for bedtime.

The agents left Marcus Hawkins' apartment by 2:00 PM, and from there they headed back up to Thibodaux. After a quick check-in with Sheriff Mickens, they drove up to Chackbay and their rooms at the Swampy Inn, where they'd rendezvous with Agent Weirdlee when she got there.

* * * *

The religious demographics of Louisiana are diverse in their Christian heritage, with Protestants and Catholics composing of close to ninety percent of all those affiliated with a religion. In the New Orleans area, meanwhile, it's said that approximately fifteen percent of the population there follows some form of the local voodoo religion, aptly referred to as "New Orleans Voodoo."

It was not that difficult, therefore, for Joanna Weirdlee to find others who practiced the belief as Marie Corbet did—she being a spiritual woman whose faith alone guided her, rather than any genuine, gifted intuition. Finding authentic, empowered casters and seers, on the other hand, proved to be much more of a challenge. In the end, Weirdlee perceived just one in the city. And that woman, the Haitian-born Angelea Diviner, refused to see her, declaring the witch from Salem a non-believer and a heretic.

It was a fruitless journey for Weirdlee, who drove back to Chackbay with no more knowledge of the region and its players than when she'd started out that day. Still, she knew she had to see the old voodoo queen, Zarah Devillier, in the woman's own domain. That was always the visiting witch's task: You go to the venerable queen, not she to you. And so, for Weirdlee, certain preparations had to be made. For the Salem witch would not be visiting Devillier as a mere federal agent.

She would instead be calling on her as a fellow sister of the Craft.

Arriving at the Swampy Inn, Weirdlee noticed her colleagues' rented black Ford Taurus in the parking lot. She would have to confer with Nicks and Fielding about their case before preparing for her journey into the Grand Bayou, so she met them first at their room.

The Swampy Inn hosted eighteen rooms—hardly enough to justify anything larger than a small cafe for dining. The three agents quickly arranged to meet there, where they'd review everything over coffee and tea.

The cafe was staffed by a single person—a young woman on this day—who acted as the server, bartender, and cook all in one. The woman, named Tracy, took the men's order of coffee and Weirdlee's order of tea, and returned with their drinks in quick fashion. She then went off to tend to the small bar area off to right side of the place, where two men sat. The cafe on this late Sunday afternoon was otherwise empty of patrons.

This marked just the second time Weirdlee had been partnered with Nicks and Fielding—who themselves had only been partners since that previous spring—and so the colleagues still felt a degree of unfamiliarity with each other as a team. Weirdlee, in particular, had set herself apart from the two men by oftentimes going it alone on her assignments. Nicks found this habit of hers troubling, and he genuinely worried about her safety. She was not only a beautiful woman—an inviting target for any depraved individual—but also very much new to working in the field as an FBI agent. Her first assignment with them, in fact, was her very first in the field, having previously been assigned to International Operations at the J. Edgar Hoover Building in Washington D.C. For whatever reason, Assistant Director Ledds had wanted her role to change at the Bureau. And so now she was "out in the wild" with them, and very much exposed to the less savory nature of society. Some might call Nicks a male chauvinist for feeling the way he did about his female colleague. And some might be right about that. But deep inside, he also had another feeling entirely coming into play.

He was growing quite fond of her.

"The more I think about the spread of the park that day," he said to his two colleagues as they sat at a small, round table inside the cafe, "the more I think how easy it would have been for that boy to just walk off on his own, or get taken from there."

Fielding gave Nicks a curious look. "You're really goin' towards that angle, and not him fallin' in the river?"

Nicks eyed his coffee. "Yup. That kid may have only been four, but he was brought up in that area—just up the road, in fact. I think it's pretty unlikely he wouldn't know not to go near the water."

"Maybe a croc dragged him in," Fielding quipped, before correcting himself, "I mean, alligator."

Nicks winced, considering the idea. "Mmm, somebody would have heard that. Even if the kid didn't scream, the 'gator would have been thrashing around."

Fielding shrugged. "Yeah. Maybe. But there was a lotta shit goin' on there that day."

"There's something else," Weirdlee cut in.

The two men looked at her.

"I'm a little troubled by something."

"What's that?" Nicks asked.

Weirdlee sipped her tea. "So far, I'm not seeing the boy with the other three they found."

Nicks, misunderstanding her, agreed. "Yeah, that's true. He'd be the only little kid, if he were connected to the others. But we haven't found very many bodies yet, and there's dozens of missing kids in this state."

Weirdlee shook her head. "No, that's not what I meant."

The two men looked at each other curiously.

"I can't *see* him," she went on. "I can't see him with the others."

Fielding gave her a screwy look. "Aww, what're ya talkin' about—some kinda hocus-pocus?" He looked at Nicks, jabbing a finger at Weirdlee. "I told ya, partner. She's got that witchcraft thing inside of her."

Nicks waved him off. "All right, hold up." Then he said to Weirdlee, "What do you mean by not seeing him?"

Weirdlee frumped back in her chair. She shook her head. "I know you don't believe," she said, and she glanced at both men. "Why do you think Mr. Ledds put me with you two? Do you honestly think I'm some kind of hotshot investigator? Do you think I'm a great interviewer? Or maybe I'm just good at finding rooms for us to stay at."

"I'm not actually sure why Ledds put you with us," Nicks replied. "I thought maybe for training."

Weirdlee scoffed. "Training? Really? Is that all?"

"Maybe," said Fielding.

She leered at him. "Then in that case I would just get a partner—just like Nicks got *you*."

"Hey—wait a minute," Fielding protested. "You tellin' me I need trainin'?"

"*I'm* telling you you do," Nicks cut in. "Now let's knock it off and get back to where we were."

Weirdlee gave Fielding a cool glare before continuing where she'd let off.

"As I was saying," she said, "I have certain abilities that even I don't fully understand. But I *do* know—and so does Mr. Ledds—that I'm most often right about what I sense and see. That's one of the reasons he recruited me."

"A witch…" Fielding muttered incredulously, staring at Weirdlee. Since their first meeting, he'd suspected that something was very different about the woman. He'd told Nicks as much. Then, after learning that her hometown was none other than Salem, Massachusetts, he simply put two-and-two together and added it up on his own. He looked again at Nicks and cracked a smile. "See? What I been sayin' all along; we got us a real-live, honest-to-goodness witch."

Nicks gave him a tired look before turning his attention back to Weirdlee. "Look," he said to her with an air of doubt, "I tend to think of things a little more reasonably. I'm not going to dismiss anything if I think it can help us somewhere down the road, but as far as any psychic ability goes, I've heard both sides, and I have to tell you, I'm skeptical about anyone who says she can see the future or tell somebody their fortune."

"I'm not a fortune teller," Weirdlee corrected him. "I don't do magic tricks, and I'm not here to amaze anyone with my intuitive abilities. I'm here to help solve a case, just like you and Daniel are."

Fielding shrugged. "Why you gotta use our formal names all the time? Can't I just be Danny and he be Sam? Or is there some kinda witchy thing goin' on with that?"

She looked back at him plainly. "What...*ever*."

"So what about the kid?" Nicks asked, getting back to their investigation. "Why is there something wrong if you can't see him with the others?"

"To me," she replied, "it just means that there's no connection there."

"So," Fielding surmised, "he coulda been dragged off by a 'gator."

Weirdlee hunched her shoulders. "Maybe."

Nicks leaned back in his seat. He was uncomfortable with Weirdlee's paranormally-based suggestion, and had a different idea of his own.

"I still think anything's possible at this point," he said. "But here, check this out..."

He took both his own coffee cup and Fielding's and lined them up, one behind the other, and then grabbed Weirdlee's tea cup and added it at the end. "Make pretend these are the booths or tents at the park that day." He grabbed a pair of salt and pepper shakers at the center of the table then and set them to the left of the line of cups, positioning them at spaces between the cups. "These are some trees." Lastly, he put a spoon at the end of the line of cups, to the left of the shakers. "Here's some kids playing in the park."

With his jerry-rigged model complete, he put his hand off to his right and made a fist. "Now, here's Mr. Hawkins, the father of the missing boy," he said, shaking his fist. "And the kids, over there, are playing at the far end of the park."

"Which he can't see from where he is," Weirdlee guessed, eyeing the setup.

"Right," Nicks confirmed. "But he told us earlier today that he saw his son playing with some other kids, off in the corner of the park. That's why he figured everything was okay."

"So, he fibbed about seein' him," Fielding said. "So what? Maybe he's just coverin' his ass."

"Maybe so," said Nicks, drawing in his hand.

"Or," supposed Weirdlee, "the layout could have been different than here. You're just guessing about the scale and such."

Nicks pointed at her. "That's true, too."

"So," asked Fielding, "what are ya sayin', partner? That he coulda been involved in his own son's disappearance?"

Nicks drummed his fingers on the table. "Not sure. But it's possible. He's got a terrible attitude, I know that."

Fielding sneered. "The man don't love his boy. No guy who talks like he did loves his boy. All he cared about was not gettin' blamed."

Nicks sighed and leaned back in his seat. "We can't rule out anything, like I said." He took up his coffee cup and sipped from it. "What about you?" he asked Weirdlee. "You interview those two women today?"

"Ms. Corbet," Weirdlee replied—flaring the *aire* at the end of her name. "She had nothing to offer. She never did, unfortunately."

"What do you mean by that?" Nicks asked.

"She's a fake. Just a wishful thinker."

Fielding sat back, smiling and amazed. "Holy...you mean you don't believe *everyone's* got the power?"

"It's true," said Weirdlee. "Ms. Corbet has her faith, and she's true to it. And she believes she has the gift. But all she's really done is made a lot of people believe she can help them, without actually doing anything at all."

"The police said she helped 'em out," Fielding said. "I know it's a bunch of—" he looked at Weirdlee. "You now what I mean."

"She means well," said Weirdlee. "And the police probably interpreted her so-called visions in just the way they wanted to see them. But that's all it ever was. That's all it ever could be."

Nicks wasn't surprised.

"What about the other woman?" he asked. "The old lady?"

Weirdlee sipped her tea. "I haven't spoken with her yet. I'm going to see her tonight, actually."

Fielding sat back. "Tonight?"

"Where?" Nicks asked.

"At her home."

"Out in the swamp?" asked Fielding.

"That's where she lives," Weirdlee replied matter-of-factly.

"Oh, no you're not," said Nicks. "Not alone. One of us is going with you."

Weirdlee leered at him. "Don't you tell me—" she started. Then she changed her tone. "I can handle this, Samuel. I need to talk to her alone."

"Why?" he asked her.

"Because..." Weirdlee answered, pausing. "There are things that I can learn from her, but only if it's us two, alone. She won't open up with an audience in the room."

"It's not worth it," said Fielding. "Too dangerous for ya."

Weirdlee shook her head. "She wouldn't do anything to me. The detective we talked to earlier said as much himself. She and her sons are strictly small-time hustlers."

Nicks frowned at that. "There's always a first time for big time, Special Agent."

"Sam," Weirdlee urged, "Let me do this. I *need* to do it. She won't tell us anything if you or Daniel are standing there right next to me."

"How do you know that?" asked Fielding.

She looked at him directly. "Because I know her."

"Excuse me?" Nicks said, surprised.

She shook her head at him. "I mean I know of her *kind*. I know where she's coming from, Samuel. We're like...sisters of the cloth. Is that the right term?"

Fielding shrugged, still unsettled by the matter. "I dunno 'bout this..."

"Are you planning to let her know you're coming?" Nicks asked. "Or are you just party-crashing?"

"I'll call first, if she's got a phone. I'll ask the captain for her number. If not, I'll crash."

Nicks considered things for a moment while Weirdlee kept her eyes on him, anticipating.

Fielding, meanwhile, wasn't nearly as undecided on the matter.

He said to Nicks, "You're not seriously considering letting her go it alone, are ya?"

Nicks eyed him, not answering. Then he looked once more to Weirdlee. "All right," he said to her. "You go." Weirdlee's eyes lit up before he continued more sternly, "But you be sure and make it clear to the old woman and her boys that me and agent Fielding, here, know where you are. We know where, and we know when. And we'll be expecting you back at a certain time, too."

Weirdlee chuckled at that. "I sure will, dad."

"You're crazy," Fielding said to Nicks. "Lettin' her go like that."

"We'll be waiting," Nicks replied to him. He looked back at Weirdlee. "Two hours. Total. You get out there. You chat. You get back."

Weirdlee nodded gratefully. "Understood."

~ | ~

-5-

The Lair of Zarah Devillier

It was dinnertime when Zarah Devillier and her sons pulled into the driveway, arriving at the home of the man she'd been god-worshipping for the better part of twenty-something years.

Paul Basil—or Marcel Unate' as he was better known by some—lived in a small, white, two-story house on a dirt road coming off of Route 631, just south of the town of Paradis. Basil had lived there for very many years. The place itself was run-down, and thick weeds overgrew a flat, open yard all around.

Zarah left her son, Lucien's, old VW Beetle and walked ahead with a stilted gait as she approached her long-time lover's front porch. There, Paul Basil sat in a rocking chair, buck knife in-hand, whittling away at a long, slender stick. The man—dark skinned and muscular, and younger looking than his forty-something years—looked up at Zarah with a bored expression. *Oh*, how he had tired of that wrinkled, broken-down wretch's visits.

"What you doin' here, old woman?" he asked her.

She smiled at him, showing off what remained of her yellowed, worn teeth. Their days of lovemaking had actually ended many years before, after Basil had woken up one day to notice that his once-lovely priestess was getting to be quite the ugly hag, while he himself could still entice women as young as teenagers into his bed with his sinister charms. These days, the old lady stopped by every now and then, mostly to remind him of their past years together—years when she used to be very important to him. She still wanted to be important to him, too—even if only to help him find others who might satisfy his wanton desires, and so in that way make him pleased with her.

"Come to see ya, let ya know I got somes girls for ya," she said to him. She gave a nod behind her. "Ya boys are here."

Basil stopped his whittling. He set his knife and half-whittled stick on his lap and eyed Zarah coolly. "Tell me about the witch," he said to her.

She laughed wickedly, slapping her frail hand to her lap. "No playin' wit' youz, Marcel," she said breezily. She looked back at the car, where her sons had gotten out but stayed put where they were. "You ain't gonna say 'Hi' to your boys?" she asked Basil. "Theyz come out here to see their pappy."

Basil cast his eyes to the young men there. Lucian, the oldest of the three, stood by the driver's-side door appearing indignant. Korram, the second oldest, stood at the far side of the car. He looked down submissively when his father eyed him. Damon, the youngest, meanwhile, was a special case. He just stared off in an empty gaze, the same as always. Just as Weirdlee had seen them earlier, all three men wore their hair in dreadlocks, each in various states of unkempt repair.

Their father looked back at Zarah. "Just tell me about the witch."

Zarah sighed. "Always business..." she muttered.

The old woman made her way up the porch steps then—five in all—to get onto the porch. She stepped closer to Basil, then slowly lowered herself down to sit on the floor, cross-legged, by his side. Settled there, she looked at him with sad eyes, and said to him in her old, crackly voice, "I miss you..."

"Get on with it, Zarah," he said in return.

She licked her lips, contemplating her words.

"Girl is from Salem," she said, a tinge of hurt in her voice. "She comes with Feds."

Basil sneered at her. "I *know* that, old woman. I can sense that much. What kind of a witch is she? What do you feel from her?"

Zarah laughed lazily. "You worry..."

"Shut up," he snapped at her. "Tell me what you know."

She leered back at him, finally bothered by his ill treatment of her. "She a hedge," she replied. "She ain't nothin' to go worryin' on. She got some powers, but no steerin' in her. She got no formal learnin'."

"Is she a seer?"

"No."

Basil eased back in his chair upon hearing that, mulling things over in his mind.

"She a deceiver, though," Zarah added. "Likes to play tricks on people's eyes. She a healer, too."

Basil frowned, entirely unimpressed by the latter trait. "All Anglo witches are healers," he said with a sneer. "That is why they are weak."

Zarah laughed again. She said through her chuckling, "You can have her, Marcel. Take her to the bayous."

"No!" he snapped back. "I've got other plans for her."

Zarah lost her sense of humor and looked at her former lover, seriously. "Whatchu mean, other plans?"

Basil eyed her coldly. "She'll be coming to see you tonight. She'll be asking questions. You tell her to come to me."

"*Yes…*" Zarah replied, her eyes flashing. "For the spirits."

"No," Basil corrected her. "For *me*. You tell her that only I can give her what she truly needs. Only I can make her a complete woman."

Zarah looked at him in despair. "You," she whispered, "want her for your own?"

"She *will* be my own," he insisted. "You tell her that she will never be a whole witch until I give her that power. Only then will she see all that she needs to see. Only then will she be complete."

Zarah stared at Basil as it all sank into her mind. It would be her task, of all people, to deliver the witch into his possession. And then she, the witch, would be his next lover, as well. And perhaps even his bride.

"Don't forgets 'bout me, Marcel," she whispered to him, her heart aching. "Please…"

He looked back at her coldly. "Just do as you are told."

* * * *

Joanna Weirdlee busied herself in her darkened room at the inn, prepping herself for her trip into the bayous. Gone was the modern, professional appearance of a federal agent. In its place, the Salem witch wore a more traditional, full-length brown pattern skirt, stitched together by her own hands, and a white cotton blouse, finely embroidered about the neck and sleeves. She wore brown leather boots on her feet, and on her wrists she wore a pair of fine silver bracelets, each imbued with its own charms. Around her neck, she'd draped her usual pentacle necklace, and, on this night, she also wore a second necklace with an egg-shaped silver amulet. Her long, dark red hair fell naturally behind her shoulders.

The room itself was decorated for ceremony: Four candles—one green, one yellow, one red, one blue—were set on her dresser, each one lit. Beside them all, to the right, was set a deck of tarot cards, faced down except for three of them, which were laid out in a vertical line to the right of the deck. The three cards were the Seven of Swords, a reversed Justice, and the Moon. Several slim, tall white candles were set about the room in different places for added illumination, as well. Finally then, she had set before her dresser's mirror a thick white candle that represented the spirits, and which gave light to any reflections there.

Weirdlee checked her looks in the dresser mirror, then went over to her bed to gather up some other things she'd need for her journey. A black cloth pouch lay there, filled with soil from her hometown. Her Bureau-issued Glock-23 lay there as well, kept in its holster. Weirdlee took the pouch and tucked it into a pocket sewn into the hip of her dress, where she also kept her smartphone. She grabbed the pistol then and clipped its holster to the left side of her skirt's belt, with the weapon's grip facing forward.

Finally, she went to the closet and fetched a brown cotton vest, this being decorated with fanciful embroidered designs of trees and flowers. She put it on, and checked to ensure that it at least partially hid her holstered weapon.

A knock on her door got her attention.

"Yes?"

"Agent Weirdlee. It's me, Agent Fielding," said her colleague on the other side of the door.

"Just a minute," she replied.

She hurried over to her bed's nightstand and turned on a lamp there. Then she went over to her dresser and blew out all of her ritual candles. She walked across the room, then, blowing out the other white candles along the way, before finally coming to the door. She unlocked it and opened it.

A smiling Fielding stood there, still dressed in his suit and tie. His eyes lit up at the sight of his pretty colleague.

"Wow," he marveled. "You look fantastic."

She smiled back at him. "Why, thank you, sir." She waved him inside. "Come on in."

She stepped back into the room, and Fielding followed her inside. He looked about the small room, right away smelling the candles.

"You been burnin' somethin'?" he asked her.

"It's candles," she said as she returned to her dresser. She grabbed the candles and showed them to him.

He nodded as he came to the foot of the bed. "Ahh, I see." Then he looked at the dresser, there to see the tarot cards laid out.

Even knowing Weirdlee to be a practicing witch, it still hadn't hit him until he actually saw, there before him, the tools of her trade.

Weirdlee asked him, "Is Samuel ready to go?"

"Uh, yeah, just about," he replied. He pointed to the cards. "You really believe in that stuff, huh?"

She looked back over her shoulder at him as she put her candles away in a dresser drawer. "Of course I do. You should, too."

"Yeah..." Fielding said thoughtfully, eying the cards. "Well, what're they tellin' ya about tonight?"

She patted her hands on her skirt, then approached the cards. As she picked up the three facing cards and put them back with the deck, she replied, "They're telling me to watch my back, and to be careful." She turned around to look at Fielding directly. "And don't be trustful of those I meet."

He stared back at her. "Shit," he said under his breath. "Maybe we should go with ya, after all."

57

She smiled at him. "Don't worry about me, Daniel." Then she lifted her vest to show off her holstered sidearm. "I've got both faith and firepower coming along with me."

Fielding smiled and laughed at that. "Good thinkin'— God and guns is a good combo." Then he remembered something. "Oh," he said, and he reached into his suit pocket to retrieve a small photograph. "Got a picture of the boy, here."

Weirdlee placed her tarot cards in the same dresser drawer she'd put the candles, then she came up to Fielding to take the photograph. "Thanks," she said. She slid the photo into the sewn pocket where she'd also put her cloth pouch and phone. Then she started for the door. "Shall we be off, sir?"

Fielding turned to follow her. "Sure thing, partner."

The two of them met Nicks in the parking and all three hopped into their rented Taurus. Nicks drove, taking them out of the little town and on over to the Bayou L'Ours, where they crossed the river bridge there before turning into a driveway and arriving at a parking area belonging to the river's east bank docks. There, the agents were met by the owner of a local tour company called The Bayous Experience, who'd been notified by Nicks beforehand that they were coming by that evening.

"I don't normally rent out boats to folks, 'less'n either me or one of my boys is in 'em, too," said owner Morgan Husk to Nicks after greeting the agents. Husk was a tall, potbellied man in his late fifties. He wore a straw fedora on his balding head and chewed on a toothpick as he spoke. "But...I guess considerin' things, I can let some G-Men take one out for a little ride."

"G-Woman," Nicks corrected him, jabbing a thumb to Weirdlee. "Agent Weirdlee, here, will be out for a couple of hours."

"Two hours, huh?" Husk said. He looked at his watch, which currently read 7:15 PM. "It'll be dark in a little bit." He glanced at Weirdlee, and then to Nicks. "You sure you want her goin' out there and then come back in the dark? That's kinda dangerous."

"How big is the boat she'll be usin'?" asked Fielding.

Husk pointed off behind him, toward the docks. "I got a boat with an outboard that I use for taxiin' around. She can use that." He looked at Weirdlee. "Where ya headed?"

She replied, "The, uh, Grand Bayou—the river junction there?"

Husk mulled things over in his head. "Hmm...that's about two miles, one way. That's a lot of gas. I'll have to charge ya for that."

"You got a light or a lamp she can use to stay on course after it gets dark?" Nicks asked.

Husk nodded. "Yep. I'll toss that into the deal, no extra fee."

"How much is it for the boat, then?" asked Fielding.

Husk looked back at the river. He toyed with the toothpick in his mouth as he tallied up the time and expenses. "Two hours...four mile trip...half of it upstream...let's see...uh, I guess about eighty bucks 'ill do it."

"*Eighty bucks?*" Fielding complained.

"Yeah. Eighty bucks," said Husk. "And that's a bargain. You tellin' me the federal government can't afford an eighty dollar expense?"

"We'll pay it," said Nicks. "You'll take a card, right?"
"Sure."

Husk led the FBI agents to the riverside. There, they came to a small dock that ran along the bank. The dock was just wide enough to keep the boats tied up there, away from the shore. Four boats in all were docked there—two fanboats, a larger boat with a swivel seat at the bow, and

Husk's little flat-bottomed "taxi" boat. He walked along the dock to get to that one. The green-colored boat, the agents saw, had an outboard motor attached to the back. This was a small, four stroke, 2-horsepower affair, probably sufficient for short trips, and would probably get Weirdlee to her destination in good enough time. As the boat was small, it rested in the water much lower than the dock itself, which was high enough to be level with the larger boats there. Husk took Weirdlee's hand and helped her into the little craft. He joined her in the boat then, where he showed her how to operate the outboard. After a quick tutoring, he started the engine for her, then got himself out of the craft and back onto the dock.

"I'll fetch that spotlight for ya," he said to her. Then off he went.

Nicks came over to the boat and knelt down beside it. He put a hand out to Weirdlee, and she took it in her own.

"Be careful out there, Agent Weirdlee," he said to her, gently gasping her hand. "I want to see you back here healthy, okay?" Then he smiled at her. "I'm kind of getting used to you, you know," he said with a wink.

She returned his smile. He was much more handsome when he smiled, she thought, and she wished he did it more often. She whispered to him, "You're sweet."

She turned then and looked out onto the river, off to the south where she'd be heading. "I'll be all right, though, Sam," she said. "I won't be too long."

Husk returned with a spotlight—a small, portable lamp with a spring clamp extension on it for mounting. "Here ya go," he said to Weirdlee as he knelt down next to Nicks. He reached down with it and handed it to Weirdlee. She took it. "Just clamp it to the side of the boat on your way back," he said, "and point it on ahead of ya."

"Thanks," she said, setting it on the floor of the boat.

The helpful owner then hoisted himself back up to his feet and untied the boat from the dock. He tossed the line into the craft. "Good luck," he said to her.

She smiled. "Thanks again."

Nicks stood back up. He was joined then by Fielding, who stood by his side as the two men watched Weirdlee power-up the boat and then maneuver it out onto the river. She appeared to have no problem handling the craft, hinting of her experience at managing such a thing before.

After she'd gone a good ways upstream, Husk turned to the two agents, saying to Nicks, "We can go into my office and take care of our business, gents."

Nicks kept watching Weirdlee, though, as she passed further into the distance.

Fielding gave him a swat on the arm. "Come on," he said to him. "She'll be back in no time."

Nicks eyed the little boat for a moment longer, still, before turning to look off at the other boats moored at the dock.

"How much to take out another one of your boats?"

* * * *

Weirdlee kept the boat throttled at a leisurely cruising speed, cutting into the slow moving opposing current. The banks along either side of the river were a thick tangle of aging, overhanging trees and gnarly vines, with tree roots and branches poking out from the water in places, so she steered the boat along the middle wherever and whenever she could. Her eyes wandered about the scenery as she motored along, too, gazing at the wilderness all around her. And over the hum of the boat's motor, she listened as best she could to the calls and chirps of nature's creatures, and to the delicately churning sounds of the water moving beneath her little craft.

When most people came to this region, and they looked out at the forests here, listening to the sounds of nature and feeling the hot air caressing their faces, they distinguished nothing in particular outside of the wilderness as a whole. The trees, to them, were not individuals, but rather parts of a much larger, more intimidating mass of living, breathing nature.

The bayous.

For Weirdlee, though, each tree or bush she beheld was, on its own, more than just a mere living plant amongst many. It was a *being*, set upon this earth by nature, and very special in its own place in time.

Divine, it was, on earth and into heaven.

Weirdlee understood this presence well. She was an unusual sort of person in her own right, having always felt much more at ease in the company of nature than with others of her own kind. With friendships rare in her childhood, and parents who considered their daughter "disturbed" in a fashion, Weirdlee had led a mostly reclusive life, with only her recruitment into the FBI and her having to uphold to its binding obligations keeping her from a more solitary, secluded life. Even with that, though, she still felt very much alone in her beliefs and insecurities.

The shadows of the forest hung heavily upon the water as the low-lying sun gradually slipped behind the unseen western horizon. There was a peacefulness out there, Weirdlee sensed, that extended far beyond any measure of human perception. Nature remained, no matter how polluted by man, untarnished in its presence and purpose.

She closed her eyes, and then took in a deep, intoxicating breath of fresh, warm air. She listened intently for the voices that would occasionally come to her, guiding her along her life's path. On this evening, though, so far, there were none.

Opening her eyes, she saw just ahead of her a small islet protruding from the center of the river. She stayed to the left of this and continued on her way. Something in the air chilled her then as she followed another turn in the river, bending once more to the right. The peaceful presence, once so reassuring to her, seemed to give way to a more troubling sensation.

She was, she sensed, being watched.

Zarah Devillier's property was close by, she estimated. She slowed up then, lowering the throttle, before pulling out her smartphone from her dress pocket. Tapping over to a GPS map, she quickly checked her position. A left turn into an inlet cove was just up ahead of her. This would lead, after just a short distance, directly to Devillier's property.

Weirdlee motored ahead slowly as a sense of foreboding crept over her. Spirits, she sensed, lay trapped in the realm of dusk, and were trying to call out to her. She could barely perceive them in her mind's eye, but they were there. Tormented souls, they were, desperate and wretched. But were they inviting her to come closer to them, or begging she leave right away? She could not discern.

Finally arriving at the inlet's opening, Weirdlee killed the boat's motor, allowing, momentarily, the little craft to drift back with the current.

She stared off into the inlet. The shadows there seemed strangely more dark and heavier. She clutched onto the amulet that hung from her neck, then, and whispered a guarded affirmation.

"I am blessed and protected on my journey..."

Her gaze remained on the inlet for a few seconds more, her mind searching for helpful signs, but still envisioning only the voiceless spirits, all of whom seemed more distant, now, as if having been left behind. Her boat, meanwhile, being led off by the current as it was, presently neared the tangled riverbank. She broke her gaze, noticing this, and then powered up the motor to maneuver back away from the shore. Moving ahead at a slow speed then, Weirdlee navigated into the inlet cove.

The shadows deepened. Her eyes wandered about her dreary surroundings—the ancient, towering trees, their branches and viney entanglements reaching out over the inlet's banks, appearing like ghosts reaching out from the blackness. She listened, too, to the chattery creatures of the approaching night, barely perceptible under the drone of her boat's motor, as they told the story of an enduring sadness that rested there.

Treachery. Hopeless despair.

Innocence lost.

Ahead of her then, Weirdlee saw the inlet opening up into the more oval-shaped cove itself. She knew from her earlier study of a satellite map that Zarah's abode would be on the far side of this, set deep within the woods.

She motored on.

After another minute, she perceived the far bank of the cove through the deepening night air. There, she spied a small, weatherworn and broken dock, appearing just big enough to accommodate a couple of smaller-sized boats. One boat—a small one like her own but lighter in color— already lay moored there. As she came nearer to the dock then, she saw that the boat was tied to a wooden mooring post that also doubled as one of the little dock's support beams. She throttled down her small craft, then killed the motor while turning the boat to port, thus letting it drift purposefully toward the end of the dock. Taking hold of her own mooring line, she waited for the boat to make contact before leaping onto the dock. She secured the boat line to the mooring post.

Standing on the dock, Weirdlee took a moment to glance about at her surroundings. At first, she saw little more than dense forest growth all around her. Then, at the head of the dock, she spied a thin path that led into the wilderness. She stepped closer to the path's beginning, and there noticed an old, red gasoline can set off to the side. The scent of its contents wafted in the warm early evening air.

Time to check in.

She fetched her smartphone from her dress pocket. Navigating to her texting app, she tapped a message to Nicks.

Arrived at location. Going to her house now. ttyl

Not waiting for a response, Weirdlee tapped off her phone and tucked it back into her pocket. It would be the last time she would make contact with Nicks, she knew, until after her rendezvous with Devillier—however that turned out to be.

Taking in a breath then, she started off down the heavily wooded path.

As she walked along the shadowy way, a creepy sensation, growing with each passing step, forewarned the FBI agent of some manner of treachery ahead of her. She knew, already, that Zarah Devillier was sickly in her mind, and that her boys were in all likelihood similarly corrupted. She hoped then that this foreboding feeling was merely a manifestation of that.

A couple hundred yards into the bog, Weirdlee discerned the outline of what surely had to be Devillier's home. This was a tall, narrow, box-like structure, with a steep-angled, triangular roof that sagged, like a tired nag, from years of neglect and disrepair. As she approached still closer, she slowed her pace. Her eyes remained fixed on the dilapidated home, and her mind became taken up by the myriad thoughts that filled her subconsciousness.

Weirdlee's faith allowed for every living person to live out many different realities, all with different outcomes depending on the various decisions one would make as she passed through time. For spiritual people such as Weirdlee, these outcomes could be perceived, or glimpsed, as visions while awake, or dreams if in slumber.

Weirdlee's gaze, quite unintentionally, brought her into a hazy, dream-like trance as she stood there. The old house she looked upon, with its gray, wooden siding presently peeled and flaking, and its front porch broken and rotted in places, conjured up images in the young agent's mind. The landscape, she saw, began to change all around the dwelling. The property's tall, viney trees morphed into a rich assortment of maple, oak, and birch. The flat, swampy land of the bayous grew into a sloping hillside covered with a carpet of ferns and newly fallen autumn leaves. And all of this, surrounded by a thick, New England forest.

Yes...she was home again!

Her gaze moved then to the left side of the old porch, where she saw an elderly woman sitting in a wooden rocking chair. Much to the agent's surprise, she saw that the woman wore a dress not dissimilar to the one she herself presently wore. The old woman's long, scraggly hair, gray with age, fell wildly behind her shoulders, and she stared off into the wilderness, unmoving.

To Weirdlee, this woman's worn, weary expression appeared profoundly lonely, as if saddened by some great emptiness trapped inside of her soul.

She looked *so* old. Far beyond her years.

Weirdlee's heart sank inside of her. For she understood, then, that this old woman she beheld—this frail, empty soul, drained of all life and vitality—was none other than herself. One of many possible lives she would live. One of many possible outcomes. And Weirdlee, in this particular life, had remained alone throughout all her years, and had grown old in complete solitude. She lived in the deep forest, a lonely hermit in a wilderness rarely visited by others. And there, Weirdlee perceived, she would pass on into the hereafter, long forgotten by all she had left behind.

The loud creaking of a door swinging open interrupted Weirdlee's vision. She snapped out of her daze, and brought her attention to the front porch and then to the front door of Devillier's home. There, from inside, an old woman came forth. At first, Weirdlee took the woman to be herself again. But after quickly shaking off that illusion, she saw instead the same woman she'd seen earlier that day at the Bayou L'Ours.

It was Zarah Devillier.

The old woman wore a raggedy, plain black dress. Her face, neck, and arms were all caked in a layer of gray, half-dried mud. Her stringy hair, likewise, was matted with the stuff.

Zarah grinned wide. She extended her arms out to either side, and she greeted Weirdlee in a loud, crackly voice.

"Joanna Osborne! Welcome to my humble home!"

Weirdlee looked back at her, lost for words.

Zarah pointed off behind the agent then, and said to her, "Meet my precious boys. They are *so* glad you've come to visit us."

Remembering her peril, Weirdlee turned to look back behind her. There, she saw all three brothers standing just a few yards away. The youngest, Damon, simply stared off at the ground. The two eldest, however—Lucien and Korram—held shotguns in their hands, and each had his weapon trained on the witch from Salem.

Weirdlee's heart raced.

Remember yourself, she told herself, even as the two armed men laughed—hungrily.

She turned back to face Zarah. "I'm a federal agent," she said to her tensely. "My partners know I'm here."

Zarah shook her head at that, and she smirked at the agent. "Theyz can't save you now, witch. Here in this place, you belong to *me*." Then she jabbed a finger at her sons. "And to thems."

She laughed wickedly.

It was, Weirdlee feared, just as Marie Corbet had warned her.

Why didn't she listen to her?

But she's not a true seer!

Weirdlee tried to calm her rattled nerves. She swallowed anxiously as she stared at Zarah, but for the life of her, she could not focus. Her faith, such as it was, was all she had with her.

I am blessed and protected on my journey...

And she prayed for the spirits to deliver her from her terrible circumstance.

Please...!

Zarah coughed heavily, then cleared her throat. She blinked her eyes, recovering, and then shook her head at her visitor dismissively before looking off to her sons and gesturing with a hand for them to lower their weapons.

"Don't be so rude, boys," she said to them. "That's not how we treat our guests."

The old woman turned and walked back to the front door's entrance. She looked again to Weirdlee, and with the wave of her hand, beckoned the agent to follow. "Come, girl. Let's talk inside. You'll be safe." And she grinned. "I's promise."

Weirdlee watched Zarah re-enter her home. She turned around, then, to look back at the woman's sons behind her.

All three, she saw, had begun to walk off, back in the direction of the cove.

With a sigh of relief, the Salem witch turned back to the house, and, after a moment of consideration, followed Zarah inside.

Zarah Devillier's home was dark and uninviting. In the living area that Weirdlee entered into, there had at one time been two windows located to either side of the room to light up the place in daytime. These, however, had been boarded up by Zarah herself a long time ago. The hardwood floor was unfinished, unwashed, and stained with years of grime. On the left side of the room, a wooden stairway led up to the second floor. Next to the foot of these stairs, an open doorway led to a small kitchen. A small square wooden table took up the center of the living room, and, upon this, an oil lamp—the room's only illumination—was set and centered. Zarah presently sat in a chair at the table's opposite side, facing the front door, awaiting her guest.

"Come, child," she said to Weirdlee. "Sit with me here."

Weirdlee approached the table. While doing so, she glanced about the room, trying to make out what few details she could discern in the darkness. At the room's far end, she saw a potbelly stove with a pile of roughly-chopped wood stacked up by its side. Hanging on the right wall and set side-by-side, she saw two pictures, both painted landscapes of some unknown countryside—probably bought at a Salvation Army store, she figured. The floor sounded hollow to her as she walked along, as if the floorboards lacked any supporting base beneath them. More than likely, she guessed, the living quarters, along all of the home's most treasured valuables, were kept on the second floor, above any potential floodwaters.

There was something else about the house, as well: Weirdlee sensed, if only vaguely, that it had witnessed some terrible crime in its time.

She arrived at the table.

There, a brown leather pouch was set nearby the old woman, and a stack of tarot cards lay next to that. Three chairs took up the remaining sides—left, right, and nearside. She chose the chair to her right, and went to sit there.

Zarah put up a hand, pointing to the nearside chair whose back faced the front door. "Not there, dear?" she beckoned.

Weirdlee glanced at the chair, then off to the doorway she'd come in through. "I'd rather not have any doors behind me, if you don't mind," she said as she took her seat.

Zarah chuckled. "Good girl. Don't blame ya for that." She patted the table with her wrinkled hands. "I'd get ya some tea, but I knows you ain't stayin' long, anyways."

Weirdlee eyed her host, whom she knew—unlike Corbet—was the real deal.

"So," she said to her, "you know my birth name."

Zarah grinned wide. "Bet your ass I do. I seen you comin' a long time ago. I knew youz comin' here."

"Oh really?" Weirdlee replied, an eyebrow raised. "And do you know why I'm here?"

Zarah scoffed, as if she couldn't be bothered with such a pesky, mundane matter. "Stupid shit. Whatchu think I do for youz, girl? You want somethin' I ain't gots."

Weirdlee reached into her dress pocket to retrieve the photo that Fielding had given her. She set it on the table before her host.

"He is why I'm here," she said to the old woman. "Have you ever seen him before?" She raised an eyebrow again. "In any way?"

Zarah scowled. She looked down at the photo of little Julien Hawkins.

"That boy," she said, "look like all the other little black boys I seen. He ain't nothin' to me." She picked up the photo then and turned it about in different directions, as if evaluating it. She brought it up close to her and sniffed it, then shook her head. She tossed the photo back at Weirdlee. "Nothin'," she said. "I ain't got nothin' for ya's."

Then, quite unexpectedly, she pounded her fist on the table. She shouted at Weirdlee, "Whatchu here for, girl! Youz got the power yerself! You can see all!—All there is and all there ever be!"

Weirdlee, taken aback by the outburst, stared back at her.

"You just need some learnin', is all," Zarah went on. "You be an ignorant witch—ain't got no sense of what you is."

Weirdlee took the photo of little Julien and slid it back into her pocket. "I thought maybe you could help us," she said. "I guess I was wrong."

Zarah shook her head, leering at Weirdlee. "Youz don't need my help. Youz got the power to see that little boy yerself. You'll know, fer sure, thens, what beast done took him away."

"Beast?" Weirdlee asked, looking gravely at Zarah. "A beast took him? An animal?"

Zarah laughed roundly at that. She replied, "Beast. Animal. Devil. Spirit. What the fuck does I care what theyz call it? You got the gift, girl, but youz blind on how to use it."

Weirdlee sighed, and she considered her next words.

"You're right," she confessed. "I can't see many things— not every time I need to, anyway."

Zarah eyed her guest, quietly gauging—and testing—the woman's abilities, as the agent continued.

"I hear voices," Weirdlee said. "Sometimes I see visions, too—or images. But I never call them to me, myself. They just come to me on their own, and I never know when I'll hear or see them."

Zarah allowed herself a mild grin.

Weirdlee sat in silence for a moment, staring at the table in thought before lifting her gaze to her host.

"What can you tell me about the Curse of the Bayous?" she asked her. "Is it real?"

Zarah lost her grin. She scowled once more.

"Real? Whatchu mean by 'real'?"

"I mean," Weirdlee asked, "is it really a curse, or is it something more mundane—perhaps using a voodoo legend as a cover for it?"

Zarah smirked at her. She kept her eyes on the FBI agent, mulling over what to say—or to admit.

"The Curse is a legend," she muttered finally. "But the lives that it tooks were real, sure enough."

"Who killed them?" Weirdlee asked. "Can you see that at all? Is it more than one person?"

Zarah gauged how to answer the questions. She swirled her tongue in her mouth, deliberating her response. She sensed, too—and more importantly—that the young witch's mind was open to her.

"Why you think peoples die when they does, girl?" she asked her. "Why does little boys and girls die, and theys old mans live? Why it be that way?"

Weirdlee looked back at her, unsure of what she was asking. "I...suppose..." she started, "we all make decisions that eventually take us there."

Zarah pointed at her, wagging her finger accusingly. "You a witch, alright. You be'a thinkin' you can change ya's fate by changin' youz mind. Is that it?"

"I think so." Weirdlee nodded. "A right or a wrong decision can change your whole life's path."

Zarah jabbed her finger at her. "WRONG!" She slapped the table hard. "It ain't like that at all, you silly witch! It ain't like youz gots some kinda control over things, and can change it all whenevas youz want to."

"I'm just saying—"

Zarah slapped the table repeatedly. "No, no, no! It ain't that ways at all!" She huffed and tossed her hands up dismissively at her guest.

Weirdlee looked at her coolly. "I don't believe in unbending fate. And I don't believe little boys and girls are fated to die at a certain time or a certain place. We can help them."

"We's do help them, girl," Zarah said, leaning forward in her chair, "by keeping them on they's own lifeline and makin' sure they stays on course."

Weirdlee tried to focus on their conversation, but even as she looked at the old woman, her eyelids weighed heavily on her.

"You can't change fate," Zarah went on. "But youz can sees what comes of 'em. You can see the fate of the victims. If only youz ain't so dumb in your ways."

Weirdlee sighed. This back and forth wasn't getting her anywhere. She stretched herself in her chair, suddenly fatigued from the long day.

"I've come here," she told Zarah, "because you are hopefully wise in the ways of the voodoo faith, and I need your second sight to help us solve a mystery. That little boy I showed you has gone missing from his home. We believe he's been killed, but we don't know how—or maybe *why,* if it turns out to be a crime."

Zarah stared directly at her. "Cuz youz lookin' in all the wrong places, girl. I ain't gots no answers for you—not any that woulds help you." She grinned. "But I knows someone who do."

Weirdlee leaned closer to her. "You do?"

The old woman nodded. "He a powerful man. Very strong. Very wise. And he'll do more than just tell youz who be who and all that other bullshit. He'll give youz the power—the true power that youz ain't got on yer own."

"I just need answers," Weirdlee said wearily. "I'm not interested in anything else."

Zarah grinned. "Don't you lie to me, girly witch. We both knows youz got the gift, and that's for sure. You just ain't got the knowin' for what to do with it. You can't sees alls you supposed to see. But he's can help you. He's can show you how to be a *real* sorceress. He can give you the power to sees everything!"

Weirdlee looked at her suspiciously. "What are you talking about?"

Zarah licked her lips. "Marcel Unate' is his name. And he will make you the witch youz always wanted to be. All seeing, and all-powerful." She picked up her arms, raising her hands skyward. "He will make you a whole woman, complete in all your ways!"

Weirdlee shook off a suddenly-dazed sensation, and she asked Zarah, "Can he tell me about the missing boy?"

Zarah dropped her arms. "Youz not hearin' me, witch. I says, he make you a powerful woman. He make *you* see the boy's fate."

"Me?" Weirdlee mused.

"Yes." Zarah nodded. "And you'n see all the others, too. 'Cuz no one more powerful than a witch does has the gift."

Weirdlee leaned back in her chair, pondering the old woman's words. Her weariness returned.

Zarah kept her eyes on her all the while. She sensed the young woman weakening, and that the silent spell placed upon her was having its desired effect. All that was left for voodoo priestess to do was wrap her spiritual voice around her, and then bring her in.

"Youz grows up," she said to her then, "always knowin' youz had the power. Always knowin' youz had the gift. And no one does ever love you for it. Theys not seein' how special you is. How youz heal the suffrin' of others. Make the poor rich in theys spirits. Make the old feel young again, like children in a schoolyard."

Weirdlee gazed off at the table before her...

"Youz all alone, child," Zarah went on, her crackly voice carrying along like a warm summer breeze. "All by yerself, with them voices and them spirits callin' to ya's. And youz never knows why. But theys come to youz, anyways, and theys guide you along through life, tellin' ya's who to love, and who's to hate, and who's to trust with yo deepest secrets."

Weirdlee raised her spellbound gaze, and she looked past the dim light of the table lamp, and then to the shadows beyond. Time itself, it seemed, had ceased to move in any direction at all.

"Go to Marcel Unate'," Zarah whispered to her. "Go to him, and give yerself to him freely. He's give you the power to see all there is to see. He's make you a whole woman, complete in every way."

Weirdlee stared off, unanswering, before slowly turning her gaze to the old priestess. She said to her in a lost, drifting voice...

"I don't know what you mean..."

Zarah stared directly into her eyes.

The Salem witch, she knew, was hers.

"Go to Marcel Unate'," she instructed her, this time in a firmer tone. "Give yerself to him, and he will give youz all you did ever want in yo's life. All youz ever needs."

Weirdlee stared back at her. She whispered, "I go to Marcel Unate'."

Zarah grinned. "*Yes.*"

A noise at the door caught the old woman's attention. She looked off to see her two eldest sons coming inside. They stopped after entering, both eying the FBI agent sitting at the table.

Zarah sneered at the spellbound woman herself, then looked off again to her sons.

"Get this pagan slut outta my's house. Bring her back to her boat."

* * * *

Nicks and Fielding had found a spot near a snaking turn in the river just beyond the Bayou Chactimahan, and there they waited impatiently for Agent Weirdlee's return.

Neither man took up the forward swivel seat of the fishing boat they'd rented, both instead taking a bench seat near the back. Nicks checked the time on his smartphone. It read 9:15 PM. He checked again for any new text messages, but there was nothing, still, besides her first one telling him she'd arrived there.

"Another five minutes and we're going in," he said.

Fielding looked off upstream, into the blackness of the night. "I think she left more like seven-thirty, partner."

Nicks didn't care about a few minutes' difference. "Close enough."

Fielding mulled their situation. He thought about their colleague, and whether she could really be what she thought she was in this life.

"It's a hell of a thing..." he muttered.

Nicks looked at him. "What's that?"

"Oh," Fielding said. "Just thinkin', what if Agent Weirdlee really did have some kinda special powers or somethin'. That'd be a heck of a thing, huh?"

Nicks smiled. "You think she might, Special Agent?"

Fielding shrugged uncomfortably. He didn't want to appear gullible, so he chose his words carefully.

"Not sure, really. I mean—who knows what's out there? They're only now just startin' to find stuff in the universe that we never even imagined could be true. But..." he tossed his hands in the air, "who knows, ya know?"

Nicks laughed. "I guess so."

Fielding went on. "She is somethin' special, though, ain't she? Don't think I ever met anyone like her."

Nicks smiled back at him. "Careful there, Fielding. She might be putting a spell on you."

Fielding laughed and waved him off. "Aww, nothin' like that." He gave Nicks a curious look. "What about you? Ain't you ever thought about her—you know, in a romantic-like way?"

For Nicks, that was a complicated question. Complicated because, he being the lead investigator, he was technically her superior—if not in rank, than in reporting status, at least. And while it was true there were plenty of agents who'd grown fond of each other and, one way or another, figured out how to make things work, Nicks had always felt most comfortable keeping a professional distance from his female colleagues, regardless of whatever feelings he might have had for them.

In Joanna Weirdlee's case, though, that wasn't such an easy thing for him to do. She was young and vibrant, daring and intelligent—all the qualities he found most attractive in women, and all of it wrapped up in one beautiful, five-foot, eight-inch package.

Something for any man to think twice about.

"Yeah," he admitted to Fielding. And he winked at his partner. "I think about her that way all the time."

* * * *

Agent Weirdlee awakened, her groggy mind lost in a fog of half-dreams and vague memories. She lay inside of her flat-bottomed boat, having no memory of how she'd gotten there. She sat up in the deck of the craft, her head slowly clearing. She looked about at her surroundings, uncertain of where she was. A first-quarter moon cast a dim, shadowy light on the area, and from what she could see, she was still in the bayous—*somewhere.*

She tried to remember what had happened to her at Zarah Devillier's home. The last thing she recalled, they'd been talking about the Curse of the Bayous, and did Devillier know anything of it? A thought suddenly came to her then—and she quickly patted her dress's belt. *Shit,* she swore. Her Glock-23 wasn't there!

Pushing her hand into her dress pocket, she fished around, but found only her little pouch of soil. *They wouldn't dare take that from me.* Her smartphone, however, was also missing.

She crawled on all fours then to make her way to the back of the boat, feeling her way in the darkness. Once there, she came across the portable spotlight that Husk had given her, still lying on the floor of the boat. She felt around for the device's on/off switch—the damn things were never where they should be!—and, finally locating it, she switched it on. She aimed it, first, at the boat itself, checking on its condition. The light's beam lit up the floor of the boat—and immediately illuminated one hell of a sight for sore eyes: Weirdlee's gun and smartphone, lying on the deck. She quickly scrambled over to them and picked them up. Her phone, she saw right away, had been smashed. It was dead. Turning her attention to her weapon, she checked its magazine first, discovering that it still had all of its bullets. A cursory examination of the gun itself reassured her, then, that it had been spared the phone's fate.

Next, she put the spotlight on her surroundings and slowly turned about. She saw, just beyond the black waters, a thick growth of tall, viney trees and brush taking up much the terrain, giving her little visibility.

She could be anywhere in the wilderness.

Putting the spotlight back on the interior of the boat, she checked it again, this time for any water leaks or other damage. Everything looked okay. She moved back to the rear of the boat then and cast the light on the boat's motor. It, too, appeared to be fine. Sitting on the bench seat before it, she started it up, and, much to her relief, it sputtered to life.

Still, though, she had no idea where she was.

She looked up into the night air. There, high in the sky, and only partially obscured by wispy, silhouetted clouds, was the first-quarter moon. She ran an imaginary line connecting the top and bottom tips of the orb's crescent and then followed that line straight down to the earth's horizon. That, she knew, was south. Also, since she'd already seen the moonrise prior to going to Devillier's home that evening, she knew that the sunlit face of the moon was west.

She wanted to go north, if she could. Pointing the spotlight in that direction, though, she saw nothing but a thick line of trees. She pointed the light to the water then. The current was very slow moving, but definitely running left-to-right. This confirmed for her, at least, that going right would take her in an easterly direction. She also surmised that, if this was in fact the same river she'd travelled upon earlier that night, she'd be heading right back to her comrades. And to safety.

Clamping the spotlight to the left side of the boat as Husk had recommended, Weirdlee throttled up the motor then and started downstream.

It was a lonely trip in the darkness for her. The tall trees, once seen in the daylight as solitary, noble figures, now massed together in the nighttime, forming one continuous, pitch-black blanket of shadow along either bank of the river. Only the probing beam of the portable spotlight, aimed directly ahead of the craft she rode in, showed Weirdlee any sign of her bearings. The steady hum of the boat's motor, meanwhile, masked the sounds of the evening's creatures.

The burden of Zarah Devillier's debilitating, hypnotic spell still hung heavily on the agent as she kept her eyes on the water ahead of her boat. She mulled over what had happened back there, trying to make some sense of the unfolding of events.

She suspected that she'd been compromised from the very start—as soon as she'd set foot on Zarah's property, if not sooner. That was about the time that she'd stopped perceiving signs of any kind. She should have paid more heed to the tarot cards, she scolded herself. They warned her of trickery and deceit. And yet, upon entering Zarah's home, the Salem witch had given way to the more mundane FBI agent in her, and she'd barely even noticed not being able to measure her senses.

Zarah had, by then, taken control of her entirely, and there was no telling what fowl things she'd done to her in her spellbound state thereafter. She worried at the thought of having been taken by the old woman's sons. Considering things, though, she'd likely have felt that by now—unless Zarah's spell was still at work. She would check herself physically once she returned to the inn.

And what of her colleagues, Nicks and Fielding? Should she tell them everything—admitting to them her naïve miscalculation? This was, after all, FBI business. She went back and forth with that dilemma in her mind, deliberating things. For this, she knew, was witches business, too, and this encounter would not be the last of its kind for her.

Weirdlee's gaze scanned the shadowy riverbank off to her left as she cruised on. She was beginning to recover her senses more fully, and she could feel, once more, that haunting sorrow she'd sensed earlier, and see those voiceless spirits and desperate souls drifting amongst the trees and shoreline along the way.

The Curse of the Bayous was real.

But it wasn't what everyone suspected.

A pinprick of light flashed on the water ahead of her, crossing her own spotlight's piercing beam. She focused on it, then steered her boat in the other light's direction, toward its source.

An overwhelming sense of relief came over her.

Friendship…

Motoring up to the boat that approached her, she smiled, and her heart warmed.

"Agent Weirdlee," said Agent Fielding in the darkness. "You all right?"

She waved at both of her comrades as their spotlight lit up her boat. "I'm all right," she assured Fielding—lying, of course.

Nicks came up to the head of their own boat, and he looked out at Weirdlee as her craft drew aside theirs.

"Didn't you get my text?" he asked her. "We tried calling you, too."

Weirdlee thought fast.

"I lost my phone in the water," she told him, and she frowned playfully. "Butterfingers."

Nicks eyed her, somewhat surprised by the mishap. "Well, that sucks."

"Yes, it certainly does."

The three colleagues turned their boats around then and started back downstream together in the darkness, both boats' spotlights showing the way.

Weirdlee, too, wasted no time "losing" her phone in the river.

~ | ~

-6-

Questions and Answers

The FBI agents returned to the Swampy Inn, and, it being a late hour, all agreed to call it a night, and so let Weirdlee give a full briefing in the morning. On the ride back in, she'd already given them a summary accounting of her experience at Zarah Devillier's home, including what she and the old woman had talked about and her departure from there. Left unsaid was her entrancement by Zarah and having subsequently been rendered unconscious.

That, she decided, would remain her little secret.

Weirdlee went back to her room and washed herself. She worried about Zarah's spell—wondering if it might have blocked out any awful memories or feelings of her experience there. By both physical and spiritual means, then, she examined herself, and so determined—much to her relief—that at the very least she had not been molested by Zarah's sons.

Lying awake in bed long after midnight, Weirdlee kept thinking about what she'd just been through. As inexperienced as she was, still, in dealing with other spell casters, she should have been better prepared, anyway. The old woman had been waiting for her arrival, and she was ready for her visitor. Upon reflection, Weirdlee determined that she should have summoned a blocking spell of her own, or, at the very least, closed her mind to any intuitive wanderings. But it was the lurking spirits in the wilderness that had kept her mind searching and, by so doing, left her exposed to the intrusions of another caster.

What were the spirits saying, though, she wondered? She felt such sadness inside of them. And a longing for...*what?*

Justice? Redemption?

Or was it simply to be freed?

She couldn't tell.

They spoke silently in the evening air, and they weren't necessarily speaking to her. They recounted some manner of tale, she perceived, of a time when last they lived and laughed and loved. But it wasn't meant for the living to hear. It wasn't a message at all. It was more like...a confession.

That was when Zarah must have seen her opportunity, Weirdlee determined. An open mind, curiously exploring the spirit world. Easy pickings for anyone seeking to take advantage of it.

Or to control it.

She should have known better. She should have been better prepared.

Next time...Weirdlee promised herself.

Next time, I won't be so easily fooled.

* * * *

By 7:00 AM, all three FBI agents had gathered at the Swampy Inn's little cafe for a continental breakfast. They sat a small, square table, nibbling on a light breakfast of muffins, coffee, and, for Weirdlee, tea. All three wore suits—Weirdlee a pantsuit—for their day's work ahead.

"So," said Nicks to Weirdlee, "You lost your phone after you got back into your boat. I wish you'd called me right after you left her house."

"Me, too, in retrospect," she replied. "I was just so preoccupied with going over the conversation I'd had with the old woman—till I got back to the boat, anyway—and then, when I took out my phone to text you that I was done, it just sort of flipped out of my hands," she said, fluttering her hands together, "and away it went."

"Right at the shore where you were at?" Fielding asked. "The water was that deep that you couldn't get it?"

Weirdlee nodded as she sipped her tea. "Mmm."

"Well, from what you mentioned last night, you didn't get much from the visit," said Nicks.

"Unfortunately not," she confirmed. "I didn't detect any sign of recognition at all from her when I showed her the picture of the boy."

Fielding grinned at that. "You mean physically or...psychically?"

Weirdlee smirked. "Physically. She didn't show much interest in him, period, actually."

Nicks shrugged as he finished chewing on a piece of his muffin. "That doesn't mean anything, necessarily. People sometimes feign disinterest—especially if they know more than they should."

Fielding replied, "You mean a guilty person hidin' that they know someone."

"Sure," Nicks said.

"It wasn't like that," Weirdlee insisted. "She didn't seem to care about him at all. But then..." she paused, starting to recollect, "when I asked her about the Curse of the Bayous—if she knew anything about it—I got a different kind of response."

"Like what?" asked Nicks. "Like she knew about it?"

Weirdlee lowered her eyelids, mulling over what she'd surmised. "Kind of like...she was explaining what it was, without actually *saying* she knew about it."

"Huh?" Fielding said.

"Didn't you press her?" Nicks asked.

Weirdlee was in a bit of spot there. She actually had no idea how that conversation ended, prior to her awakening in her boat.

"I didn't push the matter," she said. "I figured we could get more out of her, maybe, in future visits."

Fielding appeared troubled.

"You don't think she might be a part of it, do ya?" he asked.

Weirdlee looked at him. That was, in fact, precisely the feeling she had just then. Funny, though, how she didn't feel the same way the night before, when in the woman's presence.

"I'm not sure," she said to him. She looked at Nicks. "I didn't even consider that, actually. But she didn't sound defensive in any way."

Nicks waved a dismissive hand. "Let's not get carried away here," he said. He looked at both of his colleagues. "Remember, we're here to investigate the missing boy, Julien Hawkins, not some curse going around."

"But what if they're related?" asked Fielding.

Nicks felt pessimistic about that. "Yeah, it's possible, I suppose. But I'm just not seeing a connection so far."

Suddenly, then, a not-so-subtle reminder flashed into Weirdlee's mind. "There is someone else I can talk to," she said abruptly. "Ms. Devillier mentioned him as possibly being able to help us."

"This another voodoo thing?" asked Fielding.

She frowned at him. "Yeah. It's another voodoo thing."

"I hope this guy doesn't live in the swamps, too," said Nicks.

Weirdlee looked at him, and she stared blankly for a moment. Something very odd had just happened to her.

"No..." she said to him, becoming strangely aware. "He lives in Paradis. Just off of...route 631, actually."

Weirdlee, in truth, had no real memory of having talked to Zarah about this man, nor having learned of where he lived. And yet still, in that very moment, she somehow knew exactly where to find him.

How did I know that?

She continued her recollections. "Marcel Unate' is his name. His birth name is Paul Basil, though, and that's how he's listed at his home address."

Nicks eyed Weirdlee curiously, having noticed her distant look. "Are you all right, Agent Weirdlee?"

Weirdlee snapped herself from her reminiscing daze. "Yes. I'm fine. What do you mean?"

He replied, "You still look half asleep."

She smiled back at him and shook her head.

Fielding asked her, "So why's this guy got two names?"

She answered, "Oh, he's a stage performer—works up in New Orleans, mostly. But he also practices voodoo for real under his alias."

"Well, maybe we can all talk to him together then," said Nicks.

"No," Weirdlee snapped.

Both men looked at her.

"I'll go," she said.

Fielding sipped his coffee. "This another one of them witch-to-witch things?"

She looked back at him, expressionless. "Yes. That's what it is."

"Careful, Joanna," said Nicks. "I think you might be taking this *I-have-to-do-it-alone* thing too far."

"It's perfectly safe," Weirdlee said. "He's a night performer, so I can stop by his house this afternoon."

"We're going to be at the school this morning," Nicks said to her. He turned to Fielding. "There's a daycare center there, too, right?"

"Yeah," said Fielding. "Across the way or just down the road—somethin' like that."

"Okay," said Nicks. "We can meet up with the sheriff or Captain Phillips back at the park in the afternoon. I want to go over the layout of the place again on the day the boy went missing." He looked at Weirdlee. "You can go talk to that voodoo guy while we're doing that."

She gave him a nod and smiled. "Great."

"You gonna bring up that the kid mighta been picked up?" asked Fielding.

Nicks curled his lips, and nodded slowly. "Yyyeah. I think so. I know it's something they looked into, too, but before we put the boy into the maw of an alligator, I'd like to cover all the bases."

Fielding agreed. "Fair enough, partner."

The three went on to finish their breakfast.

* * * *

The Bayou Boeuf Elementary School was a small, single-story school serving the northern outlying communities of greater Thibodaux. Located on the eastern side of the bridge spanning the Bayou L'Ours, it was an easy walk from Kraemer Park, just down the road on the western side of the bridge.

Nicks and Fielding arrived there in their rented Taurus, while Weirdlee drove out in the Grand Cherokee she'd picked up. They parked in the school's lot, then made their introductions to the office staff before going in to see the school's principal.

Principal Henry Potter was a tall, chunky, light-skinned African-American, donning wire-rimmed glasses and wearing a neat, brown three-piece suit. He greeted all three of his guests with a smile and a firm handshake.

"Have a seat, please," he said to them, gesturing to chairs provided for their visit.

The agents sat in order—Nicks, Weirdlee, and Fielding. Nicks looked around the room. Potter's office was a small space with bookshelves taking up either wall. A window behind Potter's hardwood desk provided daylight and a view to the school's north side. The desk itself was cluttered with paperwork. A laptop computer was set to the right, and an obligatory family photo was positioned kitty-corner at the left corner. From where he sat, Nicks could just make out a smiling Potter and who he assumed to be his wife and son all standing together in the picture. The boy looked to be about the same age as the missing Hawkins boy, though he looked entirely dissimilar otherwise, with lighter skin and pudgier cheeks.

"What can either I or my staff do to help you folks?" Potter asked as he took his own seat behind his desk.

Nicks answered, "I'm just looking for a little more background information, sir. We're trying to pin down the sequence of events on the day the boy, Julien Hawkins, disappeared. Who was where, what was going on—that sort of thing."

"Sure." Potter nodded. "Well, we have that field day every year. There's some local vendors that provide some food, and a local band usually sets up later in the day for a couple of sets. Our school and Foster's Daycare, down the road here, provide entertainment and snacks for the kids."

"What kind of entertainment?" Fielding asked. "You mean like puppet shows?"

Potter furled his eyebrows. "More like badminton, sack races, and face painting. We set up some tables for various things, and the daycare center has a tent of their own, too."

"Their tent close to the parking lot?" asked Nicks.

Potter recollected. "Uhh…no, not usually. The beer tent is up there, and we try to keep the kiddie stuff away from the more adult-oriented fun."

"So, whereabouts were they set up?" Nicks asked.

"Over on the left side of the park, in a row of tents there. We had a tent there, too, for our supplies. The spots change year-to-year, so I can't recall exactly where in the row it was the year the boy went missin'. But that's why the kids were over on that side of park—and why the boy was there, too."

"Okay," Nicks said, his mind busy considering things.

"How many staff participate in the field day, Mr. Potter," asked Weirdlee.

"Ohh…that changes year-to-year, too. Here at the school, we have volunteers—office staff and teachers—who fill up their cars with gear and drive it over to the park. Some just help out with the setup and then go home. Others stay on and work the whole day, or parts of it."

"Four or five, maybe?" Weirdlee guessed.

"Oh no," said Potter with the wave of a hand, "just a couple, actually. There's two or three from the daycare center that stay on, too."

"The daycare supplies stuff, too?" Nicks asked.

"Sure. We mostly do the games. They cover the food. Although some parents will bring over some pies and cupcakes—things like that."

Nicks nodded while continuing to mull things over.

"I don't suppose you recall how many daycare folks were workin' the day the boy disappeared?" asked Fielding.

"No, I don't. That's a question for the police. They interviewed everyone who was there that day."

"Yeah," Fielding conceded.

"So," said Nicks, "let's get a time frame here. What time do you guys start setting up, and when do you usually start breaking things up when it's over?"

Potter scratched his balding forehead. "Shit, let's see. I guess we start settin' things up around nine-thirty, ten in the morning. The field day starts about noontime. Then, depending on the weather, we'll break it up around six o'clock."

Nicks went over those time periods in his mind. According to police reports, a daycare center volunteer first noticed the boy had gone missing around 5:00 PM, after Marcus Hawkins had asked where he was.

The agent asked Potter then, "Do you recall when you planned to break things up on the day the boy went missing?"

"No," Potter replied. "And after the boy was discovered missing, we broke everything up right away, anyway."

"So, around five-ish?"

"I don't recall."

"Does the daycare staff use their own cars to bring stuff over, too?" Fielding asked.

"Actually, no," said Potter.

Nicks' attention picked up on that.

"They have a van they use," the principal explained. "They do a lot of their cooking at the center and then haul it all over in the van."

"Does the van stay there all day?" Nicks asked.

Potter shook his head. "No, sir. Not usually." He looked at Nicks curiously. "What are ya'll getting on with that?"

Nicks waved it off. "Oh, no. Nothing. I'm just trying to locate all these things in my head."

"Was the van there when the boy went missing?" Weirdlee asked.

Potter shook his head again. "I don't know. I wasn't there till after the police called me."

Nicks looked over at Weirdlee. "We can ask them that when we talk to 'em." Then he said to Potter, "We'd like to talk to the staff members who volunteered that day, sir. Get some other first-hands accounts of the day."

"Sure." Potter nodded. "I'll get my secretary to contact them."

"Did you know the little boy, yourself, sir?" Weirdlee asked then.

"Julien?" he asked.

Weirdlee nodded. "Yes."

"Yes, as a matter of fact I knew him quite well. I know a lot of the kids who attend school here. And I can tell you this: He deserved a much better life than what he got. Very bright and curious, eager to learn. Just a wonderful boy. A terrible shame, what happened."

With that, the agents spent the rest of the early morning interviewing the six staffers who'd either brought over supplies to the park or stayed on to work the field day. None of them saw anything or anyone unusual. By 10:15 AM, with the interviews done, the agents returned to their vehicles for the trip over to the daycare center that was just down the road and around the corner.

"What are ya thinkin' so far?" Fielding asked his partner as he drove the two of them over to the daycare center.

"Oh, I dunno," Nicks replied. "Still up in the air. But I would like to know if the van was there or not when the kid went missing."

Fielding nodded as he eyed the road ahead of them, and then he turned left onto a side street.

"That'd be a hell of a thing, ya know," he said. "You thinkin' maybe the kid got into the van somehow and was taken outta there that way?"

Nicks chuckled. "I'm not thinking anything, Agent Fielding. Just trying to get everything straight."

Foster's Daycare came up on their left, a little ways after the street turn. Fielding pulled into the parking lot and parked their car. Agent Weirdlee, following behind them, parked next to them. They all left their cars and went into the daycare center.

Inside, they were met by the center's chief administrator, Frank Zimmer, a portly, middle-aged white man, who had gotten a call from the school that the agents were on their way.

"Good morning," Zimmer said to them with an inviting smile. He shook each agent's hand in turn. "I'm Frank Zimmer, the chief administrator here."

Nicks shook the man's hand. "Good morning. I'm Special Agent Nicks..." he gestured to his colleagues, "this is Special Agent Fielding, and Special Agent Weirdlee."

While Zimmer completed his hand-shaking routine, Nicks quickly glanced about the place. The main room was large and open, with small, open-ended play cubicles lining the far wall, each one littered with toys. A display window ran all along the wall's length. Presently, about a dozen children were playing about the place, with a couple of staffers tending to all of them.

Zimmer eyed each of the agents, uncertain as to who was in charge. "Henry told me ya'll wanted to talk to us about a case you're working on?"

Nicks—the one in charge—replied to him. "Yes, sir. We're investigating the disappearance of a little boy, Julien Hawkins."

Zimmer simply nodded, showing no sign of recollection.

"He used to come here after school each day," said Weirdlee. "About four years ago?"

"Oh." Zimmer's face brightened. "I just got this job a couple years ago. I worked out of New Orleans before this, so I wouldn't know any of the kids from back then."

"I see," said Nicks. "Well, we'd like to talk to some of the staffers who did know the boy—particularly the ones who volunteered at a fundraiser the day he disappeared."

Zimmer nodded slowly. "Okay. I'll have to talk to my senior councilor, Farrah Simmons, about that. She was here then and might know who can help you."

"Great," said Nicks.

Zimmer turned and walked off down a hallway to their left, disappearing through an open doorway. In his absence, the agents did a cursory look-about the place.

"I half-imagined a place with classrooms in it," said Weirdlee, observing the open room.

Fielding looked off to the far-right side of the room. There, he noted three rows of bookshelves, each set one after the other and facing front to back. Beside them were two short-legged, small tables, each with a couple of books on them. One had a juice drink cup set on it.

"Small town, small daycare," he said.

"Shouldn't have any problem with people remembering the boy, then," Nicks remarked.

Presently, Frank Zimmer came back through the doorway. He was joined by his senior councilor, Farrah Simmons.

Simmons was a dark-skinned black woman with short-trimmed hair. In sort of a business-casual mix, she wore a black blouse, white slacks, and black sneakers—the kind of footwear needed to accommodate all the running around she did as part of her job.

"Hi," she greeted the agents.

"Good morning," said Nicks.

"Farrah," said Zimmer, "these folks are with the FBI. They'd like to talk with some of the staff about a missing boy—" He looked at Nicks. "What was his name?"

"Julien Hawkins," Nicks said.

Simmons reacted immediately to the name. "Oh, that poor boy. I remember him."

"Well, that's good," said Nicks. "We've read all the police reports, Ms. Simmons, so we know what everyone told the police at the time. We're just trying to piece together anything that might have been missed."

She gave a nod to that. "Okay. Not sure what I could add, though."

Weirdlee asked her, "Are there any staff here who were also employed back then? Perhaps volunteering on the day Julien disappeared?"

"Oh, sure," Simmons said. "I helped bring supplies there that day, and then helped pack everything up after..." she shrugged, "after the boy went missing. Then there was Sally and Jens—two of our staffers. They worked there the whole day."

"Jens?"

"Jennifer Satchens," Simmons said. "She'll be in later in the day." She pointed to one of the staff members playing with the kids. "That's Sally Peck, right there."

"Good," said Nicks. He glanced about the place. "Is there some place we can interview people more privately?" he asked Zimmer.

"Sure," Zimmer replied. "You can use my office."

And so the interviews began.

Since she was already with them, Farrah Simmons was first on the list. She would be followed by Sally Peck and a couple of other staffers—the center's office clerk and a maintenance man, both of whom worked there when little Julien attended.

Simmons looked somewhat uncomfortable as she took a seat behind Zimmer's desk. The three FBI agents sat in chairs brought into the room just for the interviews. Nicks and Fielding took out small black notepads, and, going ahead, each occasionally took notes as the interviews went on.

"Ms. Simmons," Nicks began, "were you at the park the whole day on the day Julien disappeared?"

"I was not," she replied. "I helped load up the van with food that we'd cooked here. Then I rode to the park with the others and helped out with the set up. After I got back to the center, I went home for the afternoon."

"You rode in the van?" Fielding asked.

"Yes. Along with Sally and Jens. Burt drove us."

"Burt?" asked Nicks.

"Bernard Hipps. Our maintenance man-slash-custodian."

"Ah." Nicks nodded. "And he drove you back?"

"Yes, he did."

"Why didn't you just drive in your own car, Ms. Simmons," asked Weirdlee, "if you were leaving anyway?"

Simmons sighed, as if she were tired of the interview already. "I live in Raceland, which is that-a-ways," she said, pointing east. "The opposite direction. I'd be going back this way, anyway, so why burn my own gas?"

Weirdlee gave a nod.

"Ms. Simmons, did you know the boy, Julien, very well from the time he spent at the center?" Nicks asked.

"I did. But I'm a parent counselor, not a childcare specialist. I'd see him a lot, but I didn't interact with him very often."

"So you knew Regina Hawkins?" Fielding asked.

Simmons frowned at the agent. "Yes," she said with an air of disdain. "I knew her very well."

Nicks picked up on her attitude. "Sounds like you two didn't get along."

"Oh, no," Simmons corrected him. "We got along fine. I just..." she paused to consider her words..."I just never thought she was—what's the right way to put it without sounding too harsh? Prepared for the challenges of motherhood?"

"What do you mean?" asked Weirdlee.

Simmons sighed. She leaned back in her chair and slapped her hands on her lap. She said to Weirdlee, "Bringing up children is a very difficult responsibility, officer—"

"Special agent," Nicks corrected her.

She nodded to him. "Special agent." Then continued. "Regina Hawkins...how should I say this? She made a lot of bad choices in her life. Don't get me wrong about her— she's a very kind, warm-hearted person. But it takes more than a kind heart to bring up a child. And she didn't do herself any favors through the years."

"Are you saying she was irresponsible in some way?" Nicks asked her.

Simmons pursed her lips and squinted, considering. "I would say more like immature." She sat up straight again and clasped her hands together on the desk. "Regina's had a hard life. She was brought up in a poor home. She left school to go to work. Then she met a man—the wrong man—and got herself pregnant when neither one of them could afford it."

"Happens all the time in the good ol' U-S-A," said Fielding.

'I know," she replied with a frown. "That doesn't make it a smart choice. And in Regina's case, she wound up with an alcoholic S-O-B who could care less about being a father. Their home was absolutely toxic to that poor boy."

"That bad?" Fielding asked.

She looked at him squarely. "Did she tell you he beat her?"

"He hit her?" Nicks asked.

"Damn right he did. A lot. She'd come in here plenty of times with bruises."

"Ms. Simmons," Weirdlee said, "why didn't you call youth services?"

Simmons put up her hands. "We did. They asked questions, took the kid in for counseling, and then, when it was all said and done, back home he went. Regina finally got tired of the jerk smacking her around, anyway, and they separated. She had a restraining order against him for a little while, I guess. I think they're divorced now."

"They are," Nicks confirmed.

"It's too bad she let him take Julien to the park that day," Simmons said. "Worst bad choice she ever made."

"She wanted her son to have a father," said Weirdlee. "Maybe she wanted to give her ex a chance."

Simmons shook her head at that. "Like I said. Immature."

* * * *

"She was just the sweetest woman," said Sally Peck, when asked of Regina Hawkins. "She always felt so bad that she had to work all the time."

"Was she made aware of all the services available to her," asked Fielding, "to help single parents?"

"Oh yes," Peck said. "But she's a very religious woman, and she always said that hard work would lead to good things." She frowned then. "Sad that this had to happen to her. I hear she hasn't been to church in a couple of years, now."

"She still prays," said Weirdlee, knowing more than any casual observer ever would. Of all the people she sensed suffering around her, the witch from Salem felt Regina Hawkins' pain the most.

Nicks knew from reading the police reports that it was Peck who first reported the boy missing.

"Ms. Peck," he asked, "what made you notice the boy missing that day?"

Peck thought back for a moment. "The kids had all come to the tent to eat. We were running low on food, and I didn't want any of 'em taking too much and not leaving any for the others, so I counted heads. I didn't see him there, and so that's when I started looking around for him."

"About five o'clock," Nicks checked.

"Yes. About then."

"Did you know Julien well?" asked Weirdlee.

"Pretty well, yes," said Peck. "He was a sweet young boy. A little shy. But when he was with other kids, he always got along well with them."

"And you're sure you saw him at the park earlier that day?" asked Nicks.

"Yes, I definitely saw him," she replied. "He'd shown up with his dad. But then his father went off to the beer tent and Julien stayed with the other kids."

"Toward the back of the park?" asked Fielding.

"I think so. They played all over the place, really, but the back of the park was open, so they were there a lot."

"You know," said Nicks, figuring things, "it's not all that far from the park to Regina Hawkins' home. It's possible he could have wanted to walk home."

"Police checked there, though," said Fielding.

"Yeah, but he could have started out that way," said Nicks, "and then maybe got picked up."

"Or maybe made it as far as the bridge," Fielding surmised, "and, playin' there, maybe fell in?"

"Yeah," Nicks agreed. "Possibly."

Sally Peck felt otherwise. "Julien wouldn't just take off like that," she said. "He was a good boy—his momma taught him to do as he was told. And unless his father told him to walk home, I don't think he'd do it on his own."

"Well, you never know," said Nicks. "We can't discount anything at this point." He redirected his questions. "What about the other people working there, Ms. Peck," he asked. "It was you and another daycare volunteer, right? Were the school volunteers nearby you?"

"Yeah," she said. "They had a tent a couple'a spots down from us. But they spent most of the time walking around, playing with the kids."

"They were with the kids?" asked Weirdlee.

"A lot of the time, yeah."

"Did you know the school volunteers?" asked Nicks, jotting down notes.

"I recognized them. I'm not sure on some of the names, though."

"What names do you recall?" Nicks asked.

"Well, there was the principal, Mr. Potter. He helped 'em get set up. I think he left afterward, though. And Terry Stevens was there—I think the whole time. And a couple others were there, too, but I don't remember their names."

"Ms. Simmons told us she helped out with the setup, and then left for the day?" asked Weirdlee.

"Yeah," Peck recalled. "She was in the van with us. She helped us unload everything and get set up, and then she left with Burt, our maintenance man. He drove the van."

"Did you happen to notice if the school staff were with the kids just before five o'clock?" asked Nicks.

"Oh, gosh, I can't remember. But the kids came runnin' over to our tent, so I imagine someone fetched 'em."

"Okay, Ms. Peck," said Nicks. "Thanks."

After a couple of more fact-checking questions, the FBI agents finished their interview with Sally Peck. Next in the office came the daycare's office clerk, Mary Sullivan. She was a young woman—in her early twenties. She'd only been at the park for an hour or so on the day Julien disappeared, having spent the rest of the day at a family picnic. The agents kept their interview with her brief before moving on to the maintenance man, Bernard Hipps.

Hipps was a burly man, with thick, curly gray hair that carpeted his arms and chest. His head, by contrast, was bald. He wore a black tank top, and throughout the interview he'd flex his muscles while casting admiring glances at the lovely female agent in the room.

"Why ya'll investigatin' the kid now, for?" he asked the agents. "He done long-since been pooped outta some 'gator, ya know."

"Really, sir?" said Nicks, unimpressed by the man's poor choice of words.

"That kid got too close to the riverbank," Hipps said. "He fell into the muck, then into the river. Them 'gators done waitin' for him the whole time. They's always waitin' for some dumb fuck to fall in, then git themselves some breakfast."

"Well, Mister, uh...Hipps," Fielding said, "we'd like to see if we can at least confirm a few things, anyway."

Hipps looked at Weirdlee and winked at her. "Hey, sweet stuff."

She looked back at him plainly and didn't respond.

'Sir," said Nicks, examining his notepad, "when you drove out to the park that day, you had—what was it?— three people in the van with you?"

"Uhh..." Hipps counted in his head. "Yeah. I drove Sally, Jens, and the boss, Farrah, out there."

"The boss?" Fielding asked. "I thought she was a councilor here?"

Hipps nodded. "Yeah, but she's been a senior staffer for a while, now, though. Basically in charge of things when the big boss ain't around."

Nicks jotted that down.

"After you drove Ms. Simmons back to the daycare," Weirdlee asked, "did you stay there the whole time before going back there later on?"

He smiled at her. "Sure did—well, *almost* the whole time. I went to Trevor's for lunch."

"What's that? A restaurant?" Fielding asked.

"Naw," Hipps replied, giving Fielding a bothered look. "It's like a, uhh, Applebee's or somethin'. Got a bar area and some tables, too." He shook a finger at Fielding. "I didn't drink no beers, though. Just had a Coke."

"And how long were you there, Mr. Hipps?" asked Nicks.

"Oh, shit..." Hipps considered, "maybe an hour, hour-and-a-half."

"Then you went back to the daycare center?" Weirdlee asked.

He smiled at her again. "Sure thing."

Nicks kept his eyes on his note-taking. "When you did go back, was it because you got called out there, or did you just go back on your own?"

"I got called back—about five-thirty or so. Jens called me, all upset, sayin' the cops were there and the boy had gone missin' and all."

"When you got there, can you remember who else you saw there—both from the daycare and the school?"

"Well," Hipps said, "Jens was there, o'course, and Sally was still there, too. I don't rightly know the school folks too well, but I know some by they's looks. There was a few there, I guess."

"Was the principal there by then?" Nicks asked, knowing from the police reports he'd read that Potter had gone there upon hearing about the boy.

"He showed up a little after I did, I suppose," Hipps replied, before chuckling hysterically. "That poor ol' fella. He ran off to the riverbank, there, just a' wavin' his arms and all in a panic. I never seen a man so out of sorts."

"He was pretty upset, huh?" Nicks said.

"*Ohh*, yeah. He was runnin' all over the place."

"Was Ms. Simmons there when you arrived?" asked Weirdlee.

Hipps shook his head. "Nope. She came by about, oh, closer to six-thirtyish, though. I was puttin' away stuff in the van after the cops'd talked to me. She pulled into the lot a couple cars away from me."

"She upset, too?" Fielding asked.

Hipps squinted his eyes and put on a pondering expression. "You know..." he said, recalling, "she seemed pretty settled, actually. Like it's just business as usual."

"The police had already called her and talked to her," Nicks said to Fielding. He asked Hipps then, "She went straight to the cops there, did she?"

"Uhhh," Hipps droned, trying to recall. "Not sure. But she was the opposite of the guy there—the principal. Potter. She didn't seem bothered by the shit goin' on at all."

"Did you ever hear Ms. Simmons talk about Regina Hawkins?" asked Weirdlee.

"Me?" Hipps said, jabbing a finger at himself. "Nope. Never heard nothin'."

Nicks took out his smartphone and checked the time. It was 11:20 AM. "What time does your colleague, Jennifer, usually come in?" he asked Hipps.

"Oh, she comes in after lunchtime. About one o'clock."

Nicks gave a nod, and put away his phone. "Okay, Mr. Hipps," he said. "I think we're all set, here. Thank you for your time."

Fielding seemed taken aback by his partner's abrupt ending of the interview. He kept his surprise to a simple raised eyebrow at Nicks, though.

Hipps nodded, and he looked at Weirdlee one last time with an eager grin. "Sure 'nuff."

After Hipps had left Zimmer's office, the three agents talked.

"You didn't have anything else to ask the man?" Fielding asked Nicks.

"He doesn't know anything else," Nicks replied. "I got what I wanted from him, anyway. We know who was at the park before six-thirty, and who wasn't." He flipped his note pad closed and tucked it into his suit jacket pocket. "I think we'll stick around here for lunch and wait for this Jennifer, uh, what's-her-name to come in." He snapped his fingers and looked at Weirdlee. "Oh yeah. Before I forget. Can you call up Ms. Hawkins and ask her for the name of her babysitter?"

Weirdlee replied, "Sure."

"I'm not really suspecting anything there," Nicks went on, "but if the boy did make it back home..."

Fielding nodded, getting his meaning. "Coverin' all the bases."

Nicks winked at him. "Exactly."

Weirdlee asked, "You want me here for the next interview, too, or...?"

"Nah," Nicks said. "You can head out for your interview with that guy. Get yourself some lunch, first, though."

Weirdlee smiled. "Sounds good."

~ | ~

-7-

Deceptions

[Channel 4, Eyewitness News]
*The FBI is in Lafourche Parish this week
investigating the case of four-year-old
Julien Hawkins, first reported missing
three years ago in the Bayou L'Ours area.
The FBI is not commenting on their
investigation, but local authorities have
confirmed to us that there are currently
no new leads in the case. Law
enforcement experts we spoke with,
meanwhile, have speculated that the Feds
may be performing a review of police
procedures undertaken in the case. Julien
Hawkins went missing in a community
park next to the Bayou L'Ours, in
Kraemer, on July 11th of 2011. Police at
the time had concluded that it was likely
the boy fell into the nearby river, which
directly abuts the park. No remains or
any other evidence were ever recovered.*

* * * *

Jennifer Satchens arrived for work at just after 1:00 PM. She was greeted right away by Frank Zimmer, who let her know about their visitors from the FBI, and that they wanted to talk to her about the day Julien Hawkins disappeared. He escorted her to his office, where Special Agents Nicks and Fielding were waiting. She took her seat behind Zimmer's desk as the administrator himself left the room.

"I'm kinda confused," she said right off to the agents. "I thought the boy died in the bayou?"

Nicks pulled out his little black notepad and pen and set the notepad on his lap. "We're just trying to get everything straight, Ms. Satchens. We're trying to establish, a bit more clearly, a timeline of events leading up to Julien's disappearance, and then figure out what happened afterwards."

Satchens nodded, unsure. "All right. I'll try to help out."

"You worked at the park the whole day?" Fielding asked her. "From the time you got dropped off till after the boy went missin' and the cops showed up?"

"Yeah, that's right. I was there the whole time."

"Ms. Satchens," Nicks asked, "when did you first recall hearing that Julien was missing?"

"Oh..." Satchens considered, "wasn't till after the cops showed up, actually. I'd asked Sally what was going on."

"Was that about five o'clock?" Nicks asked.

She nodded. "I think so."

"You stayed by the daycare's tent pretty much the whole day?" asked Fielding.

"Yeah, I served food and bottles of soda and water. I had breaks, ya know, but that was pretty much my day."

"I suppose there was a lot of chaos going around after the boy went missing," Nicks said.

"Sure," Satchens agreed. "Everybody wanted to find that boy."

"And, uh, Ms. Simmons came by in her own car—what was it, six-ish?" asked Fielding.

Satchens nodded. "About that, I guess. She'd come by earlier in the day, too—before all the shit happened."

"She did?" Nicks asked, surprised. "You mean, when everyone first got there, she helped you all set up."

"Well, that, sure. But then also I think around three or four o'clock she stopped by to check on us. I swear I remember seeing her."

Nicks and Fielding both looked at each other. The former said to his partner, "Not asking the right questions, I guess." He turned back to Satchens. "You can't remember if it was three or four o'clock, though?"

"Try to remember," Fielding urged her.

Satchens thought for a moment longer. She shook her head. "No...I'm sorry. I didn't check the time. But I know she was going back to the daycare center. Maybe Burt saw her there."

Nicks glanced at Fielding and gave him a nod. They'd confirm that with Hipps afterwards.

"Now try to think back," Nicks asked Satchens. "Do you remember noticing any of the volunteers going missing that day—maybe someone you thought should have been there, but wasn't?"

Satchens frowned, shaking her head as she answered. "I'm sorry, sir, but I was new back then, and didn't really know anyone too much. I wouldn'ta known who was supposed to be there and who wasn't."

Nicks tapped his notepad with his pen, resigned. "Okay, Ms. Satchens. Thank you."

* * * *

The road to Paradis from the Bayou L'Ours followed south along Route 307 for close to ten miles as it took a geographical detour around the flood basin of the Bayou des Allemends. The route then met up with Route 90 at the former's southern end. From there, Route 90 ran back up northeast for another six miles before coming to the town of Des Allemends. Paradis lay just four miles further up the road.

For Special Agent Weirdlee, it was a long, thoughtful drive—and a spiritual one, as well. She'd started out with a purposeful mindset: She would go to Paul Basil's home, talk to him about the missing boy—ask if he saw or maybe perceived anything that could help the FBI's investigation—and then perhaps also mention the Curse of the Bayous, just in case there might be any connection there. But as the drive wore on, her thoughts drifted away from the mundane here-and-now, and so on to less comforting recollections of her seemingly long-ago upbringing in the years before.

Young Joanna had been a lonely child, growing up with parents who at times felt embarrassed by their daughter's odd behavior. "Don't talk to people, dear," her mother would say to her when they were out and about. "Don't say those silly things about the spirits and nature. People will think there's something wrong with you."

People did. Weirdlee—or rather, Joanna Osborne, still, in those days—was often ridiculed by her classmates as she went through elementary school and then on to high school. "Psycho," some would call her. "Retard," by others. The skinny, timid girl who sat by herself, mumbling prayers or chants that she'd made up and rehearsed on her own, was an easy target for the bullies of the day, both girls and boys. Her parents, far more embarrassed by their daughter than concerned for her, considered home schooling for their daughter just to keep her out of the public eye more thoroughly. Later on then, as she grew old enough to be left at home on her own, her parents thought it better to keep her there to "watch the house" while they themselves went out socializing.

There were no family reunions. There were no big birthday parties. There was only just Joanna, always on her own. And, of course, she had her witchcraft, which she'd taught herself from a very early age. She'd read about witch covens, too, and how they practiced the craft as a family. But she being the reclusive sort of girl, Joanna never felt comfortable enough about joining one. She had her own, special beliefs, and would practice these on her own, becoming what is commonly known as a hedge witch.

After high school, Joanna's parents—who deep down truly did love their daughter, but felt hurt and heartache for the way she'd come to be—deliberated about sending her away to college. Would she be able to get along on her own and take care of herself? Probably not, they decided. But her grades all through high school were actually quite good, and so her parents also had every reason to believe she could still be successful in life—if only she could grow up and get away from that pagan nonsense.

The family had money, so they also had options. And after the usual go-around with school admissions, testing, and—why not?—scholarship and grant applications, Joanna was finally accepted at Brandeis University, which was perfectly located just a ways down Route 95 from their home in Salem, so she wouldn't need to move away.

Still, the elder Osbornes worried for their daughter. She had grown into a strikingly beautiful young woman, and, regardless of her quirks, many a young man had expressed his desire for her company. It had started during her junior and senior years in high school, when some of the very same boys who'd taunted her in their earlier grade levels then approached the leggy beauty hoping for some reconsideration. Perhaps not surprisingly, she shunned every one of their advances, her memory of their cruelty towards her still vivid in her mind.

But, her parents fretted, would she be able to keep the guys she met at college at bay, and resist her own youthful yearnings?

The answer to that was, predictably, not for very long. Joanna attracted the attention of a handsome young man right off, and, throughout her first semester at school, their after-school sexual escapades would often continue far into the later evening hours. This very much angered her parents, who worried terribly for their daughter when she'd come home so late at night. Fortunately for both them and for her, however, this wouldn't last for very long. By the arrival of spring, and upon entering her second semester at Brandeis, the thrill of having a first, true boyfriend had largely left Joanna. She bored of the young man's adolescent ways, and he, for his part, bored of her homespun witchery and solitary meditations.

Her next two years at Brandeis turned out to be largely uneventful, with just a date here and a romp in the sack there getting her by. Her witchy ways, too, had become well known to both her classmates and her professors. School administrators had caught wind of her abilities, as well, and so eventually did that very secretive organization known as the Central Intelligence Agency.

For Joanna Weirdlee's powers (she had legally changed her name in her junior year) were seemingly very real.

Unfortunately for the CIA's purposes, though, the girl was unable to call upon her powers of second sight at will. The visions she saw and voices she heard just came to her, unawares. And even then, they came only as hints and riddles, rather than clear, distinct perceptions. She did have a rather remarkable power of deception—a tricky tool that, on its own, the Agency unfortunately had little use for. And so, they felt, without the ability to see into the future in a predictable way, her reliability would always be held in question, and therefore her usefulness to them always limited. Plus, there was also the matter of her personality, which the Agency found to be somewhat indiscrete and overly casual for their culture.

The CIA, then, passed on the witch from Salem.

Weirdlee came to the end of Route 307, and from there turned right onto the main highway of Route 90, leading north. The land about her opened up to flat, farmed fields, with just a thin line of trees bordering either side of the route. The air was hot and still.

She drove on.

FBI Assistant Director Marvin Ledds first heard about Joanna Weirdlee from a friend of his at the CIA. The friend had mentioned that the Agency—or "the Company" as he called it—had come upon a quirky young woman with some unique, but unfortunately unreliable, abilities. Too bad, the friend quipped to his FBI colleague, because she otherwise had the smarts and the looks to be a very useful operative.

Ledds took the last comment to heart, and was on the earliest flight to Boston the next day.

If professional pairings had a level called "love," then for Ledds and Weirdlee, it was love at first sight. Ledds absolutely adored the young redhead, and she found him, after just a short acquaintance, to be quite the fatherly figure in his relationship with her. So well did the two hit it off, in fact, that Ledds had little trouble in convincing the exuberant Weirdlee that the FBI was the place for her to be.

"You are a healer, Joanna—we both know that. Who better to help those who've suffered from terrible crimes? Who better to bring them peace? You were put on this Earth as a gift to us all."

Very heady words, indeed, for a woman who'd spent most of her young life shunned by all of those around her. And Ledds meant every word of it.

Soon enough, then, after joining the FBI, Special Agent Weirdlee *did* help the suffering. She healed them of their pain and, with Special Agent Nicks leading the way, brought them justice so long denied. There was so much potential in the Bureau for her, she found. So much to offer. If only, she wondered, she could truly harness her inherent intuition, and so finally be the complete witch she had always longed to be.

She looked into her future as she drove along. There was a wholeness there, she sensed. She needed only to trust in those who would give it to her. And one of them, just then, spoke to her, even as she traveled north to meet him.

I await you...

She smiled at him longingly.

Come to me...

Weirdlee drove through the town of Des Allemends, her mind settling on the task at hand.

You will give yourself to him, the old woman's voice reminded her. *You will surrender yourself to him, and only then will youz be a complete woman, in every way.*

Weirdlee kept her gaze ahead of her as she passed north, toward the outskirts of Paradis.

She whispered to herself, entranced by Zarah's spell. "I go to Marcel Unate..." She belonged to him fully and forever, she knew. And she would surrender herself to him when she arrived at his home.

My Joanna, he beckoned her once more. *Come to me...*

Weirdlee's heart raced with excitement. She gripped the steering wheel of her Grand Cherokee, her mind awhirl with visions of finally being with her true and only lover!

Marcel! she called to him in her mind.

She pressed the accelerator, speeding onward.

I must go to Marcel!

Speeding ahead along Route 90, she glanced about, suddenly aware of her surroundings.

Take a left onto Route 635.

It was just up ahead of her.

Taking the turn, she drove to the end of what turned out to be a short road, and then turned right to head north again on Route 631.

Soon—very soon—she would be with her lover.

As she raced on, the flat countryside passed by her, appearing like images of a life being left behind. She swallowed anxiously, keeping her gaze straight ahead of her. Memories conjured in her mind then, both sad and happy, and the distant future came to her, as well, drawn up by the hand of Fate itself.

So many endings. So many paths to wander across and explore. The old, lonely woman in the woods. The beggar. The lover. The powerful queen! All of these tragedies and fortunes, any one of which could be the one future that came to her, someday.

What is going to happen to me? she asked herself desperately, suddenly confused and alarmed by the myriad visions flashing about in her delirious mind.

Finally, then, her visions settled on a single scene as it slowly materialized. A frail, elderly African-American man looked up at her. He lay on a white bed, in a small room hazily lit by the rays of a sunny morning. She herself appeared older as she stood by his bedside, holding his aged hand in her own. Her once dark red hair, which she'd always dyed in years past, had given way to her natural brunette tresses.

The old man smiled at her in a very warm and fatherly way. He said to her in a weak voice, "I am so proud of you."

Joanna looked down at him, heartbroken. She said then to the man who had recruited her and given her a life she would always be thankful for, "I love you."

The old man smiled brighter, for he truly felt the same.

His eyelids drew closed then, in a final, peaceful repose.

Joanna fell upon him, and she wept openly for a very long time.

The brakes of Weirdlee's Grand Cherokee screeched aloud as she brought the vehicle to swift, shuddering halt by the side of the road. White-knuckling the steering wheel, she gasped for air, stricken by the memory of a future that might never come to be.

My God! she said to herself as she regained her senses. *What was I thinking?*

She looked off to the road that stretched ahead of her. There, she suspected, was a part of the answer, for whatever good or ill. She might very well be driving into a trap, she knew, and she might still be under Zarah Devillier's lingering spell, compelled by the old woman to go on. But the voodoo priest, Basil, she now sensed, was a part of this tragic mystery, for whatever role he played.

And so, whether compelled by Zarah or by an unyielding sense of duty, Joanna Weirdlee pulled back onto the road and continued on.

* * * *

Paul Basil drew back the curtain of his kitchen window and peeked outside at the Grand Cherokee just then pulling into his driveway. He smiled, and he watched as the vehicle parked close to his front porch. Stepping away from the window, then, he approached the front door to greet his visitor.

Weirdlee stepped out of her car, and she surveyed the old house she'd arrived at as she shut the car door behind her. The white, two-story home was set on an overgrown lot that appeared in dire need of tending to. The front porch, she saw, was worn from decades of use, with faded white paint flaked off in long chunks along its floor planks and trim. An old rocking chair was set on its left side. Something else, as well, besides the physical disrepair to the place caught her attention.

Despair.

The same sensation she'd felt when she approached Zarah's house the other day.

Loneliness.

Emptiness.

Danger.

The front door on the porch opened then, and a tall, muscular black man greeted her.

"Good afternoon," he said to her without a smile.

Weirdlee retrieved her ID billfold from her pantsuit's jacket pocket as she walked up to the porch's steps.

"Mr. Paul Basil?" she asked him.

He nodded slowly, his eyes examining her. The woman appeared to have no idea why she was really there.

"Yes," he answered. "That's the name I go by, for some."

Weirdlee flipped her billfold open and showed him her FBI credentials. "I'm Special Agent Joanna Weirdlee, sir, with the FBI."

Basil grinned in a entirely smug way.

"I know who you are," he said to her coldly, "Joanna Osborne."

Weirdlee stopped.

"You think I cannot see?" Basil quizzed her. "You think I had no idea you were coming to me?"

Weirdlee stared back at him for a moment. The man, she realized just then, was a genuine conjurer, the same as Zarah Devillier.

Look past his voice when he speaks, she told herself. *He will try to entrance you.*

She asked him as she put away her billfold, "You know why I'm here, then?"

He nodded in answer.

"Then perhaps you can help us?" she asked.

He eyed her coldly for a moment, sizing her up. He'd noted her Boston accent, which he found quite sexy. Oddly enough, though, she didn't appear to be in any way transfixed by him, as he'd assumed she would be.

Perhaps Zarah's spellcasting from afar was not working on her, as promised.

The old hag!

"Why don't you come in?" he asked her. "I've got some coffee."

She gave him a perfunctory smile. "I'm a tea drinker, actually."

He smirked at her as he stepped back inside. "Got that, too."

After he re-entered his home, Weirdlee stood there on her own for a moment, deciding what course to take. The man obviously wasn't going to talk to her outside, in the open. She placed her hand on her chest, where, underneath her blouse, she wore her amulet. Through her clothing, she held it firmly in her fingers.

Protect me from evil.

She felt, as well, the comforting presence of her Glock-23, holstered as it was to her belt underneath her jacket. That on its own helped her to make up her mind.

She made her way up the stairs then and to the front door, which Basil had left open. She peered beyond it, to look inside. There, a small, square table was set at the center of what she saw was the kitchen area. Basil was inside, placing a cup of coffee and, she presumed, a cup of tea on the table. She noted that he placed her tea at the far side of the table, with the chair there facing the door she was presently at—a move perhaps to quell her anxiety of having doors behind her. She looked to her left, there to see a hallway that perhaps led to the living room of the house. A flight of stairs was there, too, leading up to the second floor.

"Come inside, Ms. Osborne," Basil beckoned her. "You've come a long way out here looking for answers, and I have lot of them to offer you."

Avoid his words...

She stepped into the kitchen. The air around her suddenly thickened, and for a very brief moment, she felt light-headed. Recovering quickly, she said to Basil, "I don't have much time. My colleagues are expecting me back."

Of course they are, thought Basil. *But you belong to me, now.*

Weirdlee stepped over to her tea and took a seat there. Basil joined her, sitting opposite her.

"So..." Weirdlee began, "did you know my birth name before or after Ms. Devillier told you about me?"

Basil scoffed and laughed at the question. "I don't need that old woman to tell me anything," he said. "I'm a powerful high priest, on my own. You will learn that about me, soon enough. You will learn that I see, and know, many things."

Weirdlee eyed him plainly. "I hope so."

She reached into her jacket pocket then and pulled out the small photograph of Julien Hawkins. She placed it on the table and slid it over to Basil.

118

"What can you tell me about this boy?" she asked him.

Basil looked down at the photo. As he did so, Weirdlee detected no sign of recognition in his demeanor.

"He's just a boy," he said to her. "What about him?"

"He's gone missing, for a few years, now. Can you see him in your mind? Do you know what's become of him?"

Basil scowled as he eyed the picture. Then he looked up at Weirdlee. "The boy is dead."

"What?" Weirdlee said, taken aback.

"The boy is dead. I see nothing but blackness. What did you think I would see?"

Weirdlee stared down at the picture, shaken by Basil's frankness. "I..."

"Why did you come to me, woman?" Basil asked.

She looked up at him. "To see if you can help us to—"

"No!" Basil cried out. "You do not need me. *You* are a witch. *You* can see anything you wish!"

"But I can't," she replied.

Basil put his fingers on the photograph and flicked it back at Weirdlee. "Because you are weak, woman. You don't understand what you are—or what you can be."

Weirdlee focused her thoughts on her questions. Basil was trying to sidetrack her, she knew.

"Does the boy's death have anything to do with the curse?" she asked him.

"Curse?" Basil replied. "What curse are you talking about?"

"The Curse of the Bayous. You know what I mean."

Basil laughed. He slapped his hand on the table and scoffed aloud, "Curse of the Bayous, my God! Curse of the Fearful, more like it! Curse of the Weak. Curse of the Fools. It is the same no matter where you go. People do stupid things—things they soon regret. Walk on thin ice. Jump out of an airplane. Once you are there, there is no turning back. The curse, if you think there is such a thing, is the curse of all humanity. We are all going to die, sister diviner, each in our own time, and at a place God chose for us long before we were born. Our fates are sealed."

"What happened to the boy?" Weirdlee asked, keeping to the matter at hand.

Suddenly, then, she felt light-headed once more. She shook her head and drew herself back before recovering her senses.

"Was he murdered?" she asked. "Was he killed by someone?"

Basil stared purposefully at his visitor. He looked deeply into her mind. She was fighting him, though.

Only I can make you a complete woman...

Weirdlee swallowed, perceiving his message, and she wiped her brow with her fingers. Her eyes met Basil's then, as he smiled back at her.

"I can give you all that you'll ever want or need in your life," he said to her. "You will never be a complete witch without my knowledge—my gift, to you."

Weirdlee trembled, unable to take her eyes away from Basil's own. "I can't..."

"You must," he told her. "Or you will forever be weak and lost. You will never know the full wisdom and power of your craft." He leaned in closer to her. "Innocents will suffer—and for no reason. The guilty will go unpunished."

His words, seeming more like whispers, filled her mind as he spoke, and quickly overwhelmed her senses.

"There is only one way for you to find true peace in your life. You must learn what the Invisibles have said to me about life, and know that only I can give you that knowledge. Only I can make you a complete woman...in every way."

Weirdlee closed her eyes, and she prayed...

Listen to the spirits. Water, air, fire, and earth...I hear the spirit Mother Earth, she is calling to me. Blessed are the keepers of my soul...

Basil leered at the witch as he continued.

"Wherever you are in your life, you will always return to me, and you will always know that only I can give you the gift that will set your spirit free." He slowly stood up from his chair. "You will join with me, Joanna Osborne, and I will give you everything that life can offer you." He stepped away from the table, and then walked over to the front door. "I am your teacher, your protector, and...you know this to be true...your God-given lover."

Weirdlee breathed in deeply, and all around her, the world drew silent.

"You belong to me, now, Joanna Osborne, witch from Salem," Basil growled. "I am your keeper."

Weirdlee, though, never heard this final commandment.

"I have to go, now," she replied instead—and in an unexpectedly coherent tone.

Basil spun around to face her. "What did you say to me?"

Weirdlee looked back at him, appearing to have recovered all of her mental faculties. "I can't accept your offer, Mr. Basil. The price is just too high."

He snarled at her, and shouted, "You can never go back, Anglo witch! You are *mine!*"

She remained unmoved by his declaration.

"I have to go, Mr. Basil," she replied. "My life belongs only to me."

Basil leered at her. He wasn't about to let this woman to go. Not now.

Turning to the door, he latched its bolt lock secure.

"You belong to me, now," he said once more. Then he turned to her again, looking at her gravely. "Get your ass upstairs."

Weirdlee stared back at him. Her predicament was such that the man stood a mere twelve feet away from her, and also in front of the very door she needed to get through. She was armed, yes, but she would still have to gain some space between herself and her assailant in order to have enough time draw her weapon. Out of the corner of her eye then, she could see, to her right, the hallway leading to what she perceived to be the home's living room area.

Basil sensed her intention.

Instantly, Weirdlee bolted up from her chair and raced off—and Basil sprang after her! They met at the hallway's entrance, Weirdlee clawing at the grip of her Glock-23 as he grabbed a hold of her, bear-hugging her. He spun her around violently then and slammed her into the wall.

"You are mine!" he cried aloud, holding her firmly.

Weirdlee screamed defiantly, "*NO!*"—and struggled desperately in his grasp.

He pounded her twice more against the wall, and then spun her around, yanking her down so as to pull her to the floor. She pried herself away, though, and—with all of her might—she lunged forward in a turning move that threw her attacker off balance, finally breaking his hold on her.

Then, in that very instant—she was gone!

Basil spun himself about, glancing every which way. *What the hell?*

"Hold it!" Weirdlee called out.

Basil turned about to face the corner of the living room they'd come into. There, standing in a firing stance several feet away from him, Weirdlee held her Glock-23 in both hands, aiming it squarely at the thick of Basil's chest.

Deception!

The Voodoo King swore at himself. He should have known better.

"Step away from the hallway," Weirdlee demanded.

He sneered at her. "I am your only chance to be whole, woman. You will never shoot me!"

Weirdlee adjusted her aim and she squeezed the trigger. The Glock *popped* loudly—sending a bullet whizzing by Basil's head and blasting into the wall beside him.

"I *might*," she declared in an emotional voice.

Basil eyed her. She was clearly unnerved, and, he decided, not to be tested. He stepped away slowly to the center of the room.

"All the way back," Weirdlee demanded, gesturing with her pistol.

He continued to the front side of the living room.

Weirdlee kept her aim on him as she strode back into the kitchen. Basil followed behind her in a casual gait.

"You'll never get away from me, Salem witch," he told her. "You leave me now, I will haunt your dreams until you return."

"We'll see about that," she said as she made it to the door. "Stay inside, Mr. Basil. I don't want to have to shoot you."

He laughed at her. "You slut witch. You are only delaying the inevitable. God has made his choice."

Weirdlee left the house and hurried down the porch steps, all the while keeping her Glock-23 pointed at the doorway behind her. Only when she'd made it to her vehicle did she lower the weapon while opening the driver's side door. She hopped into the Grand Cherokee and set her pistol down. Quickly retrieving her car keys, she started up the engine. She looked back at Basil's house, to see him standing at the front door, watching her.

"Heretic!" he yelled at her. "You'll never escape me! So long as my eyes look into your pagan soul, you will see me in your dreams, and I will have you!"

Weirdlee shifted the vehicle into reverse and then punched the accelerator. The Cherokee's wheels spit dirt and dust into the air as it raced back down the unpaved driveway. She turned the wheel then and shifted the gear into forward, then punched the pedal once more.

Basil watched the Salem witch race off in a cloud of dust. He huffed indignantly before turning and walking back inside. Returning to the kitchen table, he picked up his cup of coffee and drank from it. Then he looked down at the table, there to see the photograph of the little boy that Weirdlee had left there in her desperate scramble to escape from him. He set his coffee down, and then picked up the photo, eyeing the image of Julien Hawkins thoughtfully.

The devil's work is a terrible thing, he said to himself.

And he had a phone call to make.

-8-

The Curse of the Bayous

Jeremiah Hillard first met up with Malton DeMures, a local voodoo practitioner living outside of New Orleans, in the early springtime of 1907. Hillard, a young man in his late twenties, worked as a doctor in the small city of Houma, some ways off to the south, and was somewhat of a spiritual idealist, believing that a combination of medicine and faith could cure just about any malady befalling mankind. The doctor and the voodoo priest hit it off right away, and would often spend hours discussing the various religious philosophies of the time, including all of the numerous taboos of the Christian faith, in particular. Hillard was brought up a Protestant, but while going through medical school he came to question many of that branch's teachings. Still being a spiritual man, though, he knew there had to be an as-yet undiscovered truth regarding the nature of life and the universe.

DeMures, consequently, easily drew him into the voodoo faith, introducing him to many of its tenets and folklore. Seduced by its magickal allure, Hillard soon began to wonder if he could use voodoo as a means of enhancing his more mundane medical procedures. So it was that he and DeMures began to experiment with

125

different combinations of natural remedies, pharmaceuticals, and ritualistic incantations, in a quest to find the answer.

The results were mixed. Some patients—nearly all of whom were unknowing of the true nature of their treatment—recovered from their sickness or injury convincingly enough to allow for Hillard and DeMures to attribute their return to health to their new methods. Others, meanwhile, simply sank further into illness. And some even died.

This all frustrated Hillard, who, as 1907 passed into 1908, grew increasingly convinced of the powers of voodoo, despite their methods' inconclusive findings.

"I must unlock the secrets of the Invisibles," he told his colleague. "Tell me more of these spells, and what avenues I might follow to call the spirits directly to me."

DeMures laughed at his colleague. "You do not speak to the *loa* on your own terms, sir. They are a part of nature itself, and will speak only to those whom they regard as their mortal agents on Earth. When I, myself, call to them, I merely *ask* for their presence. *They* decide if they will come and listen to my pleas."

"I have seen their power," Hillard said, "and I have seen them heal. There must be a way to harness this power, and so bring back those who have been denied their health and happiness. I tire of seeing death come to the undeserving. Why should we not use the spirit world for our own ends— if those ends be just and good?"

DeMures snarled and declared, "You do not make demands of the spirits! They will smite you down!"

"God gave us this Earth," Hillard argued. "He gave us stewardship of the lands, and he made us the keepers of the creatures that roam here. Why should we not then call upon his spiritual minions to aid us in our duties?"

"You dare challenge the way of things?" said DeMures. "What you speak of is heresy!"

"Voodoo itself is heresy!" Hillard declared. "Only by Divine Will has its followers seen the light and so blessed themselves in the eyes of God."

"What would you have the *loa* do for you?" DeMures asked.

Hillard approached his partner, standing face-to-face. "I want to summon them," he said, "to heal the innocent, and to punish all that is evil in this world."

DeMures scoffed. "And who are you to decide what is evil and what is simply an act of nature?"

Hillard turned away, frustrated by DeMures' intransigence.

"I will find the secrets of the spirits myself if you will not help me," he said. "I will unlock their powers, and I will wield my magick in my own, righteous ways."

"You are a fool for trying." DeMures sneered. "You will not succeed."

Hillard turned back to his once friend and now rival. "You just try to stop me."

* * * *

For the next several weeks, Hillard worked alone in his free hours, conjuring the spirit world as best he could by devising his own potions and elixirs and reciting incantations he'd learned from local lore. In particular, he summoned the *Ghede loa*—the spirits of the dead—whom he surmised would be the most helpful of any in aiding him in his plans. First off, he communicated with the spirit Baron Kriminel, patron of death and criminals, who left him unanswered on most occasions.

"Punish the wicked, for they are impure!" was Hillard's plea to him.

He summoned Maman Brigitte, too, the wife of Baron Samedi (whom Hillard suspected was none other than Kriminel himself), asking for her aid, as well. She was, in his opinion, a vile thing—barely presentable even to those who admired her, and otherwise disgusting in her appearance, and with a swearing tongue that offended him greatly. Nevertheless, she was also a powerful spirit and all-knowing in things concerning death and dying, and so he knew he needed her.

She, however, never did come to him.

The hag!

In time, Hillard's medical practice began to suffer as patients and professional colleagues alike left him. He drew increasingly isolated from the world around him, until such time as he feared he might be losing his mind.

Followers, he told himself then. *I need worshippers by my side!*

Surprisingly, they wouldn't be hard to find.

Throughout the 18th and 19th centuries, Louisiana voodoo mixed with mainstream French Catholicism, with voodoo practitioners adopting many of the latter religion's symbols and beliefs. (The famed mid-19th century voodoo queen Marie Laveau, for instance, was said to have held her own public rituals after first attending Catholic mass each Sunday.) Hillard personally detested Catholicism, but realized that many local Catholics—particularly those of African-Caribbean descent—might find solace in his notion of justice for the dead and for the punishment of those perceived to have strayed from the word of God.

He was right. Racism and hostility towards the minority classes in Louisiana was rampant in the early 20th century. And, as it was so often denied them otherwise, people would invariably pray to God, asking for His justice instead. Hillard's newfound Voodoo-Catholic spiritualism would thus create a doorway through which

God's will could be channeled, and so His judgment finally realized.

By the start of 1909, Hillard's faithful followers numbered in the dozens, and the doctor-turned-priest himself had grown obsessed with learning more and more about the powers and virtues of the voodoo faith. He explored its many paths into the spirit world, and devised his own spells to accommodate his plan of one day using the might of the *Invisibles* to usurp the mundane rule of man. And, alas, he also put upon himself a determination that, regardless of what cost it may incur, any means he saw fit were so justified in doing right by the world.

Fight fire with fire. Fight darkness with darkness. Fight evil with...

Hillard turned his mind to the black arts of voodoo. His followers soon joined him. Together, he told them, they alone would determine right from wrong, innocence from criminality, and good from evil. Theirs was a righteous cause, he lectured, and God was on their side.

All while this went on, Hillard was, unbeknownst to him, being watched from afar by his former colleague, Malton DeMures. The voodoo priest abhorred Hillard's perversion of his faith, and had been working the whole time to counter the white man's designs. Alone in his shack along the banks of the Bayou des Allemends, he chanted and sang his incantations as he turned to the *loa* to save humanity from this terrible scourge in the making.

> *I beg of you, oh spirit world!*
> *Hear my pleas—my fateful words!*
> *His days be damned, his soul be burned!*
> *His end shall come, this end so earned!*

His prayers, though, went seemingly unanswered. Hillard's faithful ranks continued to grow in the wilderness of the bayous. His followers tended to his needs, and they obeyed his unearthly commands.

Punish the heretics!
Justice for the followers of God!

It was in the summer of 1909, then, when Hillard first learned of DeMures' treachery against him.

"The fool," he sneered. "I have outgrown him by ten-fold. His prayers will get him nowhere!"

But still, the white priest determined, an enemy was an enemy. And he wasn't about to let DeMures carry on with his ways.

A plot was thus hatched, and Hillard gathered his minions for a trek into the bayous and an evening of retribution. They found DeMures in his shack on the banks of the Bayou des Allemends. He decried their presence there—the authorities would learn of this intrusion! But at the turn of the 20th century, law and order in the bayous was still very much in the people's hands. The authorities, alas for DeMures, were far out of his reach. And so Hillard ordered DeMures be bound and carried off deeper into the wilderness, where any cries would surely go unheard. DeMures swore and cursed the entire way, vowing that justice would one day come to Hillard and his blinded followers.

As a full moon rose high in the evening sky, Hillard ordered his prisoner tied to a post by the banks of the river des Allemends. He unsheathed a blade from his belt, and he stood close before the bound and helpless DeMures.

"Heretic!" he cried out to his foe. "You pray to the same spirits who betray the word of God!"

Hillard's followers, all surrounding the two men on the bank, chanted in the night:

> *God is mighty, God is great...*
> *All who live will meet their fate!*
> *God is mighty, God is great...*
> *All who live will meet their fate!*

"You are the Devil!" DeMures cried out. "God will not forgive you!"

"Blasphemy!" Hillard yelled in turn. "Heretic! Burn in hell!"

And with that, he grabbed hold of DeMures' hair, and he took his blade and cut into DeMures' forehead—carving, in deep cuts, a bloody letter H.

DeMures cried out, "Damn you!" and leered angrily at his tormentor as blood streamed down his face, saying to him, "Jeremiah Hillard! I curse you and all your servants to a life of misery and darkness! You and all who follow in your path shall walk blindly into Death, unknowing, and so meet your fate under the eyes of God!"

Hillard scowled at him, and he spat on his face. "To hell with your gods!"

He turned from DeMures then and walked away. "Kill him," he said to his followers, too cowardly to commit the deed himself.

His followers quickly obeyed. Blades drawn and hatred boiling in their souls, they fell upon their victim in a mad frenzy.

As DeMures' tortured cries filled the air, Hillard took in a breath, knowing well that he'd crossed a line from which he could never step back. From this day on, he and his followers would be, by their own declaration, the assigned agents of Fate itself, there to deliver God's wayward children to the heavenly everafter, and so returning them to the Kingdom of Heaven.

He told his people then: "We are but the facilitators of God's own will. And it is written that all who live on this Earth have already had their fates written by His hand. Their end has been cast before they ever opened their eyes. We, the faithful, are merely their shepherds, guiding them on their way."

Hillard's reign of terror in the region thus began. Not mass killings, to be sure, but instead an abduction here, and a killing there. Just enough sordid treachery, it was, to immerse his people in their own equal share of guilt, and in so doing, ensure their loyalty.

And their slavery.

All the while, as this unfolded, the *loa*—who appeared to have abandoned DeMures in his tortured misery—watched these wicked despicables, and so judged them from afar. They would not intervene directly; only priests and priestesses, the mortal agents of the *loa*, had such powers, they being of the same blood as their brothers and sisters. Rather, the Invisibles held divine influence over the natural world—the wind and water and the earth itself. It would be from these places, then, that their retribution would one day arise.

Hillard, as the supernaturals already knew, was no genuine priest himself. This much had always been true. Oh, he'd truly believed he was delivering justice and that his work was for a greater good. But for all of his efforts and wanting, he had never been properly schooled in the ways of magick. The Gift he'd so longed for was never given to him, nor ever even offered. His spells, thusly, for all of their rhyming beauty, were in reality quite powerless. He had no intuitive skills, nor unearthly ability to control the minds of others. Everything he did was a con job. A sales pitch to his followers.

And of this, he was well aware.

As August fell away to September, Hillard decided to lead his followers southward, farther into the watery wilderness of the bayous. There, upon a small, swampy island in the midst of the mighty Mississippi River's meandering delta, they built their compound, where, Hillard determined, they would build their own colony of true believers.

Time, however, would not be on their side. For brewing in the Caribbean that season, a hurricane in the making blew its way northwest. And by the twentieth day of that month, the vast storm had passed Cuba and so arrived at the northern coast of the Gulf of Mexico. On the 21st of September then, the hurricane slammed into the Louisiana coast, nearby Grand Isle at the mouth of the Mississippi delta, and from there followed a path inland that led it directly to Hillard's budding colony, east of Golden Meadow. The storm's one hundred-mile-an-hour winds blew asunder anything in its path, natural or manmade. Storm surge roared inland for two miles, inundating the bayous there entirely.

Hillard stood upon his island's high point, braced against the storm's mighty winds, shouting defiantly at the spirits who'd betrayed him!

"Damn you all! We will survive! You will not destroy us!"

His followers all screamed and fled as best they could from the burgeoning waters. Their fates, however, were already sealed as the island was brought underneath the waters. Nearly all who had once lived there perished there, and for many days thereafter the alligators feasted on their remains.

Hillard's own body was swept out to sea, never to be seen again.

One child, it came to be, survived the watery disaster. Even the spirits, in all their divine rage, could not bring themselves to smite her down. The daughter of a follower, this nine-year-old Anglo girl had found her way up to higher ground just to the northwest of Hillard's doomed island. As the storm quelled and the waters began to recede the next day, then, she trekked northward until at some point along the way she got picked up by a family, and so was taken to the little village of Larose.

The young girl, named Marah, had become an orphan. She spent the next few months, going into 1910, under the state's care before a couple from Houma finally adopted her. They raised her then as their own, seemingly in peace.

Marah, though, had never forgotten her birth mother's teachings, even at such a young age. So, after some years had passed, she took up the voodoo again as a teenager—at first only secretly, and then later on in the open. Her new parents—good Christians they be—scolded their daughter for her practices. But they could not sway her from her adopted faith.

As a grown woman, Marah traveled the region, selling herself and her enchantments to others to get by. She—unlike Hillard—had acquired the power of intuition from birth; it was in her blood and in her soul. So it came to be, then, that after just a few short years, she had risen to become one of the most influential voodoo queens in all of the southern bayous. She had, by twenty-eight years of age, a following rivaling Hillard's own from a generation before, and her mind became consumed with otherworldy, delusional aspirations. She croaked and chanted her incantations, filling hours and days in various states of self-induced euphoria.

"I sees the world through my eyes, and my childrens follow my soul into the hereafter. Take my hands, my childrens, and bring the salvation of the Lord into your souls."

Entering her late thirties—and by this time having already fallen into madness—Marah took in a young man nearly twenty years her younger, and, at thirty-nine years old, gave birth to her only child.

Zarah Devillier had come into the world.

~ | ~

Heretics! Heretics young and old!
Here we comes to git yours souls!

-9-

The Intruder

"Ms. Simmons."

Special Agent Nicks approached the counselor in the hallway at Foster's Daycare.

"Yes?" she replied, turning to him.

Nicks came up to her, followed shortly by Special Agent Fielding.

"Can I ask you a couple more questions, please?" he asked her.

She looked at him in a standoffish way. "I, uh...I guess so. What is it?"

"My partner and I," he began, pointing to Fielding, "were talking with your colleague, Ms. Satchens. She mentioned something to us that never came up during our conversation with you."

"Oh? What's that?"

"She mentioned that she'd seen you earlier in the afternoon on the day the boy, Julien Hawkins, went missing. She guessed around three or four o'clock?"

"Ohh..." Simmons recalled, nodding. "Yes, I did stop by there for a minute before going back to the center."

"So, you drove past the center to get to the park, and then drove back to the center?"

"Yeah," Simmons said, matter-of-factly. "I just stopped by to see if they needed anything. They said they were all set, so I went back to the center."

"Who'd ya talk to?" Fielding asked her.

Simmons put up a hand. "*Whoaa*," she said in protest. "You accusing me of something?"

"Hold on," Nicks replied. "We're just trying to fix our timeline of events, that's all."

She looked at him suspiciously, and then replied to Fielding. "Sally. I talked with Sally."

"Okay," said Nicks. "About what time was that?"

She answered, still annoyed, "Sometime after four, I guess. Maybe four-thirty."

Nicks gave her a nod, followed by a reassuring grin. "Good enough. Thank you."

The two agents went on their way.

Next on their fact checking trip was a revisit with Hipps, who corroborated Simmons' story of her returning to the center, which he gauged to be at around 4:30 PM. Sally Peck, furthermore, recalled the counselor briefly stopping by.

Once they were back outside of the daycare center, Fielding asked his partner, "So, what do you think of all this?"

Nicks answered him while taking out his smartphone. "The kid disappeared between about four and five o'clock, is what I'm guessing. Anytime earlier than that, I think one of the volunteers playing with the kids would have noticed him missing." He tapped on his phone. Weirdlee had gotten herself a new smartphone after "losing" her other one, and it was time to give her a call. He navigated to her number and then tapped the green call button. While waiting for her to answer, he said to Fielding, "I want to check with everyone who was there again and see if they heard any cries or any other noises going on about that time."

On the other end of his call, Weirdlee picked up. "Weirdlee."

"Agent Weirdlee. What's your status?"

Weirdlee had just made good her escape from the clutches of Paul Basil, and was still on the road. She hadn't even checked her smartphone's caller ID as she kept her eyes fixed on the way ahead of her. She glanced down at the phone's display, then, to confirm who it was.

Sam Nicks.

"Sam," she said, "I'm on my way back."

"You talk with your voodoo guy?"

She rolled her eyes and sighed. "Yeah. I saw him."

"Okay," Nicks said. "What about the babysitter? Did you get her name from Ms. Hawkins?"

Weirdlee closed her eyes, annoyed. She'd forgotten to do that.

"No," she moaned, half-expecting a *why not?* from Nicks. "I haven't called her yet. I'm just heading out."

"Don't worry about it," Nicks said. "We'll give her ring. We're right here, anyway. Why don't you just meet us at the inn and we can compare notes there."

She nodded, relieved. "Sounds good, Sam."

"Good," he said with a grin. "See you there."

He tapped off his phone then and looked at Fielding. "You got Ms. Hawkins' home number?"

Fielding instinctively padded his smartphone's belt clip. "Yeah—uh, just a sec. The sheriff gave it to me."

Fielding made the call then.

* * * *

For Special Agent Weirdlee, it was a long drive back to the inn. Thoughts of how she'd almost been subdued—*again*—swirled in her mind. She knew she'd been compelled by dark spiritual means to go to the voodoo priest. Yet even so, she went to him.

Why?

She worried, as well, that she might still be under Devillier's spell, however so remotely. If that were the case, then she was in a tug of war with not just one spiritual mind, but two. For Basil, she knew, would be trying to bring her back to him—he would make good on his vow, if he could.

I'm too weak, she feared. *How can I keep myself from the both of them?*

She worried, at that point, about actually being a liability to her colleagues. If she were compromised, she might jeopardize their investigation altogether. She might even be aiding the guilty parties, if Devillier and Basil turned out to be somehow involved.

I'll tell Nicks what happened, she decided then.

Maybe she wasn't ready for the field, after all.

* * * *

Nicks and Fielding got the babysitter's name from Regina Hawkins. Ms. Sara Ann Biddle, now twenty-one years old, worked these days as a checkout clerk at a grocery store. The agents stopped in and talked with her for about twenty minutes. Nothing terribly useful came out of their conversation, however. The young woman adored little Julien, and was heartbroken when she'd heard of his apparent death, she said. She was puzzled, as well, that the federal government would be looking into his case, but appeared to be quite happy about it, just the same. "I hope you find out what happened to Julien," she said to the agents. "Poor Miss Hawkins deserves to know."

Their interviews done for the day, the two agents drove back to the Swampy Inn to meet up with Weirdlee.

Weirdlee was waiting for them upon their arrival at about 4:00 PM. After going back to their rooms first to freshen up and take care of personal business, the colleagues met up again at the inn's little cafe.

"Maybe we should think about going to a restaurant around here," Fielding said as the three sat down at their table. He took a menu in hand and held it up. "More like a snack bar, here."

"We can eat later," said Nicks. "Let's just go over what we got, for now."

They all agreed.

After ordering and receiving their drinks—the usual two coffees and a tea—Weirdlee started on her briefing.

"Well, I found Paul Basil's home okay," she said with an air of reservation in her tone. "I asked him about the boy, first, and then I asked him about that curse that's going around—thinking maybe they're connected."

The two men listened intently as she carried on.

"He didn't seem to recognize the boy, and he said he didn't know anything about him."

Fielding curled his lip, nodding. "What about the curse thing?"

She looked down at her tea, studying the hot, dark water. "I don't think they're connected. At least, I don't think the boy's disappearance has anything to do with the curse."

"Okay," Nicks said with a nod. He eyed Weirdlee suspiciously then, sensing from her staring eyes that there was something more she might add to her story. "Is something wrong, Agent Weirdlee?" he asked her.

She looked at him, debating in her mind how to put things.

"Sam." she finally said. "I...had to fire my weapon."

"What's that?" Fielding reacted, alarmed.

Nicks sat up straight in his chair. "What happened?"

Weirdlee took in a deep breath and exhaled. "He tried to grab me, Sam."

Fielding was incredulous. "Are you kidding me?"

Nicks put his hand on Weirdlee's wrist and beckoned her, "Tell us what happened, Joanna. Everything."

She shook her head. "It's my fault. I put myself in a compromising position. I went into his kitchen and he was able to corner me there. I was just thinking about the case—I wasn't concerned about myself at the time."

Part of which was true, but not really.

She went on: "He blocked my way out, and then he went after me. We struggled for a little bit, but I was able to get from him and get to my weapon. I fired a warning shot."

"One shot?" Nicks asked.

"Yes."

Nicks turned his hand, palm up. "Lemme see."

Weirdlee retrieved her Glock-23 from her belt holster and handed it to Nicks. He inspected it, ejecting the ammunition clip and checking the rounds inside. As Weirdlee had said, only one round was missing. He cleared the weapon then before sliding the clip back in its place. He handed the gun back to Weirdlee.

"You'll need to file a report on that," he told her.

"I know."

"You didn't hit him," Fielding checked.

She shook her head. "No. Just a warning shot for him to back off."

"You should have called us right away," Nicks said.

"I'm sorry," she said. "I just wanted to get out of there."

Nicks turned to Fielding. "Call up the locals out there. Have 'em pick this guy up." He looked at Weirdlee. "What town were you in?"

"Paradis," she said. "Spelled like paradise, only no 'e' on the end."

"Okay," Fielding said with a nod. He got up and stood off to make his call.

Weirdlee looked at Nicks. "Sam, I'm sorry. I—"

He waved her off. "Don't, Joanna. Don't apologize. If you were a ten year vet, I'd be pissed." Then he smiled at her. "You're still wet behind the ears, though, so we'll chalk this one up as a learning experience. I'm just glad you're okay. He didn't hurt you, did he?"

She smiled uneasily. "No," she whispered. "I'm okay."

The whole truth, for her, though, was much more troubling. But getting into all of the witchery and supernatural aspects of her predicament would only make the entire situation far worse than it already was, she decided. Let the magick stay out of the story, at least for now.

"What was his name?" Fielding asked Weirdlee while talking on his phone.

"Paul Basil. B-A-S-I-L."

Fielding repeated the name in his phone, then got on with his call.

"You get anything else from him before things went bad?" Nicks asked.

Weirdlee looked at him thoughtfully. "I'm not sure," she said, "but I had a sense that he was guilty of *something*. I just had a very bad feeling the whole time I was there."

"Your woman's intuition again?" Nicks guessed.

She smiled. "Something like that."

"Well," Nicks went on, "we didn't get much from our interviews, either. We talked to the babysitter. She never saw the kid the day he went missing. She doesn't know anything, I'm pretty sure of it."

"Sam," Weirdlee said then, regaining her professional composure, "if the boy did end up in the water, we might never find out what happened to him. This whole region is one big flood zone. And it *was* three years ago."

Fielding returned from his phone call and sat back down at the table.

"They're pickin' him up now," he said.

"We'll finish our interviews tomorrow, I guess," said Nicks. "If we can't find anything else, though, we'll probably have to hand it back over to the locals."

Fielding looked at him, resigned. "Never did have much to go on," he said. "Too bad. Poor kid deserved a better shot at life than what he got."

Nicks eyed his partner thoughtfully, the same sentiment weighing on his mind.

"Yeah."

The agents wrapped up their meeting and then everyone jumped in one car to go a restaurant for what Fielding called "some real food." It was a quiet dinner, with not much said by any of the three. The evening ended early.

* * * *

The waxing moon had risen high in the late evening sky above the shadowy bayous. A warm, still air lay on the land.

Any peace at this hour, however, lay shattered by a haunting, chanting song that no living soul would ever want sung in her name.

"Soul of time! Soul of time! Bring the wind and make her mine!"

Paul Basil, standing bare-chested, his face painted white and a black top hat resting on his head, sang loudly in the night.

"Lift my spirit past the trees! Tonight I live within her dreams!"

He danced about the riverbank of the Bayou des Allemends, his mind consumed by the casting of his magick spell...

Witch's wonder! Pagan's soul!
Make her mine—where spirits go!
Ooo-Ma-Ma—Oh, Halo-Da!
Ah No-Mano, Ani-La!
I don't see no witch's brew,
stoppin' me from takin' you!
Here I stand, and here I fly,
Oh sister caster, dreamin' mine!
Oh, La-La, La-Dano-La!
I am yours, and you are mine!

So the living spirit of Paul Basil carried into the night air, whisking itself across the wilderness like a quite breeze, while all the time he chanted and danced by the waterside...

Miles away, where the peaceful evening remained quiet and still, a sleeping Joanna Weirdlee lay in her bed, resting after a day in which she hoped she'd escaped the clutches of a terrible outcome.

She hadn't, though, after all.

In the imposed dream that came to her, she wore her hand-stitched witch's dress, and she entered into a darkened room whose space was lit by just a dim, red-hued lamp light. This was a bedroom, and in its midst was a large, elegantly adorned bed, finely laid out with red-and-gold blankets and white pillows. And, in the bed already, his covers drawn to his waist, a naked Paul Basil lay waiting for her.

He put a hand out to her. "Come, my lovely," he beckoned. "Come to me."

She approached him, her eyes never leaving his. She knew her fate that evening.

Arriving at his bedside, she brought her hands up to the buttons of her blouse and slowly unbuttoned her top. Basil watched her admiringly as she drew the shirt off her shoulders and let it fall away. She kicked off her shoes next, and then unfastened her belt and slid her dress down, letting it fall to the floor.

Basil smiled then as she unfastened her bra and peeled it away, revealing her young, full breasts to his eyes.

She was a beautiful prize, indeed.

Removing her panties last, Weirdlee then crawled onto the bed, and, on all fours, approached her lover. She kissed him with her soft, red lips, and he in turn kissed her deeply, his lustful heart pounding in anticipation of what was soon to come. Taking hold of her then, he brought her to him roughly, and the two of them writhed in each other's hungry embrace, before, at last, they made sweet love long into the evening...

* * * *

Weirdlee sprung out of her slumber with a shout. She flew out of her bed, terror-stricken and mortified.

"Never!" she cried out.

She threw on her bathrobe and ran over to a cushioned chair in the corner of the room, hopping onto it and curling herself up protectively. She clutched onto herself.

My God!

146

Basil had made good on his promise. He could come to her anytime he wished!

She closed her eyes and shuddered as she sat there. The much-dreaded notion that she might actually fall under the voodoo priest's will suddenly became all too real for her.

Or...

Had she already fallen to him?

She felt sick inside.

A knock on the door got her attention, and she snapped her eyes there.

Who could be here at such a late hour?

"Who is it?" she asked.

"It's me, Sam Nicks, Joanna."

A rush of relief came over her. She leapt from her chair and hurried to the door. Unlocking it, she threw it open. There Nicks stood, himself still fully dressed and stoic looking, as usual. It occurred to Weirdlee then that the hour must have been something earlier than what she'd assumed.

"Sam," she said to him, her mind still clouded. "What time is it?"

"Oh," Nicks replied, estimating, "about eleven-thirty. Sorry for the late knock."

"No," she said. "It's okay. What's the matter?"

"I, uh, just wanted to let you know, the cops went to Paul Basil's home earlier, but he wasn't there. They checked his workplace, too, up in New Orleans. They said he hadn't been there, either. They'll check again tonight and then again tomorrow morning. But it looks like he might have taken off."

Weirdlee swallowed, shaken by the news. "I see."

"Keep your door locked and your gun close by," Nicks said. He looked at her then, noticing her bothered expression. "Are you okay?"

147

She nodded quickly. "Yes. I'm okay." Then she glanced behind her. "I...just had a nightmare."

Nicks nodded uneasily at the reason. "All right."

Then, she said something quite unexpected to him.

"Would you like to come in?"

He hesitated.

"Maybe," she went on, "talk for a little bit. I'm not very sleepy right now." She looked at him with a concerned expression. "Are you?"

Nicks kept his eyes on her. The woman was clearly troubled, and something was up, he knew.

"Not too much," he answered with a smile. "Let's talk for a little while."

She returned his smile, all so very pleased. "Okay."

Nicks stepped inside then and Weirdlee closed the door behind them.

The two agents talked then for well over an hour, about their lives, their childhoods, how they got into the Bureau. It was a warm and, for Weirdlee, very welcome and wonderful conversation.

One, she thought, she never wanted to end.

-10-

A Presence in the Mind

Early that morning, the special agents met outside of their rooms and there decided to hit the road for breakfast. Since they would be going their own ways afterwards, they took their own vehicles—Nicks and Fielding their Ford Taurus, and Weirdlee her Grand Cherokee. They arrived at Rita's Kitchen, a small cafe down the road along Route 20 that served traditional Southern fare in the morning and more common American dishes such as sandwiches, hamburgers, soups and salads for lunch.

Inside, the agents found a small table off to the side of the place. Nicks kept a curious eye on Weirdlee, who'd been acting strangely since the night before when they chatted.

"So," he said, getting on with business, "I think we need to re-interview some of the staff at the school and then maybe have another interview with Ms. Simmons. I also want to see if we can identify all the parents who may have been there that day."

A waitress showed up at their table as Nicks continued. "I want to try to connect every kid that was there to a parent or guardian."

Fielding raised his eyebrows. "*Whew*. Lots of kids mighta been there, partner."

"Yeah, I know."

"What are we havin', folks?" the waitress asked.

The agents stopped to get their orders in. Fielding asked for eggs and grits, Nicks ordered eggs, bacon, and toast, and Weirdlee chose oatmeal. They also ordered their usual two coffees and a tea.

The waitress left to get things started.

"I'd like to see if we can narrow down the time frame of the boy's disappearance," Nicks went on. "The five p.m. discovery of him having gone missing is our hard endtime. Let's see if we can find people who might have seen the boy earlier—maybe three or even four p.m."

"I think it's amazing that a kid that age can go unnoticed for so long," said Fielding. "He was right there with the other kids, for Christ's sake."

The waitress returned with a tray that held Weirdlee's tea, a small milk decanter, a carafe of coffee, and two empty cups for the men's coffee. The agents waited for her to set everything down and be off again before continuing.

Weirdlee poured a small portion of milk into her tea and stirred it. "Maybe," she opined, "it was so obvious to everyone the boy was in good company, nobody took notice of it." She looked at Nicks. "It happens, you know. When you don't see anything out of place or strange, you just ignore the usual."

"Yeah," Nicks said, agreeing. "And it just gets shoved out of your memory."

"Sure," said Fielding. "Like seein' the same people at work all the time. Just can't remember exactly when ya'll seen 'em, or even the day."

Nicks frowned, considering things. "That doesn't make our job any easier."

"Shit," Fielding swore with a chuckle, "it makes it *a lot* harder."

Nicks stared off—his mind mulling things over. The waitress, meanwhile, returned with Weirdlee's oatmeal.

"Your breakfasts will be right out," she said to the men.

Nicks and Fielding said their "Thanks" and the waitress left.

"Maybe," Nicks mulled, "we're asking the wrong questions."

Fielding eyed him curiously. "Whaddya mean?"

Nicks sipped his black coffee and set his cup down before elaborating. "Instead of asking people if or when they saw the boy," he said, "let's try a different tack." He looked at both Fielding and Weirdlee with an eager glance. "Let's ask the volunteers and some of the parents if they can remember who *they* were with that day—and what they were doing the whole day."

"Aren't we doing that already?" Fielding asked.

Nicks shook his head. "We were asking them *why* they were there, more like. And let's not go about this as if we're looking for suspects, either. People might have a better time of recalling things if they focus only on what they themselves were doing the whole day—no one else. And I mean minute-to-minute—trace their steps and activities, from the time they arrived, to the time they left."

"Shit," said Fielding. "That'll still be tough."

"Yeah," Nicks said, "but let's give it a shot."

He looked over at Weirdlee then, still concerned for her well-being considering what she'd gone through the other day. "Hopefully we'll hear this morning about your voodoo priest," he said to her. "Probably just out on a bender last night."

She looked back at him, managing a weak smile.

Soon afterwards, the waitress returned with the men's breakfast. The agents chatted a bit more before Nicks divvied up their assignments. He and Fielding would go back to the school and the daycare center and begin interviewing the volunteers again—this time asking them for a complete walkthrough of what they did on the day Julien Hawkins disappeared. Weirdlee, meanwhile, was tasked with finding out which parents attended the outing. Then she could start contacting them.

It was a big job for everyone, and one that Nicks expected would take at least a few days to accomplish. But there was little else the agents could to do, otherwise.

* * * *

"Well, the staff is all working," Henry Potter said to the agents visiting him in his office. "But I suppose they can spare a few minutes to talk with ya'll again."

Nicks and Fielding sat in a couple of chairs before the principal's desk. "We don't want to take up too much of their time," said Nicks. "We're just trying to wrap up the sequence of events and where everyone was."

"Sure," Potter said. "I can have my secretary set up some times. What—fifteen minutes apiece?"

"That sounds good," said Nicks.

"Okay then," Potter replied, sitting up straight in his chair. He clasped his hands on his desk. "I guess we might as well start with me, while we're here."

"All right," said Nicks. He took out his little black notepad then and flipped through a couple of pages to get to a blank page. Then he retrieved his pen. "We can start from the beginning, I guess. Did you show up at the school first before going to the park, or did you arrive directly at the park from home?"

Potter took in a sigh and gathered his thoughts. "At the school. I helped out organizing everything and makin' sure the staff had what they needed."

"And then you went to the park?" Nicks asked.

"I did. Just for a little bit."

"That was earlier in the morning?"

"Well...I guess around ten in the morning."

"Were there any parents and kids there at that time?" asked Fielding.

"Oh, no. The place was dead. It was just us and a few others. I don't even think the beer tent was set up yet."

"Were the daycare center volunteers there yet?" Nicks asked.

"Yessir. I do recall them being there. A couple of 'em, anyway."

Nicks jotted that down.

"Now," he asked while writing, "the outing itself started at, what, noontime?"

"Yessir."

"You didn't stay there until it started?"

"No. I had my staff there, and this wasn't their first rodeo. I was havin' some family issues at the time and I needed to get home for a little while before coming back."

"Nothing serious, I hope," Nicks said.

"My wife and I had separated. We had issues."

"Oh, sorry to hear. Work it out?"

"Eventually we did, yes."

"You live far away from the school, do ya?" asked Fielding

"I live in Houma, Special Agent, about twenty-five miles south of here."

"So, you didn't come back until the end of the day?" Nicks asked. "Or did the police call you?"

"No," Potter said, "I actually came back to the school around two o'clock. The wife and I ended up havin' a spat, and I just said the hell with it and headed back up north. I had some work to do at the school, so I went in and got that done till I got the call."

"Was anyone else at the school?" asked Fielding.

"Uhh," Potter thought, "I don't think so. I let myself in—turned off the alarm and then turned it back on once I got inside. Went straight to my office."

"And you stayed here the whole time, until the police called you?" Nicks asked.

"Yessir. It was the most frightenin' call I ever had in my whole life, I'll tell you that."

Having apparently been away from the park the entire day, Nicks figured there would be nothing further gleaned from the principal. He concluded the interview, and then asked to see the other staff members who worked that day.

The rest went much like the others. But Nicks was able to conclude that nothing out of the ordinary had occurred at the park prior to the boy's disappearance and that, importantly, little Julien had been seen by mathematics teacher Terry Stevens as late as 3:30 PM.

Stevens presently took his turn with the agents in a study hall room. They first went through the whole day, starting from his arrival at the park that day and ending with his departure that early evening. Then they backtracked to when he last recalled seeing Julien.

"I was with him, back in the field where we'd set up a badminton net. He was right there with us."

"Playin' badminton with ya'll?" Fielding asked.

"No," Stevens said with a shake of his head. "He wasn't much into playin' sports or games and such. He was off by the path, by the woods, there. But the badminton was set up right there, too."

"How far away was he from you?" Nicks asked. "Do you recall?"

"Ohh," Stevens mulled, "not far 'tal. Maybe a dozen feet or so."

"So he was basically right there with you."

"Sure. Close enough."

"Okay," Nicks went on, "and that was later in the afternoon?"

"Yeah. Maybe three o'clock or so. Maybe later."

"Three-thirty, maybe?" Nicks asked.

"Yeah. Maybe."

"So how long was you and the kids playin' badminton back there?" Fielding asked.

Stevens sighed. "Ohh, Jesus, I dunno. Maybe an hour, from start to finish."

"When you called it quits," Nicks asked, "did all the kids leave with you?"

"I, uh—I dunno, actually. I got called away for about ten minutes. They thought my car got backed into in the parking lot. Then when I was headin' back, I saw the kids leavin' the badminton and headin' on over to the tents."

"You left the kids there alone?" Fielding asked.

"No," Stevens said. "There was a teacher there. The one who told me my car got hit."

"Who was that?" Nicks asked.

Stevens mulled that one over, muttering, "I...uh..." while adjusting himself in his chair. "I think it was Liza Harrington."

Nicks checked his notepad, flipping through the pages to get to the teacher they'd talked to earlier in their interviews.

"Try again, Mr. Stevens," he said. "She was back home with her husband and kids by then. She told us she left the outing at about two o'clock."

Stevens looked confused. "She did?"

Nicks nodded.

Stevens sat there for a moment, appearing genuinely baffled.

"I, uh—I just don't know, then," he said. "I can't remember." He looked at Nicks and Fielding helplessly. "I swear I thought it was Liza. Now, though, I don't know. But I know the person who told me my car got hit stayed with the kids."

"Think, Mr. Stevens," Fielding said. "Take your time. You were playin' badminton with the kids, and someone came up to you."

"Yeah," Stevens recalled.

"It was a woman?" Nicks asked.

Stevens nodded slowly. "Yeah..."—but then caught himself. "*Wait.*"

Nicks and Fielding exchanged a glance before looking back at Stevens.

"I think it was a man's voice, now that I think of it," Stevens said. "But kinda soft, like he was..." he shook his head, "Aww, I dunno."

Fielding looked back over at his partner, not knowing what to make of Stevens' screwed up memory.

"Think back, Mr. Stevens," Nicks said. "When you looked at the person talking to you, who did you see?"

Stevens struggled to recall.

"I..." he said, squinting his eyes and staring off, as if trying to pierce the fog of the past. Then he looked directly at Nicks. "It *was* Liza Harrington," he insisted. "I swear to God that's who I saw." Then he twisted his expression. "But it didn't sound like her 'tal."

* * * *

Weirdlee began her assignment by going through police records searching for any parents interviewed by the cops on the day of the outing or thereafter. After this, she contacted the various teachers and daycare center staffers who'd been at the park that day, asking them about any parents they might have seen there.

It was a truly daunting task she had. Literally dozens of parents had been at the park throughout the course of the day—either from the start of the event or coming and going at various times afterwards. The list was long and it would take days to go through all the names. Days, she knew, of dealing with Basil stalking her every move.

And nights of him visiting her in her dreams.

After a long day of traveling about and getting a few interviews in, Weirdlee arrived back at the Swampy Inn where she met up with her colleagues. Nicks told her then that the Paradis police had still not located Paul Basil. There was little doubt, they concluded, that he was on the run.

The agents talked for a bit more, comparing notes and such, before all three retired for the evening.

For Weirdlee, this was no easy thing to do. She could not simply go to bed and close her eyes. *He* would surely be waiting for her, she knew. Instead, she turned to the only thing she ever trusted in her life: Her faith in the Craft.

Moving her bed aside in her room, she drew, in ceremonious fashion, a sacred circle upon the carpeted floor. Around its perimeter she sprinkled soil from her hometown, Salem, and then prayed to the spirits of Mother Earth to watch over her. Upon her dresser, she lit three white candles.

Later on then, when it came time for her to rest, she lay down within her circle, curling herself up in a fetal position, protected—she hoped—from any grievous harm that might befall her in the night.

This would be Joanna Weirdlee's ritual each evening, unbroken, until such time as the spirits at last came forth to make their stand, and so proclaim their agent from amongst the world of the living.

-11-

Angelea Diviner

Zarah Devillier sat in the back seat of her eldest son, Lucien's, Volkswagen Beetle, lazily watching the urban scenery pass by as Lucien drove them through downtown New Orleans in the early morning hours. Her second eldest, Korram, took up the front passenger seat, and seemed entirely bored by the journey. It had been a long trip for the elderly Zarah, but she was glad to be finally revisiting the old neighborhoods she'd once known so well in her long-ago youth.

She hadn't been back to the city for going on sixteen years—ever since the mambo woman-turned-voodoo queen Angelea Diviner cast her out following several rather tense confrontations. Zarah had stayed away from here all this time, knowing full well she could not match the power of the more cerebral and mentally secure Diviner. She was back on this day, however, to meet up with the still-at-large Paul Basil, who'd high-tailed it out of Paradis after his altercation with the Salem witch.

Basil had friends in the city, both from his performing job and from the drug dealing he still did on the side to keep him in good money. It was friends from the latter trade who'd found him a vacant basement room in an old tenement building on the city's east side to shack up in for a couple of days. After things had cooled down a bit then he'd make his way west, he figured, to fresher hunting grounds.

First, though, the corrupt voodoo priest still had business in the bayous to wrap up, and he needed to set things straight with his long-time partner and former lover before he did so.

As they turned onto Royal Street, Lucien glanced about, his childhood memories returning to him. He said back to his mother, "Momma, this is where we played ball when I was a kid."

Zarah nodded dismissively. "Yes, dear. Just keep driving. Your momma's thinking."

And she *was* thinking. She wondered why Basil had called her, demanding that she drive up to the city to see him. She knew he was on the run, but going up to New Orleans was risky for the both of them—her because of Diviner's influence, him because of the cops.

Lucien turned onto Franklin Avenue. They had almost arrived at their destination when Zarah reached forward and smacked Korram on the backside of his head. "And don't you boys be givin' no back talk to the man when we get there, you hear? We be talkin' business."

Lucien scowled. "S'always business, Momma. He don't love us."

"Shush, you!" she shouted back. "You be respectin' youz daddy. He's got the power, and youz be next in line, if'n youz watch yerself."

"He a bad man, Momma," Lucien went on. "Doin' bad things."

Zarah snarled back at him. "I said shush your mouth. Or I's be shushin' it for you."

That was no idle threat, either, coming from a woman with the Gift who'd already done it to one of her boys before.

Lucien drove on without another word.

A little further along, he pulled up in front of two small, two-story buildings, both tucked in tightly amongst a row of others that lined each side of the narrow street. He got out of the car along with his mother. Korram was about to follow their lead, but Zarah stopped him just as he opened his door.

"Youz stay here," she said to him. "Stay in the car. We be back."

He stopped and eyed his mother, disappointed, before reluctantly shutting the door.

Zarah and Lucien started off then.

Walking between the two buildings they'd parked in front of, they followed a narrow, crumbling brick walkway that led off to the back. Hurricane Katrina had wreaked havoc on the city just a few years before, and the sedimentary damage was still evident in the old urban landscape. Zarah walked in a stilted way, her steps hobbled by age. She led her son along to the back of the buildings before turning to her right and heading into a narrow backyard. There, a flight of wooden stairs zigzagged up the backside of the building, she saw, which was where Basil had directed her to go. Before they got to the staircase, though, a familiar voice called out to them.

"Old woman," Basil said to her in a stern tone.

She and Lucien both stopped in their tracks. They peered through the steps and railings of the staircase, from where the voice had come. There, Paul Basil stood in shadows under the stairway.

"Come here," he said to them.

Zarah smiled at her former lover. "Marcel," she said to him, and she approached him. "I's here for you."

Basil waved for her to come ahead. He glared at Lucien then, who walked behind her. "You bring the retard, too?" he asked her, meaning Zarah's youngest, Damon.

Zarah put on a hurt expression. "Aw, Marcel. Why you says that 'bout him? He's your boy, just like these be." She waved back at Lucien.

"Never mind about that," Basil said. He turned his glare from Lucien to Zarah. "You get followed?" he asked her.

She shook her head vigorously. "No-no. I checked and I watched—I watches 'em with my's mind."

Basil frowned at her. "Fuck'n. That's what worries me. You ain't so powerful no more, you old bat. What the fuck happened with that pagan bitch you sent me? She was supposed to be controlled."

Zarah answered, "I had her, Marcel—I did. And I's told her to go to youz. I says to her, 'You go to him, and you give yourself to him.' And she was on her way. I sent her to you."

"Fuck you did," Basil swore. "I couldn't cast her. I tried to put her under but the bitch almost shot me instead."

Zarah swallowed, her eyes never leaving Basil. Her old body chilled then as a dark vision suddenly crept into her mind.

She knew at the very least what had to be done.

"We havin' to kill her, now," she said to him. "We *gots* to kill her, Marcel."

Basil glared back at her. "We ain't killin' her, ya dumb hag—what the fuck are you talkin' about? That bitch is *mine*. My property. I own her ass."

"She a witch!" Zarah cried out. "She gots the Gift. She gonna kill us all!"

Basil reached out and slapped her hard across the face. "Shut your fuckin' mouth!"

Lucien made a move to protect his mother. Basil leered at him. "Back off, boy," he said, jabbing a finger at him. "I ain't no old man, and I will kick your fuckin' ass."

Lucien stopped, and Zarah grabbed him. "You stay," she said to him. "You mind your daddy."

"Momma," he began.

"Shush, now," she said to him. "It's all right."

"Gimme the keys to your car," Basil said to them.

Lucien leered at him. "*My* car," he asserted.

Basil snapped his fingers at him. "Gimme the keys."

"Whatchu want 'em for?" Zarah asked.

Basil scowled at her. "I got business down south. I got some shut-up money comin' to me, first off, and then I'll be gettin' me that pagan whore, too."

"She's ain't gonna go with youz," Zarah insisted. "She gots the Craft in her, and she ain't gonna go."

"I'll find her, old woman, and I'll drag that bitch by her hair, if I have to."

Zarah looked back at him with a hurt expression. Very many years before, she herself had been the object of his desire. Now, though, she saw, clear as day, the Salem witch would be replacing her at Marcel Unate's side.

She muttered to him, "You don't love me's no more."

He glared back at her coldly, because it was true. Then he turned to Lucien. "Gimme the fuckin' keys."

Lucien stared at him. He asked his mother, "Momma?"

Zarah scowled at her former lover, who was now casting her out. She said to Lucien, "Give him the keys."

Reluctantly then, Lucien pulled his car keys from his pocket. He gave them over to Basil, who snatched them quickly from his hand.

Basil said to Zarah, "Better get yourselves outta town before Diviner catches you here."

"You takin' my car," Lucien said to him. "How we goin'?"

"Catch a bus," Basil snapped. "Or swim."

He turned away then and started off. "Don't wanna see you again, old woman," he called out. "Don't need you no more."

Zarah watched Basil with an anguished expression as he walked away and slipped around the corner between two buildings.

An emptiness, unlike any other, overcame her heartbroken soul.

"We's on our own, now, boy," she mumbled to her son.

Basil came out to the road and quickly spotted Lucien's Beetle parked at the curb. Inside of it, still sitting in the front passenger seat, was his son Korram, waiting. The estranged father walked up to the driver's side door and opened it. As he hopped in, Korram looked at him, surprised.

"Get out," Basil said to him plainly.

"Daddy?" Korram said. "Where's Momma?"

"She's comin' out," Basil said. "Get the fuck outta the car."

Korram looked at him, confused, before turning to look at the building that his mother and brother had gone behind earlier. There, he saw Lucien walking out, his hand guiding along their aged mother.

"Get out!" Basil scolded him.

Korram got out quickly. He slammed the door shut behind him and then ran off to join his brother and mother.

Basil started up the car and put it in gear, then gunned the gas pedal and sped off down the street.

"Momma," Korram said, still bewildered as he came up to his mother. "What's goin' on?"

Zarah kept her gaze on Lucien's Beetle as it sped away.

"Your daddy's leavin' us," she said to Korram. "He be leavin' your momma for a younger woman." She sneered then. "Just like they's always do."

The old woman stood there for a moment, quietly contemplating their situation with a degree of concern—knowing, as she did, that she would have to get herself and her boys out of town quickly before Diviner's followers tracked them down. No doubt, she figured, Diviner herself was already well aware of her presence in the city.

They would have to move fast.

Just then, though, a speeding taxi came to a screeching halt in front of the building they stood by. Out of it leapt the driver first—a dark-skinned black man—followed quickly by another, lighter-skinned black man who'd been in the back seat. This man, wearing a black biker's vest, walked briskly to the Devillier clan.

"Get in," he said to them firmly. He opened his vest to show a revolver tucked under his belt. "Let's go."

Lucien and Korram glanced at each other nervously, then looked to their mother for guidance.

Zarah grasped a hand from her sons into each of her own. "Steady, my boys," she said to them in a shaken voice.

She looked off then to the taxi parked at the curb.

"The spider has captured the flies."

* * * *

Joanna Weirdlee got up early and was on the road well before her colleagues stepped out of their own room that morning. She hadn't slept very well at all—worried that she might encounter Basil yet again in one of her tortured dreams. She started the day as she figured she would the next couple, by interviewing families who'd been at Kraemer Park on the day little Julien disappeared. There would be a lot of mileage between those interviews, too, and so it would be a very tiring day before it ended.

Back at the Swampy Inn, meanwhile, Nicks was puzzled by Weirdlee's taking off before they'd all gotten together for their usual breakfast powwow. Her assignment for the day already discussed the night before, so she really didn't have to report in to him before she left. Even so, she'd seemed troubled ever since her incident with the voodoo priest, Paul Basil, and Nicks was beginning to worry about her. Something else, he feared, may have happened to her—either at Basil's home or earlier at Zarah Devillier's. She could deny it all she wanted, but the truth was more than evident in the way she'd been behaving the past couple of days.

After a quick breakfast, Nicks and Fielding planned their day. They would wrap up their interviews with the staff at the school and the daycare and then call up Weirdlee to help her out with the parent interviews. Some of them could just be interviewed by phone, of course, but most of them would need to be talked to face-to-face, which was always the better way to do these things. There were literally dozens of people to go through, however, and so this part of the investigation, much as Nicks had determined earlier, might take days to finish up.

"Everything we do," Fielding said to his partner as the two men walked to their car, "leads right back to that boy goin' into the drink. One way or the other."

Nicks opened the driverside door and hopped into the seat. "We'll see," he said as he slid his keys into the ignition and then started up the engine.

Fielding got into the passenger side and looked at Nicks. "I mean, even if he was abducted, you know what happens to most kids when they're abducted. It ain't ever for good reasons."

Nicks turned and gave Fielding a long, contemplating look. "I know," he finally said to him. "And if that's the case, then we've got us a murderer to catch."

He backed the car out of its parking space then and started out.

Fielding cast his gaze off to the small, stilted homes that crowded the street as they drove along.

"The Curse..." he muttered to himself, recalling what Weirdlee had mentioned before.

"Maybe that's what it's all about, after all."

* * * *

The basement corridor the party had come to was dark and musty, and filled with a lingering odor of swamp water due to the periodic flooding the region endured. The taxi driver and his partner led Zarah Devillier and her two sons along, pushing them at times while at others simply urging them along.

At length, they turned a corner and came upon a flight of stairs that led up to the building's first floor. They would not be ascending them, however, as instead the taxi driver opened a door set off to their left. He beckoned the Devillier clan inside.

The group of them passed through the doorway and came into a small, dimly lit room, its walls adorned with portraits and *veves* representing the various spirits of the voodoo faith. In each corner of the room, a tall, standing lamp was placed, with all four lights combined providing the room's only glow. A small black desk was set, centered, by the far wall of the room. Several thick candles were set on this, each colored either white, blue or green, and all in various states of melting from previous use. In front of the desk, facing it, were several chairs, all lined up in rows, as if in a classroom.

166

Or a church.

The taxi driver closed the door to the room, and then ordered Zarah and her sons to take up the chairs at the very front, just before the desk. They did so, with Zarah sitting in a chair at the center of the first row. Lucien sat to her left then and Korram to her right.

A very long few minutes passed as they waited there in silence. Lucien and Korram glanced around every so often, wondering what was going on. Zarah herself, however, understood her predicament all too well.

She was about to be judged.

After what seemed an hour but what was surely just a third of that time, the door to the room opened once more. From the hallway beyond then, the deep baritone voice of a man—still as yet unseen—chanted a ceremonial hymn, and he praised, afterwards, the wisdom and power of the *Invisibles*.

"All-seeing and all-knowing," his voice boomed, "their presence in Nature righteous under the eyes of God Almighty. Be it known forever on Earth and so in the Kingdom of Heaven."

His declarations finished, the man himself then entered into the room.

Lucien and Korram both turned around to look at him, and so beheld a very dark-skinned black man wearing a black robe and a black top hat. White paint decorated his face in the likeness of a skull, and in his right hand he held a long wooden staff, which he then banged on the dank stone floor at intervals as he stepped towards the front of the room in a slow, rhythmic cadence.

Following then behind him through the doorway came a tall, thickly shaped black woman, dressed in a finely made, colorful robe, and with an elegantly decorated headdress wrapped neatly about her head. Around her neck, she wore several necklaces, each encrusted with stones and fine jewels. She wore rings, as well, on all of her fingers, and from her earlobes there hung a pair of round, oversized gold-colored earrings.

This woman was none other than the Voodoo Queen of New Orleans herself, Angelea Diviner.

She strode ahead in a slow, purposeful walk behind her captain, who escorted her to her desk at the far end of the room. She kept her cool gaze set squarely ahead of her the whole time, too, never once glancing aside even as Lucien and Korram stared at her, awestruck by her presence.

Arriving at the desk, the man then stood aside, making room for Diviner to take her place in a chair behind it. She sat without so much as a word or gesture, her eyes remaining unmoved from their grim stare.

The man then pounded his staff upon the floor four times. He said aloud, "All praise the wise Queen of New Orleans, Angelea Vivia Diviner. Let none trespass upon her righteous soul!"

Zarah rolled her eyes at the declaration. Such a flourish, she bemoaned, given to a woman who in all likelihood made her living as a hairdresser.

"Madam Diviner," the priest said to his mistress, "the guilty have been summoned." He gestured to the Devillier clan.

For the first time then, Diviner turned her gaze to her old nemesis, sitting there before her, followed by a dismissive glance to Lucien and then to Korram. She looked back at Zarah then, expressionless, and spoke to her in a very calm, monotone voice.

"I warned you never to return to my city, Zarah Devillier," she said. She cast her eyes about the room, and then lifted her hands, waving them about lazily. "And yet...here you are today."

Zarah nodded nervously. She felt the woman's immense spiritual power overwhelming her own, even as she sat there before her. A hairdresser Diviner might well be in the mundane world, but in Ethereal World of Nature, she had no rival in this place.

"I's seein' my man, Marcel," she said weakly to Diviner. She glanced at her sons. "He's be my boys' daddy."

Diviner stared back at her, emotionless. "You are no longer the woman of Paul Basil," she declared. "You have not shared his bed for a very long time. And he has now chosen another to be by his side."

Zarah sneered at her. "She is a pagan! She will not go to him!"

Diviner's captain pounded his staff on the floor. "Quiet, woman!" he demanded. "Do not raise your voice to Madam!"

Diviner raised her hand, haltingly. Her eyes never left Zarah's own, though, as she read the old woman's mind, discerning from this some terrible plot being undertaken in the bayous.

"You should not have come here, Zarah Devillier," she said at length. "I warned you never to come back to New Orleans."

Zarah pressed her hands together in a pleading way. "I know youz don't want me here, Angelea—I knows that. But I's had to see my Marcel. He's their daddy," she said pointing to Lucien and Korram. "He's gonna make them strong someday."

Diviner stared back at her, then slowly shook her head.

"Your sons are powerless, Zarah. They will never have the Gift. Your family's line has ended with you."

"No!" Zarah cried out. "It's not true!"

The captain pounded his staff on the floor. "Silence!"

Cowed by his wrath, Zarah shrunk back in her seat. All the while, too, her two sons sat there, spellbound and staring quietly at the voodoo queen before them.

169

Diviner herself, meanwhile, grew more troubled by the visions she'd encountered. Zarah, she saw, was in league with Paul Basil—that much she could plainly discern. And Basil was involved in some manner of awful crime—an evil that, thankfully, the *loa* themselves had played no part in. Zarah, she perceived, had always delivered to him the innocents he required, and then he, in turn, did...*what* to them?

She could not see.

The Curse of the Bayous...

It came to her then, though more as a matter of deduction than any sort of spiritual revelation. The Curse of the Bayous—that old legend of evil turned upon itself and forever damned—was still going on. And it lay upon Devillier and Basil, after all!

"Zarah Devillier," she declared aloud, "you are doomed. Your soul has been taken by evil, and you are its slave. I had once before cast you out from this city, so that it might not be spoiled by your black magick and your poisoned ways." She seethed. "I warned you never to return!"

Zarah froze in fear. Tears streamed from her eyes and she clasped her hands in prayer. "I begs you, Angelea! I means no harm! I's only wantin' to see my man, and hopes he'll be lovin' his sons."

Diviner scowled. "He hates your sons, Zarah. He hates the innocent. He hates all that is good and right in this world. He is fallen—just like you—and has been completely consumed by darkness. The *loa* will not be kind to him, either, when his fate one day arrives."

"Ohh, Angelea, do not blame him for me!" Zarah pleaded. "I's his mentor and teacher. He wanted so much—"

"Shut up, you fool," Diviner said. "You were merely his whore and nothing more. Just like your mother before you, you gave yourself to any who could afford you."

"No..." Zarah replied, tears streaming down her wrinkled face. Her willpower—such that she had when she first entered the room—had since been stripped away by the more powerful Diviner.

"Go, now," Diviner demanded. "Go, and never return to my city. If you do return again, against my will, I will have you killed. I swear I will. Do you understand?"

Struck by the voodoo queen's harsh words, Zarah stared back at her.

Would she truly kill one of her own?

Perhaps she would.

She answered meekly, "I's understand."

Diviner scowled at her guest. Her disgust with the old woman was genuine, and her hatred of her had only grown with the passing of time.

"You are blind, you evil wretch," she said to her. "The Curse of the Bayous is upon you. There can be no escape from it. You are condemned. In their own time, the *loa* will deliver an agent to deal with you, and you will be sacrificed."

Zarah trembled at the declaration. She looked deeply into Diviner's eyes, but, for the very first time in her life, could see nothing at all.

Diviner slapped her hands together, awakening Zarah's offspring from their spellbound states. The two young men glanced about, confused by their surroundings. Diviner's captain then pounded his staff twice to the floor, so summoning from the front of the room the taxi driver and his partner.

"Remove them," the captain said.

Zarah and her sons were then taken roughly in hand and led out of the room.

Diviner watched them in silence until the door closed shut behind them, leaving just her and her voodoo priest captain alone in the room.

The captain bent low, bringing himself to Diviner's ear. He said to her: "The witch will not be able to resist Basil for very long, Madam. She is a hedge witch—on her own. If she does not have aid, he *will* one day take her."

Diviner stared straight ahead. There was nothing more that she herself could do to protect the woman from Salem, whose fate, after all, had been decided long before she was even born.

"I know."

~ | ~

-12-

Evidence

Joanna Weirdlee had spent the better part of the day visiting what turned out to be for the most part cold leads. Few of the parents who'd attended the outing on that long-ago Saturday afternoon remembered who else had been there that day. Most didn't know Julien Hawkins at all. Only a couple, thus far, had recalled seeing him there.

Presently, Weirdlee was at the home of Janet Brown, the second of the two people who remembered seeing Julien. Both women sat at opposite ends of a love seat in the living room there.

"Julien was a quiet boy," Brown recalled. "He played with the other kids—and my two kids, too—but it was more like he was just *with* them, you know, 'cause he had to be there, and wasn't really having fun with 'em."

Weirdlee nodded. She clutched her small notepad in her hands, occasionally taking things down as the two chatted.

"Did you ever talk to him?" she asked then.

"No. Not myself."

Brown herself had noted Weirdlee's accent as they talked on—though the Louisiana native mistook the agent's softened "r"s for something more like a Georgian drawl.

"How long were you at the park that day, Mrs. Brown?" Weirdlee asked.

"Ohh…maybe three hours."

"So you parked in the parking lot where everyone else did?"

"Yes. The parking was real tight, too. It's actually tough parking there every year. You know, the year after Julien went missing, we had a moment of silence for him at the beginning of the outing. It was so sad."

"I'm sure it had to be," Weirdlee said sincerely, jotting down a note in her notepad. Then she continued. "So, do you remember where you went, first, after you got there? Do you recall that?"

"Our first stop there?"

"Yes. Did you go to a particular spot—did you visit with other parents there?"

"Oh…" Brown considered. "I'm not sure. I think my husband, Joe, went right to the beer tent, though." She laughed at that. "Always the first stop for him at these things, you know."

"Yeah," Weirdlee said with a nod and a grin. "And you?"

Brown thought about that for a little bit. "I…think I did talk to a couple of parents, actually. Maybe Karen Fowler and her husband, Tom. And there was, uh—what was her name?—Sandy or Samantha. She and her husband. I don't know his name."

"Try to retrace your footsteps, Mrs. Brown," Weirdlee said. "From talking with them, did you and your husband go to any particular tents, or maybe visit with other people?"

"Well, we actually did do the rounds of all the tents— you know what I mean, the once-over to visit each one, just to see what they had."

"Sure," Weirdlee said, taking another note. "And when thereabouts did you see the Hawkins boy?"

Again, Brown took some time to sift through her memories. She gave a thoughtful expression. "I'm thinking...it was a little while after we got there, anyway. Maybe an hour after."

"And what time did you get there?"

"About one o'clock—maybe one-thirty. We go there at the same time every year."

"Think back, now, Mrs. Brown. While you were visiting all the tents, do you recall talking to any of the volunteer staff there that day?"

Brown nodded thoughtfully. "Yes...I think I talked to a couple, actually. Not sure I remember their names, though. It *was* a while ago, you know."

"Picture their faces, Mrs. Brown. Who do you see?"

Brown tried to focus, but the fog of three years gone by made it very difficult for her. "Just some teachers—I really don't know their names. And Mr. Potter, the principal."

"Did you know the daycare counselor, Ms. Simmons?"

"Oh," Brown recalled, "I think I know what she looks like, yes. And I did see her there, off and on, I think."

"Off and on?"

"Yes."

"You mean at several different times, or just a couple?"

"Uhh—a couple? I think it was twice."

"You're sure?"

Brown winced helplessly. "Not really."

Weirdlee frowned. Vague recollections weren't very reliable, and she couldn't very well go back to Nicks with a bunch of "I think so's" and "Not sure's." It was also entirely possible, Weirdlee realized, that Mrs. Brown was mixing up memories of being there at different years.

She was about to ask Brown another question when suddenly she felt a sharp, jolting presence shoot through her body. She straightened up in her chair, then went light-headed as a flood of intense passion overwhelmed her.

Brown noticed Weirdlee's red, flushed face right away.

"Ma'am," she said, "are you all right?"

He was coming for her, she sensed.

Stop it! she demanded, panic-stricken. She stood up quickly. "I have to go," she said to Brown.

"Are you okay?" Brown asked her again.

"Yes," Weirdlee replied. "Thank you for your time, Mrs. Brown." She shoved her notepad into her skirt suit's pocket and then strode to the front door. "We'll be in touch if we need anything else."

Brown got up from her seat and followed Weirdlee to the door. "All right," she said, taken aback by the sudden rush. "I hope everything turns out okay."

"Yes," Weirdlee said, her mind swirling. "So do I."

She rendered a quick, fake smile at Brown before letting herself out the door.

Brown watched her then as she hurried to her Grand Cherokee, parked in the driveway. The agent got in, started it up, and then backed out quickly before gunning it down the street.

Brown's puzzled gaze stayed on the road as the car disappeared around a corner.

"Odd..." she whispered.

Weirdlee sped down the road, her heart pounding and her entire body stricken by fear. Basil was fast approaching her, she knew, and he very well intended to claim his sought-after prize. She kept her mind focused on the road ahead of her as best she could, barely making it through two traffic lights as she raced on.

Don't let up! He'll catch you!

On she drove.

The nightmare of him subduing her kept her foot heavy on the pedal.

Move!

She raced along—weaving around several cars that drove much too slow!

He's coming for you! He's coming!

The Cherokee's wheels screeched, their rubber smearing the road underneath them as she forced a hard turn around a sharp curve.

STOP! she cried out in her mind then—her intuition taking hold.

She slammed on the breaks—just barely missing another car crossing her path. She screamed aloud, *"NO!"* as her vehicle thundered to a halt.

She'd come to a four-way stop and nearly blown through it. The car she'd come inches away from slamming into stopped, too. From out of it leapt an irate middle-aged man.

"You stupid bitch!" he hollered. "Jesus Christ! You almost fuckin' killed me!"

He sprinted over to her driver's side door.

Still stricken by her ordeal, Weirdlee glanced at the man as he stalked up to her.

"What the hell is the matter with you?" he yelled. "You fuckin' around on your phone?"

She looked up at him as she recovered her wits.

"You on drugs or somethin'?" he asked her, still fuming.

She dug inside of her jacket pocket then to retrieve her ID billfold. She flipped open the billfold and showed him her FBI credentials.

"Aww, fuckin' shit," he swore on seeing it. "You drive like that all the time?"

"On your way, sir," she replied in a shaken voice, glancing to the road ahead of her.

The man, quite unexpectedly then, gave her a concerned look.

"Hey...you all right, miss?"

She looked at him thoughtfully, in turn, suddenly aware that such a mundane thing as a near-accident had delivered an innocent soul to her side, thereby, perhaps, breaking the bond her pursuer had forced on her.

She had no lingering sense of Basil in her mind any longer.

"I'm fine, sir," she said. "Please move along. I'm very sorry."

The man hesitated at first, uncertain of what to do. "All right," he finally said then. "But you might wanna watch where you're drivin', miss."

He stepped away then and went back to his car.

After he drove off, Weirdlee sat for a moment to collect herself. Her heart still pounded with apprehension, but her mind was beginning to clear.

Suddenly then, she remembered her situation. She glanced up at the rearview mirror anxiously. Peering into the peaceful distance behind her, though, she saw nothing was there.

No car. No Basil.

She drove ahead then, past the intersection, before pulling over to the side of the road. She turned off the engine and got out of the car. Looking all around her, she saw fields of sugarcane off to her right and, along either side of both intersecting roads behind her, a thin line of bordering trees trailing off into the distance. No other cars were anywhere to be seen. She was all alone out there, she confirmed in her mind. If Paul Basil had, at one time, been close by her, then something must have warded him off— and Weirdlee very much doubted, upon reflection, that the irate man she'd almost hit was enough to compel the voodoo king to stay away.

178

Something else, she pondered, must have...

Suddenly then, a terrible sadness overwhelmed her soul. She looked off to the northwest, her heart aching in despair.

Ohh, no...

Regina Hawkins was weeping.

* * * *

Nicks and Fielding were twenty miles away from the home of Regina Hawkins when Nicks got the call. Sheriff Mickens informed him that a local fisherman had discovered a sneaker in the river just past the Grand Bayous junction, and that hey were presently taking it to Mrs. Hawkins for a positive ID.

The two special agents arrived at Hawkins' residence at about 3:00 PM. A Louisiana state trooper stood at the head of the long dirt driveway to greet them as they drove up. After showing their IDs and getting waved past, the agents continued to the mobile home itself. There, a Sheriff's Department police cruiser was parked outside, and, parked next to it, was Special Agent Weirdlee's Grand Cherokee. The agents left their car and made for the home's front door, where Mickens greeted them.

"What's up?" Nicks asked him.

Mickens jabbed a thumb inside. "Come on in."

Entering the small mobile home, Mickens led them into the cramped living area. There, sitting on a small, beat up couch, Regina Hawkins sobbed. Agent Weirdlee was there, too, sitting close by her side, an arm draped around the grieving woman's shoulder. Tears leaked from the agent's own eyes as she touched her head to Hawkins' own.

"The spirits of Heaven are with you," she whispered to her, "and they are your witnesses. You are blessed by them, no matter who might trespass against you."

Her words, however, were of little comfort to Hawkins, who wept on.

"I'm going to die," she wailed through her tears. "My baby's up in Heaven."

Weirdlee looked up to see Nicks and Fielding standing there. Her eyes met Nicks' own, and she shook her head in despair.

Nicks looked back at her. He saw in her eyes a very deep and genuine heartache, and he hoped, above all, that she had the strength to see this thing through.

Weirdlee, for her part, even in her utter sadness, felt an endearing sense of relief with the lead agent's arrival there. He was a rock to her—so very calm and thoughtful in his demeanor, deliberate and determined in his purpose. She could always count on him to be sure-minded and good in his heart.

A sheriff's deputy presently held the little boy's sneaker, which they kept in a paper bag. He handed it to Mickens so that the sheriff could show it to the FBI agents.

"She ID'd the shoe by the boy's initials she'd put on the inside heel," Mickens said to Nicks as he gave it over to him.

Nicks peeked inside the bag. The sneaker, waterlogged and frayed, was made of a red fabric, he saw, with a now-filthy white rubber trim. He examined it, turning the bag this way and that. He noticed, too, that one of the muck-soaked laces was knotted on itself, as if it had broken at some point and someone had tied it up in repair.

"You ask her about the laces?" he asked Mickens.

"What about 'em?" Mickens replied.

"Ask her about the knot in one of them," Nicks said, pointing into the bag. "See if she remembers it."

"Sure 'nuff."

Nicks then gestured for Mickens and Fielding to follow him back to the front door. When they got there, they all stepped outside.

Nicks showed the bag's open end to Fielding. "What do you think?" he asked him. "Look like it's been in the water for three years?"

Fielding eyed the sneaker in the bag and shrugged. "I dunno. Looks in pretty rough shape to me."

"We'll be takin' it to the lab in the city, Special Agent," said Mickens. "They might be able to get some of the boy's DNA out of it."

Nicks nodded, and then gave the bag back to Mickens. "Have 'em do a complete analysis—parasites, bugs, any vegetation—that sort of thing. You said someone found the sneaker upstream from here?"

"Yessir. Maybe three miles from here. Just past the Grand Bayous."

Nicks looked off to the west, toward the nearby Bayou L'Ours. "I'd like to get some water samples from the river," he said. "Here by the L'Ours bridge, and then up by where the sneaker was found."

"Sure thing."

"You search the area where the sneaker was found?" Nicks asked.

"Yeah—we figured to get started on that early in the mornin' and get us a whole day or two in for it."

"Why don't you get a police boat out there, for now," Nicks advised.

"What's that?" Mickens replied.

Nicks repeated, "A police boat. You've got one, don't you?"

"'Course we got one. You talkin' about keepin' it out there overnight?"

Nicks put his hands on his hips. "Yes, Sheriff, that's what I mean. Listen, that shoe didn't just drift upstream from the park. There could be a crime scene out there, and we've got the press crawling around and a bunch of curious civilians right behind 'em."

Mickens nodded, understanding. "Yeah, I get it. I'll see about gettin' one out there, then."

"Seems more likely the boy'd be more upstream from where his shoe was found," Fielding suggested. He made sure to keep his voice hushed as he went on. "He gets dumped, then caught up in some shit up a ways, and then...with decomp and all, the shoe comes loose and gets carried off downstream."

Nicks looked off to the L'Ours, mulling the idea. "Yeah...that's possible."

"Whatcha thinkin' then, partner?" Fielding asked.

Nicks turned to him. "I just think it's a little convenient that three years goes by without finding any evidence, then suddenly, after we show up, someone finds a sneaker." He turned to Mickens. "You said a fisherman found this?"

"Yessir."

"We'll need to talk to him," Nicks said.

"I got his phone number and address. He's a local boy—lives just west of here, down the road a ways."

"Okay," said Nicks. "It'd be helpful if he could take us back there, too, and show us exactly where he found it."

"I'll ask him."

* * * *

Joanna Weirdlee—a healer above all—stayed with Regina Hawkins for the remainder of the afternoon and into the early evening. She kept her company, comforted her, and even cooked her dinner before finally taking her leave. It had been a heart-wrenching day for the young special agent, and she felt completely drained inside—as if the vibrancy that had always been a part of her soul been had been stolen away from her entirely. She prayed to the spirits to help guide her, but the voices she'd grown so accustomed to through the years had, on this occasion, failed to come to her. She retreated then to her room at the Swampy Inn, alone and worried for what might happen to her in the days ahead. And fearful, always, that Paul Basil would return.

Nicks, meanwhile, took Fielding with him that late afternoon. He wanted to check out the area where the sneaker had been recovered before anyone might go there first and disturb the scene. Prior to leaving Regina Hawkins' home, too, Sheriff Mickens asked her about her son's knotted shoe. She replied that she'd often knotted her boy's broken laces, same as her own, but she couldn't recall if she'd knotted the lace on the sneaker they recovered.

The agents arrived at The Bayous Experience, there to rent another boat from owner Morgan Husk.

Husk greeted them in the parking lot as they got out of their car.

"Boys back again, huh?"

Nicks gave a nod. "Just couldn't stay away." He looked off to the docks by the riverside. "We'll need to rent another boat from you."

Husk smiled. "Sure thing."

Nicks kept his attention on the docks, where presently he observed an elderly white woman and three younger-aged black men gathered. One of the men was helping the old woman into a small motor boat. This woman, unbeknownst to Nicks at the time, was none other than Zarah Devillier, recently returned by bus trip from New Orleans after she and her two eldest had been dropped off at a bus terminal there by their armed escorts. Upon arriving at the dock, they were met then by Zarah's youngest, Damon, who'd brought their boat downriver from their home in the swamps.

Zarah herself was in a foul mood as she stepped shakily into her boat, swearing and fuming over what had befallen them in the city.

Nicks studied her curiously, and he wondered, recalling Captain Phillips' description of her, if this could be the voodoo woman Agent Weirdlee had met up with on their first day in town.

The family got into their boat and Damon fired up the engine.

"Sir?" came a distracting voice to Nicks.

He looked back at Husk. "Yes?"

"I said, did you want the same boat ya'll had last time?"

Nicks glanced at Fielding. "Uh—yeah. If it's available, that'd be fine."

Husk replied with a nod, "Sure 'nuff," and started back to his office to get the keys to the boat.

Just then, a dark blue Ford pickup truck pulled into the parking lot and parked close to where the agents had parked. A young man in worn overalls and wearing a tattered baseball cap hopped out of the truck. This was Evan Stewart, the fisherman who'd discovered little Julien's sneaker. Over the phone earlier, Stewart had offered to take the agents out there in his own boat, but Nicks had declined, preferring instead to go with a known neutral party.

"Afternoon, sirs," Stewart said to the agents as he approached them. "You the FBI folks?"

"That's us," replied Nicks.

Husk came out of his office. "Over here," he said to the men, pointing off to the left side of the docks where the boat with the swivel seat was tied off.

They followed.

Arriving at the dock and approaching the boat, Husk gave the keys to Nicks. "Gonna have to up the rental fee," he said to him.

"What?" Fielding replied, annoyed.

"More people in the boat," said Husk.

"Really?" Nicks said to him.

"Ya'll. My boat's just down the road a ways," Stewart offered again. "Won't cost ya nothin'."

"All right, all right," Husk relented. "Same as before."

Nicks smiled at him. "Fair enough." Then he looked to Fielding and Stewart and gestured for them to hop onto the boat. "Let's go, guys. You can drive, Agent Fielding."

The men got aboard.

The trip upriver was uneventful. Most of the way, too, they followed behind the Devillier clan, whose boat, though smaller than theirs, still had good speed to it. The sons would occasionally look back at the agents as they motored along. Korram even flipped them the bird a few minutes along the way.

"That's got to be the old voodoo woman and her sons," Nicks said to Fielding over the drone of their boat's motor. "Can't possibly be two families like that."

Fielding peered ahead of them as he kept the boat steered upstream. The Devillier's boat was about sixty yards ahead at that point. "You mean bein' interracial?" he asked.

"No," Nicks replied, keeping his eyes on the Devilliers. "Weird."

They cruised on.

The river led southwest for another fifteen minutes before the agents bypassed the same islet they'd encountered that previous Sunday when they'd followed after Agent Weirdlee. Up ahead of them, the Devilliers stayed closer to the left bank. Nicks studied them with growing interest as they eventually slowed their boat's speed and the agents' own boat then began to overtake them. A few dozen yards farther along, then, the Devilliers turned their craft into a heavily wooded inlet, and Nicks and Fielding both eyed the family as they motored on by them. Nicks looked ahead of the Devilliers' boat at this point, there to catch a glimpse of the murky cove that lay at the far end of the inlet, toward which the family was headed. Though he held no magick in his soul, the agent still felt a sense of brooding gloom in the warm, still air all around them.

"That's the way Agent Weirdlee went the other night," he said to Fielding.

Fielding eyed the inlet cove with a grim expression. He looked over at Nicks. "Some creepy shit at night, I bet."

Nicks kept his gaze on the inlet, his mind still unsettled. "Some creepy shit in the daytime."

Just a couple minutes further on, the agents came upon the junction of the Grand Bayous. This was a convergence of two rivers that merged into one as the waterway meandered northeastward, behind them, eventually spilling into the Lac des Allemands. At this point, Stewart directed them to take the river flowing in from the south, to their left. Fielding turned the boat then and motored on.

After passing by another islet farther upriver, they soon came upon a narrow cove that opened up on their right. This was the outlet of the Bayou Plat. And this was their destination.

"Hold up here," Stewart said. He pointed off to the Plat's opening. "Right there by the shore, over on the left side. Up in them trees."

"The trees?" asked Nicks.

Stewart jabbed his finger at the trees as he answered. "It was hung up in them low branches there, just above the water."

Nicks gestured for Fielding to taxi them closer to the treeline.

As the boat came in close, Fielding cut the engine, and Stewart tossed in a ball anchor to keep them in position.

Nicks eyed the tangle of tree branches that hung low over the riverbank there. In many places, he saw, they dipped into the water itself. Thick brush and tall weeds lay clumped along marshy, semi-submerged terrain beyond the treeline.

"You fish here, Mr. Stewart?" Nicks asked.

"Stew," said Stewart. "My friends call me Stew. And yeah, I fish all around these parts. This here is about as far south as I go, though."

"Oh yeah? Why's that?" Nicks asked.

"'Cause it's as far south as I need to go, sir. Plus'n...I don't really get along too well with the Chamblases. They own a place south of here."

Nicks and Fielding both turned to look southward, following the upstream course of the river. Nicks could just barely make out what looked like a treeline cutting across the river in the distance.

"What's upstream, there?" he asked. "Does the river break up into a swamp or something?"

"Naw," Stewart said. "It just keeps goin' south till it gets to the Boeuf Lake. There's a lot of streams and irrigation out here, though, that crosses it up."

Fielding glanced around. "Any roads around here?"

Stewart laughed. "Shit. You're on the only road in or outta here, chief."

"What about upstream?" Nicks asked. "Any roads up there?"

Stewart looked off to the south, then turned his gaze to the east as he mulled things over in his head.

"Well," he said, pointing eastward. "307 is off thataways. There's some roads that'll come close to the river from that, but I ain't sure whereabouts they'd be from here, though."

"Okay," said Nicks. He turned his attention back to the shoreline. "And you found the shoe—where?—in a tree or something you said?"

Stewart pointed directly at a low hanging branch whose end dipped into the murky bayou waters. "Right there. In that branch. The laces were tangled in it."

"This place flood a lot, does it?" Fielding asked.

Stewart nodded lazily. "From time to time. When we get storms and such."

Nicks said to Fielding, "We'll need to ask the sheriff to search the whole area upstream from here, following along either bank."

"How far up you wanna go?" Fielding asked.

Nicks shrugged. "All the way."

"All the way up to the lake?"

"Including the lake, Special Agent."

Fielding shook his head. "Whew, boy, partner. That's a whole lotta territory. That could take weeks. Plus all this swamp and alligators and such?"

Nicks looked at him plainly. In the senior agent's mind, when there was a job to do, any inconvenience that might be a part of it was entirely irrelevant. "I don't care."

Fielding remembered himself then—and who he was talking to. "Yeah," he said to him. "Sure enough, partner."

Nicks turned to Stewart. "Mr. Stewart," he said, before quickly recalling the man's nickname, "Stew. You fish around here pretty regularly, do you?"

"Yessir. Couple times a week, leastabouts."

Nicks looked again to the riverbank with the low hanging branches. He scanned the thick brush and weeds all around. Every so often, here and there, a plastic trash bag or an old can or bottle lay about.

"So, what made you pick out an old dirty sneaker from all of this other stuff littered around here?"

Stewart smiled proudly. "Shit, sir. I watch the TV. I know you guys were searchin' for a missin' boy out here. It's all over the news. When I was out here fishin' early this mornin', I spotted me that red sneaker. I said to myself, 'Stew, that looks like a little shoe, there.' And so I pulled in there and grabbed it outta there. I called the police and let 'em know. They met me at the docks later on."

Nicks studied the bank, contemplating things. "And this morning was the first time you ever saw that sneaker there?"

"Yessir. First time I noticed it, anyway. I don't usually go'a trash watchin', ya know. But this morning before I went out, I was watchin' the news, and Miss Kelly—she's our news girl—she says that the FBI was still lookin' for a little boy out here. And then when I was out here myself, I was just'a trollin' around and such, and when I came hereabouts, I was lookin' at the trees...and *shazoo*, there it was."

Nicks' gaze never left the treeline. "Yeah," he said thoughtfully, mulling things over in his mind.

"There it was."

~ | ~

-13-

The Fall and Rise of Joanna Osborne

In her youth, Zarah Devillier was a homely woman, rarely sought after by the men of her generation. Thanks to her mother, too—whose own poisoned mind often settled for life's lesser pleasures, drugs and alcohol—she was brought up in an impoverished environment that encouraged neither success nor any measure of self-respect. Her father left them while Zarah was still a small child. Her mother did teach her the ways of magick, and also the offshoot voodoo religion that she herself had been taught much earlier in her own life. But the mother, Marah, never encouraged her daughter to seek wonderful, wholesome things. Instead, she cared only that her daughter carry on with their wretched ways.

And so, very early on in her life, Zarah had a choice to make: Either take advantage of the natural gifts she'd inherited and make a better life for herself, or use the magick she'd learned from her mother to carry on with her family's adopted religion and way of life.

Sadly, it didn't take much deliberation on her part to choose the latter. For in the Catholic-voodoo religion of her family, she realized there was genuine power to be had. People, she'd discovered, would come to her practically begging for her favor—simply because she could see their futures and, many hoped, provide some sense of justice seemingly always denied. She would, as well, have more than her share of men, all of whom flocked to her, spellbound and at her mercy.

The elderly Marah Devillier, meanwhile—a wreck for most of her forsaken life, anyway—drank herself into oblivion, and she died alone in a rain-drenched parking lot in downtown Houma. As much as the old woman had predicted the future of so many others in her lifetime, Marah never once clearly perceived the tragedy of her own life, nor its own miserable end.

Such was the way of the curse she had inherited.

By her mid-twenties, the now orphaned Zarah Devillier had risen to become the Voodoo Queen of the Bayous. This was not as glorious a title as it appeared, however, as the region south of New Orleans, where she held sway, was actually quite sparse with potential followers, and so, even at the height of her reign, her flock numbered merely in the dozens. Still, though, much as teenaged gangs exalt in the glory of "ruling" their street corners, power was power. And Zarah's followers, at first, were devout in their newfound religion, and genuinely loyal to their high priestess.

Zarah was content with her life for very many years. She'd inherited her mother's old family house out in the bayous, north of Thibodaux, and for money she worked as a house cleaner for a local Raceland maid service for some years before eventually taking up her mother's profession, prostitution, for easier cash. This lifestyle remained the norm for several years thereafter. Passing into her forties then, Zarah's looks—never an asset to begin with—deteriorated noticeably as she turned more and more to abusing alcohol and drugs. Her practice of packing mud on her face, chest, and arms began at about this time, too. She hated the fact that she was a white woman practicing a religion followed mostly by blacks, and she'd always felt she had to go out of her way to show that her race was irrelevant—this despite the fact that none of her flock ever questioned this in any way at all. Masking herself with mud during ceremonies, then, in her mind, made her appear race-neutral.

Zarah's years, quite predictably, passed every bit as miserably as her mother's did before her. Despite her inherited gift of second sight, she'd led a wretched life, much like her mother, for several decades. Her life would only take a turn, then, when she finally made the acquaintance of a certain young man who came to her with a considerable degree of ambition of his own.

And he, just like her, had the Gift inside of him.

So Zarah Devillier met Paul Basil.

Basil was a young man, still in his early twenties, when he first met Zarah. And up to this point he had never been properly schooled in the art of the Craft. Zarah would thus spend hours, weeks, and months on end teaching him the ways of magick, until such time as he had mastered all of its supernatural powers. And soon, too, they began a passionate romance, and Zarah quickly fell in love with her much-younger lover. She brought him into her sect thereafter, and her followers quickly became convinced of his power, too, and so fell under his sway just as easily as they had come under Zarah's.

Paul Basil, however, unlike Zarah, had no intention of settling for a mere little fiefdom in the swamps. He saw in the Catholic-voodoo religion he'd adopted a much higher purpose in this life.

"We are the agents of the *loa!*" he extolled their followers. "And in the name of God, we must purge from this world all that is blasphemous in His eyes!"

Basil's words captured the will of every one of Zarah's followers. Theirs, they believed, was a most righteous cause. And though none played a knowing role in the couple's murderous ways, their souls, to a man and woman, were tainted just the same by the cruelty Basil had instilled in their hearts.

Gather the sinners for God's judgment!
Banish the heretics!

Soon, then, the young priest rose up to become Zarah's equal in the sect, and he took on the title of Voodoo King of Bayous. By this time, as well, Zarah had subordinated herself to him in their personal relationship, and so it would only be a matter of time before she surrendered control of the sect to him, too.

And all the while, as this transfer of power unfolded, Zarah truly believed that her abdication was of her own free will—that Fate itself had always meant for her to find her man and so give herself and everything she owned to him.

The bitter truth, however, was far more sinister than even the wicked Zarah could have ever imagined.

Soon after meeting Zarah, Paul Basil had discovered that the priestess, much like he, wielded the power to bend the will of others—to shape their minds. Not long after joining her sect, then, he decided that she might be useful to him in delivering both the followers and the sacrificial souls he would need for what he envisioned to be a holy mission.

First, however, he knew he had to replace her as the leader of their group. This would not be so difficult, he determined. Early on in their romantic relationship, Basil had sensed his mate's willingness to be controlled by him. She'd left herself open not only to his charms, but also to his powers of supernatural persuasion. So, with the passing of each day and night, he would slip into her mind—first by way of her dreams, and then later on via conscious entrancement—to eventually take control of her will and so convince her that he, Paul Basil, should be the master of everything in her life.

So Zarah Devillier fell to him.

Being under his control, however, soon began to affect the priestess's own ability to reason and deduce things. Her thoughts became twisted, and, at times, she would become delusional. At public events, she might explode into furious fits of rage—her rantings unnerving even her own followers, many of whom began to leave the sect as the psychological change of power from Zarah to Basil took its bizarre, disturbing course. Zarah Devillier had always been the binding force of the sect, while for Basil it was always about the mission, not the people conducting it. And so, with Zarah's collapse of sanity, the group she'd built from her own guile inevitably fell apart completely. None stayed on to bear witness to Zarah's final overthrow. The two lovers, once heads of a loyal and growing following, in the end had only each other to preach to.

Basil, in hindsight, understood his miscalculation. In his greed to have it all, he'd not considered how much he needed Zarah to have at least *some* of her wits about her. He thereafter released much of his hold on her—though by then it was too late for them to bring back their following. Both of them, too, were left penniless in the aftermath, and so Basil had to think of alternative sources of income for them. Before joining Zarah's sect, he had earned money as a petty drug dealer, and so he decided to turn back to that for his own part. Zarah, he concluded, was too goddamned ugly to go back on the street. So he got her pregnant, instead. Three times was the charm. Three welfare babies. Later on, Basil found himself a job in New Orleans—a stage act as a voodoo priest, of all things, dancing and singing for the idiot tourists. He called himself *Marcel Unate'*,

Voodoo King of Bayous—a name that Zarah herself came to so adore that she would call him that fully on her own.

Mostly released from her lover's supernatural control, Zarah would eventually regain much of her lost faculties—at least enough for her to care for her children and, of course, to recruit the wayward souls that Basil would always need to carry on with his life's mission. Basil himself, meanwhile, would grow tired of living with an older woman who'd aged quite obviously into an *old woman.* He left the home they shared in the bayous and took up residence in a rented house in the small township of Paradis. Zarah took it very hard. But still, she knew she had a job to do for the man she loved. And so she would deliver into his hands plenty of heretics in the years to come.

* * * *

"Momma, why you so mad?"

Zarah Devillier and her sons had just arrived home. The old woman stormed into the small living area of their ramshackle house and shoved an old wooden chair out of her way before turning and leering back at her eldest son. "Damn youz, ya fuckin' child! Can't ya see ya momma's bein' traded in? All I's did for him! All I's gave him! He just'a tossin' me out like a piece a fuckin' trash!"

"Momma," Lucien implored, approaching her, "we's got our house. We got each other."

Zarah pounded her fists on his chest. "Ya fuckin' ass! Ya so fuckin' stupid! You and youz brothers'll never have the magick! Ya's never have the gift! He took it all away from youz!"

She stalked across the room then to make her way to the stairway. Step by shaky step, she ascended the stairs.

The three sons stood there, each glancing at the other and not knowing what to do. They waited there in the darkened living area while their mother rummaged around upstairs. She'd gone to her bedroom, where from underneath her bed she pulled out an old square trunk. She opened it up and fetched herself a plain cloth voodoo doll from a collection there. This she planned to use for some rather nasty spiritual work coming that evening.

Yes. A certain witch was going to pay very dearly for taking away her man.

The old woman came back downstairs and stepped gingerly over to the living room's small square table—the same one where she'd hosted Special Agent Weirdlee on the weekend just past. She set the doll down beside a little black bag she kept there, then took a seat for herself. Her sons, all three trained not to bother their mother when she sat at the table, took their leave by going into the kitchen.

The brooding priestess would need to wait until nightfall before getting things started. The spirits always moved about much more readily in the darkness of night. In the meantime, she'd see what there was to see for them all in the days and weeks ahead. She picked up the little black bag on the table and opened it up. From inside, she dumped out a collection of old, dried chicken bones. She took them up in her hands and shook them vigorously. "Cast my eyes to the future," she chanted.

She tossed the bones onto the table. They tumbled about before coming to rest. Three leg bones lay pointed inward, while a small thighbone lay across on its own. A wing bone ended up off to the left.

"Mmm..." she considered. It looked to her like a sign of short times. She swatted her chest encouragingly. "Keep'a tickin', ya beater."

She brought a finger to the thighbone then and flicked it closer to the leg bones. She eyed it curiously, then leaned her head in closer and spat on the bones.

"Ehh?" she grunted.

Something didn't look right.

She gathered up the bones and she rattled them about in her hands once more. She tossed them onto the table again. The bones tumbled about as before. This time, the thighbone ended up on top of the wing bone, while the leg bones all cluttered together, their ends facing each other, similar to before. She examined them closely for a moment, and then lifted her gaze and closed her eyes, allowing her second sight to take hold.

"Ehhh..." she groaned as a vision came forth to her. She watched it patiently, its emanations drifting through her mind like a dream. As the vision passed on then, she smiled and opened her eyes.

What she'd seen with her first toss of the bones was a future cut short for herself. But she was old, she realized, and she had that coming to her. Her second tossing, though, showed another scene in her mind, entirely. She saw a bayou in the night, and lots of trees, and water here and there. And she saw alligators, too. Lots and lots of alligators. And the witch was there, her heart beating rapidly. And fear was in the air.

Alarm!

Desperation!

Another woman was there, too.

Innocence lost.

Death.

Zarah laughed hysterically, her old vocal chords cackling loudly in a fit of vile happiness.

Her sons hurried out of the kitchen upon hearing their mother. They stood by the stairwell, looking anxiously at her.

"Mind yerselves," she said to them with a sneering glare. "Cook us some dinner."

The sons all said their "Yes, Mommas" in response and then returned to the kitchen to do her bidding.

Zarah groaned again as she turned her attention back to her chicken bones. She eyed them with a widening grin as the vision she'd just seen lingered in her mind.

"Put the fear of God into youz," she whispered. "Chop, chop, little witch. Chop, chop, they do's in the bayous."

The Devillier clan ate their dinner—a concoction of a stir-fried vegetables and turkey, with Italian bread on the side and cheap wine to wash it all down. The sons cleared the kitchen table afterwards and washed the dishes, and then went upstairs to their bedrooms.

Mother, they knew, still had work to do.

Zarah returned to the small table in the darkened living area. She'd picked out a selection of black candles and placed them about in a circle on the tabletop. Sitting down, she lit the candles. She hummed, and then she sang a short incantation, inviting the spirits into the realm of the living. She picked up the voodoo doll she'd left there earlier then and passed it about the candles, letting the little flames of each just barely touch the doll's fabric.

She cackled, anticipating what was soon to come.

She closed her eyes then, and she chanted to the supernaturals:

> *Gold and black diamonds, demons of fire*
> *The faithless succumb to dark passion's desire.*
> *She, the deceiver, will live out the night*
> *Trapped in her nightmares—imprisoned by fright!*

She laughed again, unable to contain her glee.

> *Cry in your dreams while ye fight with*
> *the beasts*
> *Tonight you will die in your dreams while*
> *they will feast!*

Her eyes lit up then, and she spat on the doll. She tossed it onto the table before her.

"Die in your dreams!" she cried out.

"Die in your dreams!"

* * * *

Nicks and Fielding returned to the Swampy Inn after eating their dinner. By that time, Agent Weirdlee had already retired to her room. Nicks checked in with her, but she seemed out of place and not wanting of any company on this evening. He let her alone and told her they could discuss things in the morning. He wished her a good night's rest.

Weirdlee, however, was not so well in her mind, and there would be little rest for her on this evening.

For much of the night she stayed sitting on the floor in her room, held like a prisoner within the bounds of her sacred circle and hoping above all that it would be enough to keep her protected.

The power of the dark magick that sought her out, however, would not allow for such a ceremonious contraption to interfere with its plans. Not on this evening.

And so, after the witch from Salem lay down at last, there to fall into slumber, the wandering curse of Zarah Devillier crept into her protected abode...

Joanna wore her favorite homespun dress as she strolled across a mountainside meadow on a bright, peaceful day. She was older in this dream, her heart enriched by the love and adventure she'd enjoyed throughout her entire life. She'd had lovers, and happy times, and challenges and trials, but always she'd moved on from them, contented as she was by the blessings of the gift she'd inherited.

This was a dream she often had.

Walking along, she looked off to the far away horizon, where she spied a gathering of clouds approaching in the distance. So curious, they looked to her. She pressed on anyway, though, her pleasant thoughts keeping her company on her journey.

By the time she came to a gurgling creek at the foot of the meadow's hillside, a soft breeze had picked up around her, and it felt more like autumn in the air than the nice spring day it had been just a few minutes before. She looked off to the sky once more. There, she beheld dark clouds encroaching, low and ominous, upon the once pale blue light of day.

A storm was coming.

She eyed the clouds more deliberately then, and she sensed in their presence something possessed and malevolent.

Shelter!

She looked all about her surroundings. There was, however, nothing but a scattering of trees to either side of her and to her front, and, behind her, the mountainside meadow she'd just come along. No cover at all from the approaching weather.

The breeze picked up to a firm wind, and the air became cool and uncomfortable. Joanna wrapped her arms about herself as a chill went through her.

Protection, she told herself.

But there was none.

She darted off then into a panicked run—racing as best she could along the banks of the little creek.

The storm is coming!

Another instant passed, and she left the bank to splash into the midst of the creek's shallow waters. Darkness devoured the once peaceful light of day. Suddenly, too, the cool air grew oppressively hot and humid—as if nature itself had been twisted by some evil design. She gasped for air as she ran along, but—much to her horror—there was no sign or indication of which way to go!

"Help me!" she screamed, begging the spirits to save her from her peril.

Then, as if in cruel answer to her plea, the stony creek bed beneath her feet gave way to a swampy, muck-ridden bottom that sucked her into its thick, black mass.

She could run no more!

She steadied herself in the mire, tugging her feet out from the mud with each lunging step. And it was just then—in that most terrifying moment—that she spied a sight that quite nearly drove her mad.

Bodies. Everywhere! Freshly dead, and half-eaten. Decomposed and bloated.

She screamed aloud in horror!

Tugging and pulling herself desperately come free of the muck, she wept in anguish as the bog only sucked her deeper into its depths.

She could not move!

"Leave me alone!" she wailed through her tears. "Leave me alone!"

In the midst of the howling wind and darkness, then, the sky opened up into a torrential downpour, and Joanna cowered, like a beaten soul, under the weight of the inundation.

Nature, it seemed, had turned wholly against her.

Her fate was sealed.

And so high aloft in the roiling clouds, the ghostly face of Zarah Devillier then appeared. She laughed wickedly at her victim far below her.

"Die!" she told the helpless pagan. "Die in youz misery!"

Joanna looked up to see Zarah's apparition, and she cried out in anguish at her tormentor.

"Don't you do this! Don't you kill me! Don't you!"

And she broke down and wept on.

Zarah then cast her hand about, and so the priestess conjured forth the final act of her morbid plan.

First came the sloshing sound, alerting Joanna to her peril. Then came a snapping *clack-clack*, giving away its proximity to her.

Joanna spun about.

Alligators!

They came at her from all around—too many to escape from, and too close to give time to pray. They fell upon her in a wild, writhing frenzy—jaws a'lunging and chomping and tearing. Joanna screamed, stricken, as the animals ripped into her flesh. Her blood spattered her face and soaked her dress as she fought them off, but in vain.

Her tortured cries filled the evening air.

Far away, meanwhile, off in the waking world and hunched over her little square table, Zarah Devillier cackled away in a wicked, cold laughter, tugging and clawing at the doll she'd contrived for her evening's cruel labor: To finally put an end to the meddling ways of the witch lady from Salem, once and for all.

* * * *

The sun rose on Thursday morning, peaceful and pleasant, with barely a wisp of white clouds tingeing the pale blue sky.

Inside Special Agent Weirdlee's room, a tormented, shivering woman—who'd once been so undeniably strong and confident in both her mind and spirit—sat curled up in a corner, dressed only in her nightgown, her hands clutched against her chest. Her eyes stared ahead, still lost in the terror that she'd gone through that last evening. Her very soul, it seemed, had been stripped away from her and savaged. Gone was the familiar Agent Weirdlee known to all. There was no cheerfulness left inside of her. All of that had been stolen away by those she knew to be much stronger than she could ever be. And she knew, as well, that whether her end came by death from Zarah Devillier's incantations or by slavery under the will of Paul Basil, she was surely doomed if she stayed there any longer.

Flee!

Flee from the bayous as quickly as you may!

Leave, she told herself, and go back north to New England. Find there a refuge in the woods and hide away from those who would bring such misery to her!

Home at last!

She should have never left her home!

She closed her eyes and broke into tears. So sorrowful an end she could not have imagined just four days earlier, when all was good and right in her world.

Why did you leave me? she asked the spirits.

Why did you abandon my soul?

It wasn't fair at all!

She wiped her tears from her face and sniffled. She opened her eyes, and she stared across the room.

Such loncliness. Such solitude for anyone to have to endure on her own.

But you are not alone, Joanna.

The voice was that of a stranger.

Weirdlee glanced about, unknowing.

Go to the sea.

She had heard that voice before. But where?

Go to the sea, and live!

The sea, Weirdlee remembered, where the spirits of nature roamed freely in the clean, salty air, and where, at last, she might find some peace from the torment that raged in her soul.

I must go to the sea, she whispered.

She looked heavenward, where her gaze fixed on the spiritual world that lay largely unseen to any mortal eye, yet unyielding in its supernatural power over all that lived on the Earth.

I will go to the sea.

* * * *

Special Agent Fielding woke up, showered, and dressed in a fresh suit and tie for the day ahead of him. He stepped out of the room that he shared with Special Agent Nicks, who had risen earlier, and walked along the front patio facing the inn's parking lot to make his way to the cafe. He'd planned on meeting Nicks there, and hoped Agent Weirdlee would be joining them, too. But even as he walked past the parking lot, he saw Weirdlee just then getting into her Grand Cherokee. She wore, he saw, her homemade dress—the same one she'd worn that previous Sunday night on her trip to see the old voodoo priestess. He called out to her—

"Agent Weirdlee."

She glanced at him quickly before closing her driver's side door.

He hurried over to her.

"Where ya goin'?" he asked her.

She powered her window halfway down to answer him. "I'm leaving, Daniel," she said to him, and then started up the vehicle.

Fielding asked, "Waddya mean?"

"I'm going away, Daniel," she replied sharply. "Just let it go."

She powered the window back up. As it slid closed, Fielding asked her impatiently, "Goin' away? What does *that* mean?"

She didn't reply. Instead, she turned and looked behind her, and then backed out of her parking space. Fielding kept his eyes on her, baffled, as she shifted the Cherokee into forward and drove off. Something, he knew well enough, was terribly wrong.

Entering the cafe, Fielding spotted Nicks sitting at a small table over by the left wall, and he went over to join him.

Nicks, preoccupied studying his little black notebook, glanced up at his partner as he arrived at the table. "Morning," he said to him.

Fielding took a chair and sat down. He looked at Nicks gravely. "You and Agent Weirdlee have an argument or somethin'?"

Nicks stopped his business and looked at him. "Huh?"

"You and Joanna," Fielding repeated. "She said she's leaving."

"Leaving?" Nicks replied. "What are you talking about?"

"Just like I said. She said she's leavin'. When I asked her what's up, she said she's going away, and for me to let it go."

Nicks muttered, "What the hell..." and reached for his smartphone on his belt. He tapped and scrolled to get to Weirdlee's phone number and then tapped the green call button. He put the phone to his ear. The line connected, only to buzz six times before going to voicemail.

"Agent Weirdlee," he said, "this is Nicks. Give me a call back as soon as you can." He glanced at the time on the phone. "It's seven-thirty." He tapped the phone off and put it back into its belt case. "She say where she was going?" he asked Fielding.

"Nope. She was already in her car. I'm lucky I spotted her."

Nicks eyed his partner, concerned now about Weirdlee's wellbeing. He'd suspected she was having issues and, despite her denials, he was quite certain—now more than ever—that she hadn't been entirely forthcoming about her visit with the old voodoo woman. And perhaps about her encounter with that guy Paul Basil, as well.

He sat back in his chair...suddenly, and entirely, uninterested in the investigation at hand.

* * * *

Weirdlee drove south down to Thibodaux before taking Route 1 eastbound, which would take her through Raceland and, from there, southeast toward the coast. It was a two hour drive, at least, that would give her plenty of time to think about her life and her future.

Her short career in the FBI, she concluded, was over. That much had to be true, and it brought her no great joy in knowing that. How wonderful she'd felt when she first joined the Bureau—it was every bit as fulfilling as her new boss, Deputy Director Ledds, had told her it would be. After spending her entire youth taunted and teased and looked down upon by even her own parents, to walk the halls of the J. Edgar Hoover Building and be greeted by colleagues who treated her so kindly and with such respect and regard meant more to her than she could have ever imagined. She cherished them all, and would miss each one of them very much. But owing to her terrible experience in Louisiana, it was obvious to her that as a lone, self-trained witch in a world filled with masters of the craft, she stood no chance at all working in the field.

If anything, she figured, she was actually a danger to her colleagues.

Weirdlee's eyes welled up with tears, and she stared off down the road as she traveled on.

"Sorry, boss," she whispered to her mentor, Ledds. That sweet old man. He deserved so much more than she could ever give him. She would resign from the Bureau, she decided, and then, in her own time, travel back to Massachusetts to find a safe, secluded place there, perhaps in the beautiful forests of the Berkshires. A simple two-room cottage of a sort would do. Her parents had money, and though they hadn't gotten along with their daughter in many years, they'd still paid for her college when she needed it, and would likely give her enough for what she needed, if only to keep her away from them and their snooty Cambridge friends.

She planned her life out in her mind. She'd make her money telling fortunes and selling trinkets and homemade jewelry—whatever it took to get by. She would sit out on her little porch, year after year, and watch the seasons pass on, one after the next. And she would grow old there, safe from harm and the travails of the mundane world.

It dawned on her then that this was the same vision she'd seen at Zarah Devillier's home that day.

So the vision was true.

Children would venture out to her property from time to time, she imagined, and afterwards tell their parents about the old witch who lived out in the forest. And their parents would promptly lecture them: "Don't you go out there. Stay away from that crazy old woman!"

And so she would live out her days, till the end of her
life.

Weirdlee's drive south led her past Golden Meadow,
and then on through Leeville after that. Just before Port
Fourchon, her route turned east, heading out to Grande
Isle—and the final destination of her journey.

Her heart sank as she drove past the stilted houses that
lined the road along the way. She whispered, "Samuel…" as
she pictured her handsome colleague in her mind, already
missing him.

The houses along the road soon gave way to a less
settled part of the shoreline. Weirdlee crossed a bridge
then that led directly to Grande Isle, and she drove on
until, halfway along the little island's length, she abruptly
pulled over to a dirt parking area. There, she put her head
upon the steering wheel, and she at last broke into tears.

Her long, lonely journey to the sea had come to an end.
She was alone, at last, with the spirits, if they would have
her company amongst them.

Where have you all gone from me?

She wept as a feeling of emptiness consumed her
entirely. Her soul ached, and there was nothing for her to
do anymore, nor anywhere else for her to go.

The sea.

It called to her in her mind.

She wiped her welled-up tears from her eyes and
composed herself as best she could. Then, she looked off to
the east, toward the nearby shore of the Gulf coast.

Go to the sea.

She opened her car door and got out, as if being led by
some possession. She took in a breath, and she gazed out
at the rolling, grassy mounds that bordered the road,
beyond which lay a sandy beach leading to the shore.
Walking towards the mounds, she felt as if she were in a

dream as the soft ocean breeze buffeted her tear-soaked face.

The spirits, she knew, had summoned her.

Come to us, they beckoned.

Her heart pounded as she walked briskly over the grassy mounds. Coming to the other side, she beheld a narrow beach that joined up with the waters of the Gulf of Mexico. The deep blue sky, mottled with white, puffy clouds, watched over the waves as they gently crashed ashore.

It was beautiful.

The Salem witch looked out upon the ageless sea—the one place where, if there were any truth at all to her faith, peace might finally come to her. She closed her eyes, and she prayed.

"Spirits of nature, wise and all-seeing, I come before you and beg your guidance. There is an evil trespassing upon me, and they are too strong for me to resist any longer. I am weak..." her voice quaked, "and I don't know what to do."

This was her final plea. Throughout her young life, she had been a kind and giving woman. The Gift had blessed her, and she in turn had blessed so many others in their own time of need. Would she then fall into darkness, and forever be enslaved by those she so reviled?

The world around her slipped into a deathly silence. There was no ocean anymore, nor any sky upon the heavens.

Joanna Osborne...

A woman's voice, unlike any other Weirdlee had heard before, called out to her. Bitter it was, and with a hoarseness to it that lent to great age and hardship.

Open your eyes, the voice said to her. *See the world as it lies in the Great Beyond.*

Weirdlee swallowed. Apprehension gripped her soul.

She opened her eyes.

The sea before her had vanished entirely. In its place, a quiet evening, dimly lit by a three-quarter moon, settled over a small grove of apple trees on a rolling hillside. She was not alone, either. There were others there, as well. She recognized them right away—though how this was so, she could not comprehend.

Nearest to her stood Ezili Dantor, the spirit protector of single women and mothers. A dark-skinned *loa*, her age-worn face was marked by two deep scars on her right cheek. She wore a dark blue robe and black shawl, the latter decorated with woven golden trim. Behind Ezili stood the lean, pale figures of Baron Samedi and his wife, Maman Brigitte. The two death *loas* wore black top hats upon their heads, and each wore fine black and red clothing—Brigitte's including a woven red corset and long, black dress. Their eye sockets were hollowed and blackened with the small whites of their eyes showing at their centers. Brigitte's long, dark red hair, Weirdlee observed, also bore a disturbing resemblance to her own.

Beside Ezili Dantor stood a short, older white man. This was the spirit Belie Belcan, the patron saint of justice in the *Las 21 Divisiones*. He kept a casual, friendly gaze upon his mortal visitor.

Finally then, standing some ways off in the distance by an apple tree, the European *loa* Mademoiselle Charlotte, for her own part, kept a cool glare on Weirdlee, as if not trusting of her presence there.

"We have heard your prayers, child," Ezili said to Weirdlee in an easy tone. And so it was that Weirdlee recognized hers as the voice she'd heard calling out to her a moment before.

"You come to us, a lost soul, and you have been terribly abused."

Weirdlee pleaded, "I can't stop them. They're stalking me wherever I go."

Ezili nodded slowly. "Joanna Osborne, descended of witches from time immortal, you must carry on. Your path is filled with evil that will trespass upon you if you do not fight it with your very life."

"I tried," Weirdlee said weakly. "They're too powerful for me."

"They're not!" Baron Samedi cried out.

Ezili turned to him and batted a hand. "Shush, ya malcontented spirit! You be'a wakin' the dead." She turned back to Weirdlee then and shook her head. "Child," she said, "you have more power inside of you than you will ever know. You are a witch from a line of witches that goes back into eternity. And even in your darkest of times, girl, you were never alone in this world."

"But I *was* alone," Weirdlee insisted. "I begged for guidance. I begged for help. But I couldn't—"

"Spellcasting, is all it was," Ezili interrupted. "They made you hear silence, when there was none."

"Joanna," said Belie Belcan, in a calm, easy voice. "Do you know who those voices belong to? The ones that come to you in your mind?"

Weirdlee looked at him thoughtfully. Throughout her young life, she'd never known the identity of the voices, nor why they came to her. She shook her head.

Ezili smiled at her. "They are your very own family, child. Your forefathers and foremothers, your descendants from all time. And they come to you because they love you. They would never leave you alone—not ever would they do that to you."

Weirdlee asked, "A spell kept me from hearing them?"

"A demon's spell," said Baron Samedi. "One, if you had known, you could have tossed away as easily as I spit on the ground."

211

His wife, Maman Brigitte, grinned at her husband admiringly.

"Child," said Ezili, "the two that conspire against you cannot defeat you if you will them not to do so."

That much, of course, was very true. For though she'd failed to realize it at the time, earlier when Weirdlee had prayed to be kept from harm as she approached Zarah's home, and then afterward in demanding that Paul Basil leave her mind—"Stop it!" she'd commanded him—these things were immediately done. She simply never connected her actions to the results.

"But how did they get their power?" Weirdlee asked. "Wasn't it you, the spirits, who directed them?"

Samedi scoffed. "*Us?* Direct them? To do what? To slaughter? To maim? To butcher? Is that what you believe we do to the living?"

"Shush, now, Samedi," said Ezili with another bat of her hand. She said to Weirdlee, "People are what they are, child, whether good or bad. We can help guide them through their lives, but we don't control their minds."

"When we discovered the murderous ways of Zarah and Paul," said Belie, "we ceased hearing their prayers to us." He glanced at the others then and sighed. "Of course, that is not to say that other spirits, less righteous than we, did not take our places."

"Who controls the curse?" Weirdlee asked him.

"Curse?" asked Samedi.

"The Curse of the Bayous," Weirdlee said.

Ezili looked at Belie, knowingly, and he to her. But it was Baron Samedi who answered.

"The *Ghede* control the curse, Joanna Osborne."

Weirdlee looked at him, alarmed.

"The curse, child," said Ezili, "is the only thing that keeps those who are evil from becoming stronger."

"The Curse of the Bayous poisons the minds of its victims," explained Belie. "It blinds them from seeing that which will eventually destroy them."

"It's what has kept Zarah in poverty for all these years," said Ezili.

"And, in its own way, what kept Paul Basil from capturing you," said Belie.

Ezili looked at Weirdlee with a sincere expression. "You will defeat them, child. We know this, because they will never be blessed as you are so blessed in this life of yours."

Weirdlee looked back at her. She was only just then beginning to understand the reason for her presence there before them.

"Is that why you brought me here?" she asked her.

"Do not be afraid of the evil that confronts you," said Ezili. "Their power over you is merely an illusion."

Belie stepped closer to Weirdlee, and he smiled in a very pleasant way.

"You, Joanna," he said to her, "are more spiritual than they, together, will ever be."

"You," said Ezili, "are more intelligent than they, together, will ever be."

"You," Baron Samedi said in a deep, stern tone, "are *much* stronger than they, together, will ever be."

Belie Belcan said to her, then, "Joanna, we have brought you here before us because, unless something is done to intervene, the murder and misery wrought by the priest and priestess will surely go on. No mundane being will be able to stop them. We have chosen you, Joanna Osborne of Salem, to be our agent upon the living world. And it shall be your task to bring an end to this evil, once and for all."

Weirdlee's mind swirled.

"Me?" she whispered.

213

Ezili came closer to her, and she placed her aged hands around the witch's own, pressing her grip firmly into her flesh. She leered at her, then, as if ready to give a command.

"Joanna Osborne," she declared in a seething, defiant voice, "from this day forward and on to the end of your living days, so say we, the protectors of all that live and die in this world, you shall be our mortal hand of justice. No spell will overwhelm your mind. No man or woman may overpower your body. And all who live in darkness, or who practice evil in their time, will either flee upon your approach,"—and her voice quaked with rage— "or they will *die!*"

Weirdlee stared back at her, shaken by her words. She knew, though, that what the spirit said to her was now entirely true. For there was no worry in her mind any longer. There was no fear.

Belie Belcan said to her, "Know, Joanna, that just as the woman who opposes you represents all that is evil on this Earth, so the woman you watch over is all that is good. You *must* return to her."

"Go, now," Ezili commanded, releasing her grip on the witch. "Walk the path of life, and know that you have a gift inside of you unmatched by any who live, and that you will never be alone, ever again. Your family in the Great Beyond will always be with you."

"*I* will always be with you," Baron Samedi declared.

"I will always be with you," said Belie Belcan in his soft-spoken way.

Ezili Dantor smiled, and her tone returned to a nurturing one. "And I will always be with you, child."

Weirdlee looked at each of them, in turn, before eyeing Maman Brigitte, who stood quietly beside her husband. The *loa* of death looked back at Weirdlee, and she grinned wide at the witch from Salem. Theirs was a sisterhood that Weirdlee could not yet comprehend.

Mademoiselle Charlotte, off in the distance, meanwhile, lowered her head. She turned away, seemingly satisfied, and walked off into the meadow.

"Close your eyes, now, child," Ezili said to Weirdlee then, bringing her hand up to the witch's brow.

Weirdlee lowered her eyelids, and Ezili's aged voice faded with each passing word as she spoke on.

"Close your eyes, and know that those who care for you and who love you will seek you out, and you will know who they are."

Weirdlee closed her eyes completely, and total darkness filled her mind, before, once again, she heard the comforting sounds of waves crashing gently upon the shore.

She opened her eyes.

The sea had returned, and so too the beautiful sunshine. Everything was just as it had been before. Everything, that is, except the woman on the beach.

Joanna Osborne was reborn. She had become, at long last, a whole witch.

A complete woman in every way.

"Joanna!"

Weirdlee spun around, surprised, to see Special Agent Nicks jogging over the grassy mounds behind her.

"Sam?"

Nicks appeared entirely out of place on the beach in his dark suit, tie, and fine leather shoes.

Weirdlee smiled at him. "What are *you* doing here? How did you know where I was?"

Nicks patted his smartphone in its belt clip as he came up to her. "Tracked your phone. GPS."

Weirdlee sighed. *Of course.*

"Are you okay?" he asked her.

215

She shook her head. "I'm fine, Sam." Then she looked off behind him. "Is Daniel with you?"

"No," Nicks replied. "He picked up another car. He's going on with the interviews while we're away." He glanced all around them. "Quite a road trip for you," he said. He looked back at Weirdlee. "What did you come out here for? And why did you take off like you did?"

Weirdlee reached for his hand and took it in her own. "Sam," she implored, "please don't ask me questions right now. I promise I'm okay, and I'm sorry I left in such a rush."

Nicks was hardly satisfied with that. "Agent Weirdlee," he said to her sternly, "I can't have you taking off like you did without any word to anyone. We're in the middle of an investigation. You could've—"

Weirdlee put a hand up to his lips. "*Sam,*" she insisted, "please...let's just please talk about this another time. I'm really very sorry, and I swear to you, it won't happen again. But I need for you to trust me on this for now. I had some things I had to work out in my head, and I've done that."

"Things to work out?" Nicks replied. "Like what? Did that guy, Basil—"

"*No,*" Weirdlee insisted. "He didn't hurt me, Sam."

Nicks eyed her, trying to determine her sincerity. He remained unsettled in his mind, though. "You can't do this, Joanna. You can't continue to think and act like you're just a hired hand, here, doing whatever you want."

Weirdlee looked back at him sympathetically, for she knew in her heart that he was far more worried about her than angry.

Those who care for you, and who love you, will seek you out, and you will know who they are.

She knew.

"Can we go back, Sam?" she asked him. "I promise, no more taking off on you. And I'll tell you everything you want to know—*after* the investigation."

He looked at her, gauging his decision. This was definitely not standard procedure.

"Ahh, what the hell am I going to do with you?" he finally said with a relenting grin.

"Keep me for a little while longer," she said with a wink and a smile.

He laughed at that.

He said to her then, "How about we stop for an early lunch after we get back. I've been here all week and I still haven't had any jambalaya."

She gave him an overly-curious look. "Are you asking me out on a date, mister?"

He waved a hand. "Oh, no. Strictly business, Special Agent. We can go over the case while we eat."

"Sure," she replied with a pouting expression. "Business, as usual."

With that, the two headed back to their cars.

On the return trip, Weirdlee spent a great deal of time considering her new-found situation. She'd meant exactly what she said to Nicks—that she would tell him everything he wanted to know. There was no turning back for her, unfortunately. No going back to the way things had been before they came here. Much as she would love to have it otherwise, she knew as well that even with her head cleared of all its troubles, it was exceedingly unlikely she'd be able to stay on at the Bureau. Witches of the kind she was about to become don't usually carry badges, you see.

And they don't always obey the law.

~ | ~

-14-

On the Trail of Innocents

Paul Basil was an angry man for having been so abruptly denied his most hoped-for prize. He sped down Route 90 on his way to Raceland. There, he had important business to tend to. Shut-up kind of business.

The FBI, as it turned out, had made life harder for him than he'd expected, and he needed to make some adjustments as a result. Chief among them was a re-sourcing his income stream. As long as the Feds held a warrant over his head, his career as a stage show entertainer was over. But he'd started his career by dealing drugs on the street, and still occasionally dealt some shit on side. So, he decided, that was what he'd fall back on to keep things going. His holy mission, meanwhile—the very reason he'd done everything else in his life up until then—would still need to be taken care of.

Justice be done to the heretics. Devour the unbelievers!

Since the time he was a small child growing up in New Orleans, Basil had mixed the religious lectures of his parents with the gangster culture of the streets. By the time he'd reached his teen years, the lectures were losing out. The streets were tougher, for sure, but that's where all the action was. And he wanted to be a part of that more than he wanted to be a part of God's Plan.

By sixteen, he'd dropped out of school and was spending most of his waking hours on the streets with his friends. He learned street-level drug dealing—first as a lookout, and then later as a dealer himself—and also got himself introduced to the sex trade in the city by working the money side of it, collecting cuts for pimps. He found he enjoyed slapping around the whores who didn't cough up enough income. He also enjoyed screwing them in exchange for covering what they owed.

He'd known about the mambo woman, Zarah Devillier, since he was a kid. Then, later on as a young man, he'd see her now and then as she prowled the streets selling fortunes—or her body—for whatever she could make. She had a following back in those days—somewhere south of the city in the thick of the bayous. She also looked halfway decent back then—at least enough to fit Basil's own, decidedly low standards. He never paid for her services, having easily managed to charm his way into her bed, instead. She, in turn, talked to him about the power of voodoo, and how, coupled with Christianity's righteous way, she could guide hundreds or even thousands of non-believers to their proper places in the Eternal Afterlife. She told him, too, that she felt in him an inherent ability to be trained in the ways of magick.

He was swayed.

He told her that if she could teach him all that she knew—and if he truly had the Gift, as she'd said he did—then the power would come to him readily enough. And then, he vowed, he would join with her in leading her followers and guiding the masses to their predestined fates.

"Yes," she told him then. "Theyz all doomed! Theyz fates bein' sealed from the times theyz been born. We just the agents of the loa, deliverin' theyz and God's will."

Basil knew, though, what she really proposed to him. Cold-blooded murder.

At first, he was taken aback by the notion. Did she truly mean what she implied?

"God's will," Zarah said to him, "ain't gots no right or wrong. It just bein' what it is."

So Paul Basil got himself trained in the twisted magick of Zarah Devillier's voodoo clan. And the more he learned from her, the more he truly believed in the message she proselytized. His own designs began to fill his mind:

Punish the heretics. Offer their souls to the spirits of Heaven.

Soon after they became lovers in a more formal way, Basil was able to gain the upper hand in his relationship with Zarah. He was younger and stronger than she, after all, and had become more eager to do God's will, as well.

And so the hierarchy would turn about, and Zarah would become Basil's servant in the end.

All the while, however, the *loa* themselves looked down upon the clan, and they shunned their sordid, murderous ways. The Curse of the Bayous had poisoned their minds, they saw, and their souls were thus doomed forever.

* * * *

Basil finished his business in Raceland quickly enough—when you hold all the cards, of course, there isn't much to negotiate—and then drove back north. He'd hoped he was done with the old hag, Zarah, and could start anew with the witch, but he'd felt in his mind an abrupt termination of his will and influence upon red-haired pagan. Why the spirits would help a heretic was beyond him, but they'd turned against him, it seemed, sure enough. For decades, he'd prayed to the *Ghede loa*, only to be betrayed by them in the end!

"Damn you!" he swore as he drove on. "Damn you all! I will do God's work without you!"

Never should he have turned away from his own, true faith, he fumed. Never should he have left the Church!

He considered the witch herself as he drove on to Route 307. Her having escaped his grasp was not merely just an unfortunate turn of events. She was an empowered witch, he knew—a genuine spell caster of a kind he couldn't simply dismiss. He'd concluded that she was, at the very least, his equal in conjuring ability, and that she might thus be a challenge to him so long as she lived.

Perhaps the old wretch, Zarah, had been right all along.

As he drove northward, Basil passed by two police cruisers traveling in the opposite direction. His dark charms, however, kept them from perceiving his car, Lucien's old Beetle.

Capturing the Voodoo King of the Bayous would not be so easy for them.

Halfway up 307, Basil pulled out his cellphone. There, he noticed a voicemail message that must have come to him while passing through a weak signal area. The caller ID read *Jillian Truscott*. He smirked at the name. He'd get back to her later.

He tapped a quick dial then to call Zarah's home. The old bat had never bought a cellphone and though Lucien and Korram each had their own phones, he was not inclined to encourage their sonly aspirations by contacting either one of them.

Zarah was home. He informed her that he was on his way north, and told her to meet him on the opposite bank of the entrance to the Bayou Baton Pilon, about a mile south of the Grand Bayou. Basil had important matters to discuss with his former lover and partner in crime.

From Route 307, Basil himself would get to his destination by taking a side road that led westward to the bayou—this being the same route, in fact, that fisherman Evan Stewart had referred to while on his trip with Special Agent Nicks the day before.

Bitter plans were in the making.

* * * *

"Get yer asses into the boat," Zarah Devillier scolded her sons. All three of them would be joining her for the trip upriver to meet up with her beloved Marcel. He had returned to her! Just as she'd prayed he would, even between her curses of him, angry as she'd been.

She would show him, now, how truly valuable she was!

Lucien, Korram, and Damon all crowded onto the little motor boat. Damon piloted the craft, being the most familiar with its controls. Lucien sat quiet, scowling most of the way. He had no love in his heart for Basil, a father who had neglected and abandoned his sons a long time ago. Korram, for his part, could care less either way. He didn't like working, and his mother provided for them well enough with a roof over their heads. He, of the three, in fact, would be most likely to turn out like their dad, if he could.

Damon steered the boat west, and then at the Grand Bayou turned southward to motor upstream past the Bayou Plat, and then past a little river islet before making shore on the river's east bank.

The sons helped their mother off the boat. They traveled through the thick, marshy brush for a time before reaching a weed-strewn clearing a few hundred yards inland. There, they waited for Paul Basil's arrival.

"Youz be quiet and respectful of yo daddy when he gets here," Zarah instructed her sons. "No smart mouthin'."

Lucien sneered. "He never gave us nothin', Momma."

She snarled back. "You shush you mouth, boy. He give your momma more than you ever know. He give the whole world a lot more than you ever know."

Basil took his own time getting there. Having been there before, he knew the way. He parked his car in a small dirt lot and then sat there for time, mulling over his options. The sacrifice of heretics for the greater cause of God's will had to go on, he determined. Only from now on, with the *loa* having clearly abandoned him, he would be working on his own. And, of course, with his slave, Zarah, and her nuisance sons.

God's will. Who but God would compel him to bring forth the sinful to be judged? And He, after all, was far mightier than they, the *loa*—mere spirits in a realm created by Him.

God! he prayed inside the car, his hands eagerly gripping the steering wheel. *I am your servant, and called here to do Your will!*

He glanced off to right then—there to see, off in the treeline, the skinny, black figure of his son, Damon, standing on his own. The young man, simpleminded and, for most of his life, under the strict control of his mother, simply stared off at his father.

Basil opened the door and leaped out of the car. He glared at his youngest offspring.

"What are you looking at?" he cried out. "Don't you eyeball me, boy!"

Damon shook out of his stare and then turned and darted back into the marshy forest.

Basil scowled at him and fumed. "Son of a…"

He followed after the boy, stalking purposefully across the dirt lot and entering into the woods.

A short distance through the thick, boggy tangle brought Basil to the waiting Devillier clan—with young Damon just rejoining them there, as well.

Basil kept a watchful eye on this one. Ever since his last born had been a little boy, he'd mistrusted him. The kid had always been disturbed in a very psychotic way, and the father suspected that had it not been for Zarah's grip on his mind, the boy might have turned to serial killings on his own—and not for any holy design, either.

He might even kill his own.

Basil pointed at him and said to Zarah, "What'dya bring the retard for?"

The old woman eyed Damon with a rare expression of sympathy. "Aww, he just lookin' for his daddy, is all."

Still leering at Damon, Basil stalked up to Zarah. He said to her, "You keep that fuckin' retard away from me, Zarah. I told you before."

"He ain'ta hurtin' nothin'," Zarah said weakly. "Please, Marcel, let's make good again."

Basil scoffed, "*Good?*—Shit, I'll give you good." He sneered at her. "I came here to talk about you and me, Zarah. I came here to talk about our faith in God, and the mission we've been on all these years."

"Mission?" Zarah asked. "Whatchu mean?"

"The cause of the righteous, you old bat. I mean you bringin' me sinners to face their judgment."

"Blessins of the spirits," Zarah said. "We's bringin' dem to theyz chosen fates, is all we's doin'."

Basil scowled at her. "We need more, woman. Lots more."

Zarah brought her wrinkled, frail hands up to Basil's chest, resting them carefully there. "I gives you lots, Marcel, you knows I do."

He took her skinny wrists into his strong hands and gripped her firmly.

"I need *more*, you old wretch."

Lucien advanced. "Let her go!"

Basil snapped his eyes to him. "Back, off, boy!" he shouted, and he pointed at him stiffly. "I will strike you down!"

Lucien leered back at him. "I's ain't afraid of you."

Zarah snarled at her eldest. "Lucien! Mind yerself! Be respectin' youz father!"

Lucien stood, eyeing Basil angrily but heeding his mother's demand.

Zarah looked back to Basil. She smiled at him nervously. "I's tries to make you happy," she said. "I's always do what you says."

Basil pushed the old woman's hands away from him and turned away from her, stepping off.

"The Yankee witch," he said, "is out of our reach, now."

Zarah scowled. "Pagan whore! I told youz, Marcel. I said to youz, we gots to kill her!"

"No!" Basil yelled, spinning around to face her. "You must never approach her! You must never go after the witch again!"

"She a heretic!" Zarah shouted. "We have to, Marcel." She stepped shakily towards him. "It's ours callin' in our lives."

Basil kept an angry glare on her. In another time, he would have slapped her down and scolded her. But on this day—and ongoing for the next few weeks at least—he knew he'd need her powers more than her obedience.

He sighed, relenting to a more forgiving tone.

225

"I've lost them, old woman," he said, looking off into the forest. "The *Ghede* have forsaken us. They have betrayed the cause."

Zarah eyed him curiously. She turned her glance to her sons then, wondering if they understood the implications of what their father had said. Lucien maybe. Damon, definitely not. Korram could probably care less.

She looked at Basil. "Ours is the righteous cause," she said to him, her old mind ever so deeply influenced by his powerful presence. "Bringin' folks to theirs fates is what we's do for God."

Basil turned to her, and he grinned, quite satisfied. "Bring me more, old woman. *Lots more.*"

* * * *

Joanna Weirdlee sat with Sam Nicks at a table in a small local restaurant that Nicks had found via his phone's Siri inquiry as they traveled north. They were in Lockport, stopping there before continuing on to meet up with Special Agent Fielding. They had just ordered drinks and their lunch.

"Sheriff Mickens called me while we were driving up," Nicks said to Weirdlee.

"Oh yes?"

He nodded as their drinks arrived. The waitress set them down and then went on her way.

"He, uh, let me know that Ms. Hawkins talked with a priest earlier this morning and that they arranged for a service on Saturday for her boy."

Weirdlee looked at him thoughtfully. "I see."

Nicks sipped his iced tea. "Sort of a closure thing."

"Yeah," Weirdlee muttered. She shook her head. "Very sad."

Nicks set his glass down and clasped his fingers together on the table. "We've still got a lot of interviews to do—though I'm less sure now that any of 'em will amount to anything."

Weirdlee nodded. "Yes, they all seem to be the same. Three years ago is a long time for people to look back on. Nobody can remember anything for sure."

"There *is* something missing, though," Nicks said. "Something we're not seeing yet. The time frame is pretty tight, and I was hoping we could narrow it down even more." He shook his head. "But unless someone has a sudden revelation, I doubt we'll be able to find out what it is."

Weirdlee eyed him thoughtfully once more. There was something...

She squinted as a vision came vaguely into her mind. *Deception*...

"Something wrong?" Nicks asked her, noticing her stare.

"No," she said, snapping out of it. "I'm just wondering, if maybe more than one person was involved in this—if it *was* a crime and not an accident."

Nicks pursed his lips and nodded. "Yeah, that thought came to me, too. You know, one of the witnesses—a teacher—said that he thought he remembered a female colleague of his calling him away from watching the kids that day. But he also recalls a man talking to him, too—at the same time."

"Does he remember who the man was?"

Nicks shook his head. "Nope. He just remembers a man talking to him." Then he tapped his drinking glass. "Funny thing was, though, he said he thought it was his colleague talking to him—the *woman*. He thought the two were one and the same."

"Really?" Weirdlee said, curious.

"Crazy, huh?"

Weirdlee eyed him as her intuitive mind wrestled with the possibilities.

"Maybe so."

After eating their lunch—with Nicks finally getting his jambalaya—then chatting a bit more, the two agents left the restaurant. As they walked along the sidewalk on their way to the parking lot, Weirdlee passed by a short blonde woman heading into the restaurant. The FBI agent slowed her pace and turned, curiously, to eye the young lady walking by her.

A disturbing presence came into her mind.

Treachery.

She shook it off almost as quickly as it came to her. So many signs—so many people with their own life's dramas—intruded upon her mind. She turned again and continued to her Cherokee. She and Nicks still had a good drive ahead of them before meeting up again with Fielding.

* * * *

Jill Truscott swung open the door and strolled into the restaurant. She was in a terrific mood that day and looking forward to what she hoped would be an exciting weekend ahead of her. She'd have an early lunch first before trying to call that sexy voodoo priest, Marcel Unate', again and hooking up with him.

"Voo-doo love," she sang to herself as she found a table to sit at.

That coming weekend would indeed be a time she would never forget.

-15-

The Agent of the Spirits

Special Agent Fielding had conducted three interviews in the morning and another in the early afternoon before taking a break to join up with Nicks and Weirdlee, who'd both driven up to the little town of Choctaw, just east of Chackbay. The two agents had stopped at a cafe on the western side of town, and Fielding arrived there at just after 1:30 PM.

The cafe was a hole-in-the-wall type of place with a small counter area set off to the right, a couple of booth tables set against a display-windowed front wall, and a half dozen small, square tables scattered throughout. The wall behind the small counter had a large flat screen television bolted to it. Another, smaller flat screen TV was mounted on the backside wall. The counter's television showed a local channel, while the backside one had a cable sports channel on. The place—clearly not a tourist spot—was about half-filled with locals.

Fielding entered and quickly spotted his colleagues sitting at a table in the far left corner. After putting in a quick coffee order with a waitress at the counter, he joined them.

"Agent Fielding," Nicks greeted him.

"Afternoon, partner," Fielding replied with his exaggerated Southern twang. He glanced at Weirdlee, sitting there with her tea, and smiled at her. "Agent Weirdlee. Good to see ya."

She nodded, returning his smile. "Daniel."

Fielding grabbed an empty chair and took a seat. "So, what's the word, ya'll?"

Nicks, sitting with a coffee of his own, took a sip of it and sat back in his chair. "Word is, we're about ready to wrap things up on the road, here. After our interviews, I just want to check another couple of things out, logistically."

"Yeah," Fielding said, "didn't havin' much luck, myself, today."

The waitress came by with Fielding's coffee, and after a couple of cordial words, was off again quickly enough.

Nicks glanced around the cafe as he went over some things in his mind. He said, almost under his breath, "Seems like anyway way we look at, that kid's more than likely at the bottom of a bayou somewhere."

Weirdlee looked at him with a sullen expression. She drew her hand across the little table, placing it gently on his own. "Don't give up," she said to him. He looked at her, in turn, surprised by her gesture. "You're a good man, Samuel," she said. "If anyone can do this for Miss Hawkins, I know you can."

Fielding raising an eyebrow at the scene.

Nicks eyed her hand upon his. "Yeah," he said. He slipped his hand away and took up his coffee cup. "Sometimes, Agent Weirdlee, movies don't have happy endings." He sipped from his coffee.

Weirdlee withdrew her hand and lowered her eyes.

"Got three more people today, partner," Fielding said to Nicks. "We keepin' this up tomorrow, too?"

Nicks gave him a nod. "Nothing better to do. I think I'm going to take a trip all the way upriver, too, from where the boy's sneaker was found. The police should be out there dragging the area by now."

Fielding shrugged. "Sure bet on that one. That's a long-term project, there, partner. You seen the lake at the head of that thing? Looks like a huge swamp from the satellite view."

'Yeah," Nicks said, unimpressed. "Tough shit about that." He looked off across the room, frowning. His eyes gravitated to the wall-mounted television on the back wall, and he gave that his attention next.

Fielding said Weirdlee, "So, how you doin' today, Agent Weirdlee? Hope everythin's okay."

She gave him a weak smile. "I'm all right, Daniel. I just wish there was something more I could do."

Fielding sipped his coffee. "Don't we all."

Nicks kept his eyes on the television, quietly watching a weekend baseball preview segment with only mild interest before the show broke to a commercial.

"Hi, I'm Sandra Gregory, with Christian Adoption Services. For over thirty years, we've helped loving parents find children in desperate need of a family to call their very own. With offices located throughout the state of Louisiana, and with full state and federally-approved certification, we offer one of the finest services for parents in search of a child to bring into their lives. And our support doesn't end with the successful matching of parent to child. We offer personal counseling to both parents and children, school placement, health care planning support, and guidance in obtaining financial assistance for lower income families. We'll be there, from the very beginning of your journey to its very happy ending—and then again afterward. For more

information, please call us at 1-800-555-2940, or visit our website at..."

Nicks turned away from the commercial to look at Fielding. "Agent Fielding," he said, tapping a finger on the table.

Fielding replied, "Yeah, boss?"

"Instead of going on with the interviews, I'd like you to head out to New Orleans tomorrow morning."

"New Orleans?" Fielding replied with a smile.

"Yeah. I want you to do a search of state records. Look for any adoptions that took place from 2010 to 2012."

"Holy shit," Fielding swore. "Are you kidding me?"

Nicks shook his head. "No. And bring along our list of people who attended the outing. See if any of their names match up with the roll of adoptions."

"Shit," Fielding swore again. "That's still dozens of folks."

Weirdlee gave Nicks doubtful look. "That's a long shot, Sam—and exceedingly unlikely. There's way too much oversight."

Nicks looked at her and gave a shrug. "Maybe so. But I just want to be able to go home when this is over and say to myself we did everything we could."

Fielding leered at Nicks, trying to figure out his thinking. "So...the kid gets abducted, and whoever does it sets up fake papers or somethin'?"

Nicks tossed his hands in the air. "Just a thought." Then he slapped his hands on the table. "Look—that kid is either alive or he's dead. If he's dead, then I think he was murdered. In fact, I'm *sure* of it. But either way, unless we find some pretty solid evidence, I think it's highly unlikely we'll ever find out what really happened to him. If he is alive, though, then that means it's possible someone tossed that sneaker into the river to throw us off their trail—

someone who lives around here, and who wanted us to close this investigation."

Weirdlee looked at Nicks. She said to herself, distantly, "He hasn't been sacrificed like the others…"

"What's that?" Nicks replied.

She straightened up, glancing from Nicks to Fielding. "The Curse of the Bayous. It's not what everyone around here thinks it is."

Fielding laughed uneasily. "What're ya talkin' about?"

Nicks eyed her seriously. "You mean, you don't think he's one of the murder victims in the serial killings."

She replied, "Yes. He's not a part of that. But…" she hesitated, "He *is* connected. The same people are involved."

Fielding gave her a curious glare. "You soundin' like you *know* this, Agent Weirdlee."

She turned to him, taken by his observation. "It's true."

"Now, hold on," Nicks said, "nobody knows anything for sure. Not at this table." He reached over to touch Weirdlee's wrist. "Joanna. I know you've got a lot of faith in what you believe in, but we have to stick with what we know. This isn't about intuition. This is about facts and evidence."

Weirdlee pleaded to him. "I swear to you, Sam. I know it's true."

"Then if you know it's true," Fielding asked, "tell us what happened to him. Where is he?"

"I don't know," Weirdlee said in a pained voice. "I can't see him at all. I wish I could. But I know he's not a part of what happened to the others."

"Then how is he connected?" Nicks asked. "Are those voodoo people involved in this? The ones you talked to?"

She eyed him momentarily. "Yes. One of them is, for sure."

"Which one?" Fielding asked.

Weirdlee picked up her tea, taking a quick sip before answering. "Paul Basil."

Fielding slapped the table. "Great. The one who's on the run."

Nicks asked her, "Do you have any evidence of his involvement, Joanna, or are we still talking about your intuition, here?"

She frowned at him. "I know it's true, Sam. I can feel it inside."

Fielding eyed his coffee and muttered, "Then we got nothin'," as he brought it up to his lips to drink.

Weirdlee sat up and said to Nicks, "You're sending Daniel out to New Orleans tomorrow on a hunch. Isn't that right? How much different is that from what I feel?"

"Big difference," Nicks replied. "I'm searching for clues and evidence that might help us in our investigation. You're making conclusions based on what you think is true—in your opinion."

"And my opinion doesn't matter, does it?"

Nicks reclined in his seat, keeping his eyes locked on Weirdlee. She was making this a personal thing and being offended by it when there wasn't any need for that. "Listen," he said to her, "My only interest is in finding out what happened to that boy. I need your help to do that just as much as I need Fielding's, here, and I value your opinion just as much as his. But I'm telling you, Joanna, I just don't have time to pretend I'm a true believer in anyone else's philosophy or religion. I've just got no time for that."

Weirdlee sighed, relenting. "I know," she said. "And I'm sorry about that. It's just that sometimes I feel like I'm not doing enough around here, and I want to do more." She looked at him sincerely, offering a weak smile. "I know I've been difficult at times, Sam, and I'm sorry for that, too. I

234

do want to help you solve this case, and I just *know* you're
going to solve it."

Nicks smiled back at her. "Intuition again?"

She kept her smile and nodded. "Hopeful premonition."

"Okay, then," he said. "Let's get on with it."

* * * *

The agents talked some more and then spent the rest of
the afternoon conducting a few more interviews, each
going their own separate ways to cover more ground. By
5:00 PM, Weirdlee had wrapped up two more interviews,
and she decided to drive out to Regina Hawkins' place to
visit with her.

Arriving there, she found the woman curled up on her
sofa, her face worn from dried tears. The agent sat with her
and consoled her, and then afterward helped her finish up
some chores she'd been neglecting. Those done, Weirdlee
cooked dinner as she had before, and then sat with Regina
again on the sofa.

Happier now for having Weirdlee's company, Regina
said to her, "You're so kind to me's. I don't know why you
do this for me."

Weirdlee smiled warmly as she replied, "Goes with the
job, Ms. Hawkins. I just like to help people. And you
deserve it."

Regina smiled. "Call me Regina, please. All my friends,
theyz call me by my's first name, and youz more like a
friend to me than anything I knows."

"Okay," Weirdlee said. "And you can call me Joanna."

Regina nodded. "Okay."

Weirdlee moved her hand then to place it on Regina's
own. She squeezed it gently. "Regina, I just want you to
believe, deep in your heart, that no matter what happens,

you are truly blessed to be alive. I don't want you to ever not believe that's true."

Regina stared back at her, her own words not coming easily to her. She whispered weakly to her friend, "I don't know what I can believe, anymores. I don't know what's gonna happen to me, and I don't understand, either, why God would do this to me and my boy."

"He didn't do this, Regina," Weirdlee said. "I swear he wouldn't do this to you. God loves you—he truly does. And when people on Earth do very bad things to others, they do it against God's will, not because of it."

Regina whispered, "And he lets it happen."

"He doesn't," said Weirdlee. She adjusted herself then to face Regina squarely, and she took the woman's hands firmly into her own. "God watches over everyone, Regina, and he will judge those who have trespassed against you. They will be punished for their sins. I promise you."

Tears ran down Regina's face. "I just want to be with my boy again, and I don't want anyones to have to go through what I's been through all these years. I swear, I can't stand it no more. I just want to be with my boy, up in Heaven, where he is."

Weirdlee put her hand to Regina's face and wiped her tears. She looked into her eyes. "I want you to know something, Regina Hawkins," she whispered to her, her healing, supernatural voice weaving into the poor woman's injured soul. Hawkins kept her eyes locked on her, entranced.

"I want you to know that God is kind and loving, and he is watching over you. I want you to know that there is good on this Earth, and that the spirits of nature will bless you and protect you, always, from this day on. And the evil that has trespassed against you and that has hurt so many others in its path is going to be destroyed, forever." The witch drew her hand to Regina's own, and she held it gently. "*I* am going to destroy it, my friend. And it will never live again."

Regina, dazed by the sorceress's words, drew a curious expression. "You?" she whispered to her. "But what can you—?"

Suddenly then, the answer appeared in her mind even before she finished asking, so revealing the incredible truth to her.

"*Oh my God.*"

~ | ~

-16-

Blind Endeavors

Ibo Lele! Hear me'z calling!
Hear my's voice upon the wind!
See the souls and see the spirits!
Help me guides them from
within!

Ibo Lele, show the way!
Bring themz to their knees to
pray!
Shame on you, you devil's child!
Shame on you, your soul defiled!

I's will catch you, pull you in!
Bring your spirit up to Him!
Shame on you! Shame on you!
I's will bring you up to Him!

Zarah Devillier chanted and hobbled about in a circle in her backyard. She danced around a collection of four tall, thick black candles, all alight and surrounding a small bonfire at their center. The night lay still, illuminated otherwise by only the waxing first quarter moon set high in the cloudless sky.

Zarah's three sons sat in a line before her ceremonial ground, their legs crossed and hands set on their knees. All three stared ahead blankly, each entranced by the controlling spell their mother had cast upon them.

Lucien and Korram, in particular, had been rebellious towards their mother for far too long. Too much back talk—too much "thinkin' on theys owns," she decided. And so she captured their minds on this eve, and she enslaved them to her will from that day on, the same as she had Damon's mind so many years before. Their souls would be corrupted, forever.

The old woman stopped her stilted dancing and turned to the bonfire, shaking a finger at it angrily. "I sees you!" she cried, having successfully found a non-religious young man who, unbeknownst to him at the time, would be meeting Zarah Devillier in the coming hours, she decided.

"I sees youz a'walkin'! I know wheres you is!"

So it went on throughout the evening, as the tainted, evil spirits called upon by Zarah leant their guidance to finding for her the innocents that she and her master, Paul Basil, so needed to carry out their decades-old murderous rituals. Forty-nine lost souls—including thirty by Zarah herself before Basil came along—had met their ends in just this same manner throughout the past sixty years.

Heretics!
Heretics one and all!
Hear my's voice and come along!

* * * *

Dressed in her nightgown at the end of a very long day, Joanna Weirdlee sat on the floor inside of her room at the Swampy Inn, kept safe there within the bounds of her sacred circle. Surrounded, too, by the lighted candles of Earth, Air, Fire, and Water, she prayed first to the spirits of her family, and then afterward to the spirits who had counseled her earlier in the day. They would all be, she knew, a part of her life from that day on, and so be a part of her eventual fate.

She prayed:

> *Peace be with the night and morning*
> *On the 'morrow, sunlight bring.*
> *Guard the weak and guide the helpless*
> *Lend the weary strength within.*
> *Water, Earth, and evening Sky*
> *Shield my soul from Evil's Eye.*
> *For on the 'morrow's setting sun*
> *My voice shall carry, Justice done.*

The witch from Salem then took up and blew out each candle surrounding her, in its turn. She got up to her feet then and went to the room's dresser bureau, there to place the extinguished candles upon an empty plate. Walking to her bed, she threw up the covers and drew herself in, then tossed the covers over her.

So it was on that night, and every night thereafter, Joanna Weirdlee would sleep entirely unmolested by the evil that had once stalked her. She would dream her peaceful dreams, and, in her own time, gain within her soul a strength once known but only to the gods themselves.

* * * *

Morning on Friday brought with it a gray, cloudy sky.

The FBI agents all arose, showered, and met at the Swampy Inn's cafe for breakfast together. Each ordered his or her usual meal—eggs, bacon, toast, and coffee for Nicks and Fielding, oatmeal and tea for Weirdlee—and they ate as they talked about the day ahead.

"So, now that we all have our own vehicles," Nicks said to Fielding, "you can head out to New Orleans right away." He looked at Weirdlee. "Can you keep going where we left off with our interviews, Agent Weirdlee?"

She nodded. "Yes. Sure."

"You drivin' up to that lake this mornin', are ya, partner?" Fielding asked Nicks.

"Yeah," he said. "I'll probably spend most of the day out there. Give me a call after you get that info on the adoptions, though, and we'll meet up."

"Fair 'nuff."

So their day got underway. Agent Fielding drove north to New Orleans, while Agent Nicks took Route 307 south to the Lake Boeuf area. Agent Weirdlee, meanwhile, headed out to South Vacherie for her first interview of the morning.

Always on her mind, too, was keeping tabs on another person's progress that day—someone whose own agenda was much more dark and malevolent than her own.

* * * *

"Get yerself over there, boy," Zarah Devillier growled to her youngest, Damon. The two were on a day-long road trip, stopping by three towns where Zarah would perform her fortune telling routine for tourists and others. Her real intent, of course, was to make herself available for the people she'd targeted the previous evening in her ceremony. Six of them in all had been touched by the old priestess's spell casting, and though each would believe that his or her encounter with the fortune teller was due to little more than chance, Zarah in truth had put it in each of their minds to make their journeys to her. And so on this morning the former Queen of the Bayous sat upon her rickety lawn chair before a small fold-up card table in downtown Houma, patiently awaiting her first quarry of the day. Of her three sons, only Damon had joined her that day, as Lucien and Korram were both at their jobs.

Damon sat on a large, now-empty black travel case he'd hauled along with them on their trip to the city. The case had stored all of Zarah's magickal supplies—crystal ball, hex dolls, tarot cards—all of it garbage props to her, really, that she didn't actually need in order to conjure, but which looked awfully impressive to the fools who surrendered their money to her for their fortunes to be told.

The mother and son had first arrived at their location at 9:20 AM. By 10:05, Zarah was twiddling her fingers.

"Wha' time is it, boy?" she asked her dull-witted son.

Damon fetched his flip phone from his front pants pocket and checked the time. "Ten o'clock, Momma."

She scowled at him. "Ten o'clock?" She looked around the street and sidewalks near where they sat. "Where the fuck is that boy?"

Just then, an elderly black woman walked by. She stopped to observe the Devilliers' little setup.

"What are ya'll doing?" she asked the old priestess.

Zarah frowned at first, but then grinned at her visitor. "Readin' fortunes, miss. Wanna have youz's read?"

The woman curled her lip and considered the offer. "Nah," she said. "I don't really believe in that stuff."

She walked away.

Zarah snarled at her as she walked off. Then she turned back to her son and said, "Pack up this shit, Damon.

Somethin' musta happened to that boy, or he'da been
here."

"Okay, Momma."

The two packed up Zarah's belongings into the large
black case, and Damon hefted it along as they made their
way back to the nearest bus stop, where from they would
go to their next destination. This would be the Del Rio
River shopping plaza on North Canal Street in Thibodaux,
where they unloaded from their bus at 11:25 AM. This spot,
like the other locations they'd end up at on the day, was a
regular destination for Zarah in all her fortune telling
travels. They set up her card table at the edge of the
parking lot, well away from the storefronts that lined the
plaza. Zarah waited then for the next pigeon on her list of
heretics to be guided into her murderous web.

* * * *

Michael Prichard grabbed his keys and walked out the
door. The night shift worker had decided the previous
evening to take a drive down to Thibodaux to pick up some
rims for his Chevy that he'd seen in a shop there recently.
He strode down the steps from his apartment, and he'd
just started down the walkway to get to his car when a
woman called out to him from behind.

"Hey, Mike," she said in a cheerful voice.

He spun around, there to see his on-again, off-again
girlfriend, Sheri Stevens, approaching him.

"Sheri," he said to her, surprised to her there. "What's
up?"

Like Michael, Sheri was also a night shifter, which was
why they'd dated in the first place. Currently, though, they
were in the midst of an "off-again" phase of their
relationship, and so Michael wasn't expecting to see her.

"I was just thinking of you this morning," Sheri explained, "and thought I'd swing by to visit."

Michael gave her an agreeable nod. But then he shrugged as he recalled his trip.

"I was just headin' out, actually."

Sheri put on an exaggerated frown. "Aww, really? Where ya headed?"

Michael looked off to his car. "Just out to Thibodaux. I was gonna pick up some new rims I spotted at Chester's."

Sheri swatted her hand dismissively. "Oh, you can do that anytime. How about we hang out for a little while?"

Michael smiled at the thought of that. Seeing his girl, there, his little trip didn't seem so important to him any more.

"Sure."

"Come on," Sheri said with a wave of her hand. "Let's grab somethin' to eat. We can go in my car, if you want."

Michael gave her a curious look. Sheri had hung out the "r" in her "car," the same way them Yankees did up in Maine.

Or was that Boston?

He walked up to her and gestured for her to lead the way. "Your car's fine, girl."

The two headed off together then and Michael's life was saved, as the couple's rocky relationship—with a friendly assist from another—changed once more to "on-again."

* * * *

A long and exceedingly slow hour had gone by.

"What the fuck time is it, boy?" Zarah asked Damon impatiently.

Damon checked his phone. "Twenty till one, Momma."

She leered at him, her mind filtering through a few unsettling conclusions. Not by mere chance, she reasoned, was it that two souls she had snared so easily would then fail to arrive at their directed destinations. Either she was losing her skill as a conjuror, or someone from afar was interfering with her charms.

The Salem witch, possibly?

Never! The pagan wouldn't dare!

Zarah grumbled, "Red-haired slut..."

"Momma?" Damon asked, overhearing her.

"Pick up our shit, boy. Ain't no heretic comin here today. We gots to go to Vacherie."

And so they journeyed on, one stop after another, completing a wide circle along the southern bank of the Mississippi River and on down south along Route 90 to Des Allemands, until finally they arrived at their last stop of the day in Raceland, at 5:40 PM.

Wherever they went, though, the result was always the same: A long wait, and a no-show.

Zarah used Damon's phone to call Paul Basil while they were still in Des Allemands. The witch, she told him, was interfering with her spell casting.

"Stay away from her," Basil demanded of her, as he had before.

"But she's a' blockin' my spells from gitten yer souls. I gotsta'—"

"I said *stay away*, goddammit. You must not open your mind to her. She's got the spirits inside of her, now, and she's in bed with them."

Zarah cursed and spat. "I's ain't afraid of her! I's took her once, I take her again."

"You will do as I say!" Basil shouted. "Or I will kill you myself, you old hag."

Zarah's eyes flashed at that.

"Youz..." she grumbled, "never kill me, Marcel."

"I will," Basil said sternly. "And you will meet our God."

Zarah stared off as she held the phone to her ear.

Theirs had long ago stopped being a partnership between to empowered priests. Only just then, though, did it become clear to her who Basil truly was to her, after all.

Her master.

"I's understand," she muttered.

* * * *

Paul Basil got off the phone with Zarah and continued his stroll along Victor II Boulevard in Morgan City. To his left ran a black gilded fence fronting a small urban park. He'd just gotten past a baseball field there, then, when he spotted someone he recognized right away, standing in front of his path some ways ahead of him and joined by her companion.

She was someone, though, that he would rather not have run into that day.

He grimaced as he continued along, not shying away from the inevitable confrontation.

The woman, standing quietly as she eyed Basil approaching her, wore an intricately laced black and green dress, with a red shawl draped over her shoulders. Upon her head, she wore a traditional headdress for the season. Her black skin showed nary a sign of sweat in the heat of the late summer day. Next to her, as always, stood her trusted captain, who on this day wore plain street clothes. Basil paid him no mind, though, as he came up to them both.

"Angelea Diviner," he said to the Voodoo Queen of New Orleans in a contemptuous tone.

Diviner eyed him indignantly.

"Didn't think I'd run into you out here," he went on. "What's the matter—they kick you out of New Orleans, too?"

She kept a cool glare on him, sizing him up before answering.

"I come to talk to you, Marcel Unate'. Deliver a message."

Basil gave Diviner's companion a quick, guarded once-over. Then he eyed Diviner again, and said to her, "Message, huh? What kinda message?"

"From the *loa,* Marcel. They spoke to me last evenin'."

Basil huffed indignantly. "The spirits spoke to *you?* About *me?*"

She nodded. "Baron Samedi. He tells me last night for you to leave the souls to him. Don't you be speakin' for him."

"Shit..." Basil swore. "I don't believe you. And the *Ghede* ain't been comin' to me for years. Why would they want to talk to you?"

"He says you gone bad. You done turned against our kind. He says he gonna send the devil after you."

Basil laughed. "The devil, huh? Well, lemme tell you somethin', Angelea. I don't give a fuck what the spirits say to you. My heart is with God Almighty, now. And I am doing *His* will."

Diviner set her gaze skyward.

"Samedi," she said, "says you can redeem yourself in Heaven only by obeying his word. There is no other way."

Basil scoffed at that. "*They* left me, mambo woman. I didn't leave them. They're the ones who need to come back around."

Diviner scowled at him. "How *dare* you challenge the spirits!"

Basil simply smirked. "You just tell 'em I said to go fuck off, errand girl. My work has only just begun here. I still got lots of sinners to bring to justice."

"The Curse has poisoned your mind, Marcel. It's made you go in circles your whole life. Just look at you, now. Everywhere you go, you's on the run."

Basil leered at her. "What are you gonna do about it? You gonna call the cops or somethin'—make 'em see where I am?"

Diviner shook her head. "No. I won't call the police on you, Marcel. I don't want to see you goin' to no prison for the rest of your life."

"Aww, ain't that sweet."

"I don't want to see you in jail," Diviner finished, "because I want to see you *dead*."

Basil laughed aloud at that. He swore at her then, "Fuck you, old lady," before starting off again, walking around the voodoo queen and eyeing her coldly as he passed. "I decide my own fate, mambo woman. And I don't plan on going anywhere for a very long time."

Diviner turned as he passed by her, keeping her gaze on him as he walked off.

"You are blind, Marcel Unate'," she said to him. "Maman Brigitte is watching you!"

"Oh, yeah?" Basil said with a sneer, striding away. "Well, you can tell that nasty ol' bitch to go fuck herself, too."

He lifted his arms then and waved them about, mockingly, while shouting, "Betrayers! Betrayers, all! Left me on my own and under the eyes of God!" He laughed hysterically as he continued down the sidewalk.

Diviner kept a grim stare on him as she watched him pass around a corner, and then shortly afterward out of view.

"She is watching you."

~ | ~

-17-

Facts and Clues

Special Agent Nicks found himself knee deep in swamp water as he trudged along the banks of Lake Boeuf. He and Fielding had guessed right, and Sheriff Mickens' deputies and local town police were indeed busy scouring the area that Friday morning. A long line of motor boats dragged the shallow, marshy lake in one of several passes, while along the shoreline, officers with waders on and armed with metal-tipped poles searched the heavy weeds and bog there. Two teams of cadaver dogs were also on the scene.

The same as any gamble, everyone out there realized there was probably just a one-in-a-million chance they'd actually find anything out there, and that all of this was most likely an effort without reward. Yet even so, there was no grumbling amongst their ranks, no frustration or impatience with the job at hand. A few of the cops even went out of their way to suggest other places they might search upriver, as well.

Nicks could not have been prouder of them.

"I thought I'd find you out here," said Sheriff Mickens, himself sloshing along the bank to reach the FBI agent.

"Sheriff," Nicks greeted him.

"Talked to the state police this mornin'," the sheriff said. "They'll be coverin' the irrigation canals a ways off to the east, here."

"Appreciate it, Sheriff."

Mickens drew up to Nicks' side. He glanced around at the scene.

"So," he said, "I hear you've gone to checkin' some adoption records? Is that true?"

Nicks nodded. "It is."

The sheriff eyed him with an air of doubt. "You know, Special Agent, it's a rural community out here, for sure, but, ah, we ain't no hicks, either. Everyone out here follows the rules, as far as bureaucracy goes. You really think somebody could get away with fakin' an adoption, of all things? That's some ballsy shit. What about doctor appointments? What about school and friends and relatives?"

Nicks agreed. "I know, Sheriff. We talked about it last night. But I think there's a possibility—no matter how remote—that the boy was abducted."

"Possibly," Mickens said. "Kids get abducted and killed all over. It's sad as hell, but it happens."

"Kids get abducted for other reasons, too."

"Shit," Mickens swore. "Sex trade and all that. We're talkin' about a little boy, here. I don't—"

"Love," Nicks interrupted. "Kids get abducted for love, too."

"*Love?* What the hell are you sayin'?"

Nicks waved for the Sheriff to join him in getting out of the muck. They both trudged a few feet to drier ground.

"I've been here a week, Sheriff," Nicks explained, "and I've heard a lot of people say a lot of different things about Ms. Hawkins. Some people think she's irresponsible. Some think she's a victim. Other people think she's sweet and brave. But without exception, everyone I've ever talked to about her little boy, Julien, says the same thing about him. He's just a wonderful kid stuck in a really bad situation. *Really* bad."

Mickens nodded, understanding. "So you think someone might'a wanted to get him out of that situation."

"Yes, sir, I do. It's at least a possibility."

Mickens looked off to the lake while considering Nicks' idea. He watched the boats dragging their lines in between the multitude of little marshy islets that dotted the water's surface, and he eyed the officers along the nearby shoreline jabbing their poles into the weeds. "I hope to God you're right, Special Agent," he said. "I truly do hope you are." Then he looked at Nicks directly. "Miss Hawkins is having a service for her boy at six p.m. tomorrow. She wanted to have it a bit later on, at sunset—sort of a closure thing—but the church she's going to is having a service there at eight o'clock."

"I see," Nicks said with a nod.

Closure, though, was something he doubted Regina Hawkins would ever have in her life, as long as her boy remained missing.

* * * *

"Did you know, sir, that there were over a thousand adoptions in the state of Louisiana, just in 2010 alone?" said the incredulous clerk, presently standing behind a counter at the state building in New Orleans.

Special Agent Fielding looked back at the man with a blank expression. "No, I didn't know that."

The clerk raised an eyebrow. "And you're looking for anyone who adopted a kid between 2010 and 2012?"

Fielding waved a list of interview names he'd brought with him. "I only need to compare the names on this list with what you got," he said.

The clerk frowned at the paper in Fielding's hand. "And you brought along hard copy, too," he noted.

"Sure," Fielding said. "I printed it out this mornin'."

The clerk shook his head, disappointed. "If you'da put the names inside of a spreadsheet and put 'em on a flash drive, we coulda done a v-lookup on 'em."

"A *what?*" Fielding replied.

The clerk chuckled. "Never mind." He stepped back from the counter then and walked over to his desk, located in the middle of an office area where a few other clerks also went about their business. "I can print out each year separately," he said as he went to work on his computer.

"That'll be fine," Fielding said. "Alphabetical, right?"

The clerk grinned, shaking his head again. "Yeah, I think I can manage that for ya."

Retrieving the data took just a few minutes, and with his three lists printed out, Fielding retreated to a desk in the lobby area of the room. There, he hunkered down for his comparison search of names.

It would be a tedious next couple of hours for him.

* * * *

Joanna Weirdlee stepped out into the late morning sun after finishing yet another interview from amongst the list of parents that had been at Kraemer Park on that fateful Saturday morning when little Julien Hawkins disappeared from the face of the Earth. Wearing her favorite charcoal-colored skirt suit, she retrieved her thick-rimmed sunglasses from her jacket pocket and put them on as she walked out to her Grand Cherokee, parked midway up the short driveway. Hopping inside the vehicle, she fired up the engine and backed out, then drove down the road, her next stop already planned in her mind.

It was a laborious task she had, both in time and in energy spent. Most of the questions were the same ones, repeated again and again for every parent or teacher. She'd also occasionally talk to a kid who'd been there that day—though for the most part the kids' memories were worse than their parents. She took detailed notes, still, no matter how dull the routine.

Traveling down Route 90 as she drove south toward Des Allemands, she passed through the town of Paradis. She glanced off to her right, where, looking west, she knew the home of Paul Basil stood empty. She felt nothing inside of her. There was no hint whatsoever of his presence in her soul. And so what the spirits had said to her was true, after all: She had always had the power to remove him from her.

So this was done.

Weirdlee's powers, and her limitations, had been a mystery to her all of her life. She'd known—or at least strongly believed—that she'd had second sight since her early teenage years. It was at that time that her behavior had turned in such a way that her friends no longer wanted to see her, and also when her parents became convinced that their daughter was, to put it mildly, disturbed.

Throughout its long history, the family lineage of witchcraft had never run directly from one generation to the next. Rather, a generation here and there was skipped in the line, with some women never being gifted, while their daughters after them might be. For Weirdlee, two generations of Osbornes had passed—her father's own, and his before him—without an empowered witch having sprung from the litter. And even though her dad had recalled since his own childhood the stories of his elderly grandmother having claimed psychic powers of a sort, he never believed such a thing could be true, himself.

Then along came Joanna. Leading up to her pre-teen years, she had always been an odd sort, though she still kept friendships and retained the trust of her doting parents. It was only after she turned fourteen that nature's gift to her—those magickal ways—began to blossom inside of her. And so thereafter, the fear of her "weirdness" drew her friends farther and farther away from her, and would eventually cost her everything in between.

No friends. No sweethearts. Not anyone to confide in.

Her mother—who'd of course married into the family—was never comfortable with her husband's reminiscing of his rather strange grandmother. And so when teenaged Joanna began to show an interest in the same sort of practices, she at first grew angry with her—insisting that she stop it right away. But when, after all of her lecturing, the girl stubbornly remained intent upon adopting a pagan way of life, her mother retreated from her, both physically and emotionally, and the two never got along the same way ever again.

Joanna's father noticed the strain. He'd taken his daughter aside early on and tried to convince her that the witchcraft she'd grown so attached to was, really, just a make pretend thing that she needed to grow out of. But Joanna would still have none of it, and so his efforts, too, came to no avail.

It was sometime afterwards that her parents decided to seek psychiatric treatment for their daughter. The move, however, backfired entirely, and only made their relationship even worse than it had been before. The psychiatrist had no simple answers—Joanna was just living out a fantasy, he'd said to them, due mostly to her loneliness in life. But for her parents, they'd already determined that her loneliness was *because* of her strange ways, and not the other way around.

The distance between daughter and parents grew wider.

John and Elizabeth Osborne still loved their only child—their precious young daughter. And they wanted the very best for her, still, even though she'd disappointed them so with her candlelit ceremonies in her bedroom and bizarre spell casting rituals. It was frightening for them, really. Her classmates, all the while, had taken to taunting her in the school hallways, calling her "Weirdo" and "Broom Hilda" and "Morgana"—the latter a reference to King Arthur lore, which, ironically, bore some resemblance to her family's true lineage.

After high school and upon entering college at Brandeis, Joanna changed her last name to Weirdlee. This was half out of spite for all the name calling she'd grown up with, and half just to get away from her family name. It was at this time, too, that she dyed her naturally brunette hair dark red.

Finally, by her junior year, word of Joanna's strange abilities had spread around pretty well. And not long afterward, she made the acquaintance of the most important man in her life up to that time: FBI Assistant Director Marvin Ledds.

The rest was history.

Weirdlee took an exit off Route 90 and drove through Des Allendes until she reached the banks of the Bayou des Allemands. There, she parked her car on the side of a narrow road. She got out, then strolled along the grassy, level riverbank. Her mind drifted from her childhood to her teenage years, and then on through her short time with the Bureau. Those latter times, she thought, were her most favorite times of all.

What would become of her now?

Justice. It was more than just a word. It was, on its own, a reason for taking action—and not always for the good. That much, at least, Paul Basil had made very clear.

But Weirdlee felt in her heart that, in her role as an agent of the *Invisibles*, there would indeed be justice for the helpless and the innocent forthcoming.

And by any means she saw fit.

The witch from Salem walked up to the edge of a small wooden boat dock. From there, she looked out upon the wide, slow-moving river. She breathed in the wholesome air, and it eased her mind for a time. Then, still gazing out upon the water, she whispered into the wind, her voice carrying through the air like a dream…

> *Here I walk my pathless journey*
> *With my heart and soul I give.*
> *Bless my words and incantations*
> *Hear me, spirits, and forgive.*

* * * *

In the late afternoon, a mucky, sweat-soaked Nicks finally received the call he'd been waiting for from Fielding. The junior agent had just finished going through the over 4,000 names of parents who'd adopted kids from 2010 to 2012, and he'd scored matches on three of the names from their interview list. The names included two teachers and, perhaps not so surprisingly, one name both men were already familiar with from the daycare center.

Farrah Simmons.

Nicks told his partner to head back to Chackbay and meet him at the Swampy Inn, where Nicks would grab a shower and they could discuss their next move. He met Fielding in the café, then, where Fielding had brought along with him printed copies of the adoption certificates.

"We'll check these out today," Nicks said as he examined the certificate belonging to Simmons.

"Not sure what you're expectin', partner," Fielding said. "Can't see anyone pullin' a stunt like this—especially after a kid goes missin' like the Hawkins boy did."

Nicks eyed the certificate in his hand. "Maybe not," he said. He looked down at the signature block of the certificate, taking note of the Notary Public's stamp and signature. He recognized the Notary's name right away.

"You'd be surprised what a little sleight of hand can do," he said to Fielding. He looked at him and winked. "You believe in magic, Special Agent?"

Fielding chuckled. "Shit. You been talkin' to Agent Weirdlee too much."

Nicks sighed and tossed the certificate onto the table. "You might be right." He sat up in his chair then and looked over at a small wall-mounted clock hanging over the cafe's counter. "Let's drive out to the daycare center first and see if we can catch Ms. Simmons before she leaves for the day."

The two agents drove up to Foster's Daycare in Fielding's rented blue Chevy Impala. They reached the place at 4:15 PM, and just in time to see Farrah Simmons walking out the front door, a small black purse slung over her shoulder.

"Ms. Simmons," Nicks called out as he got out of the car.

She stopped and looked his way. "Yes?"

"Can we talk with you for a moment, please?"

She looked at both agents suspiciously as they approached her. "I...guess."

Nicks held the copy of Simmons' adoption certificate in his hand. He and Fielding both came up to the counselor.

"We wanted to talk to you about this," Nicks said, handing her the certificate.

She took it and examined it. "What's this? My son's certificate of adoption?"

"Yes," Nicks said.

Fielding said to her, "I wouldn't'ta guessed ya for the adoptin' type, Ms. Simmons."

She leered at him. "Oh really? I didn't know that only certain types of people adopted."

"You married, Ms. Simmons?" Nicks asked, looking at her left hand, which had no rings on its fingers.

"I was," she replied. "We're separated."

"I see."

"Ms. Simmons," Fielding said, "you wouldn't happen to have a picture of your son on you, would you?"

At that, Simmons scoffed loudly and shook her head at him. "You have got to be kidding me, FBI man."

"Humor us," Nicks quipped.

She looked back at him, clearly annoyed. But then, after all, there was no point in refusing them. She brought her purse around and dug into it to fetch her billfold. Taking it out, she opened it and flipped through a few photos before coming to one they requested. She flipped her billfold up to show it to them. There, a young, light-skinned black boy, about ten years of age, looked back at them with a posed, innocent smile. "Elliot is his name," Simmons informed the agents.

Nicks took the billfold in his hand for a closer look. The boy, he saw, in no way resembled the missing Hawkins boy.

"Satisfied?" Simmons asked him.

Nicks handed the billfold back to her. "I recognized the signature of the Notary Public on the certificate, Ms. Simmons."

She looked down at the paper, still clutched in her hand. "Notary Public?"

"Mr. Potter, the principal at Kraemer Elementary?"

"Oh—yes," Simmons recalled. "He did do that for me."

"Well, I just thought it was a small world, and figured we'd check things out."

Simmons smirked at him. "And...what? You thought maybe me and Mr. Potter conspired or something?"

Nicks drew up his hands. "Just the way I work, Ma'am."

Simmons closed her billfold and replaced it in her purse. "You guys are really something," she said. "That poor boy is at the bottom of a bayou somewhere, and you think somebody kidnapped him." She started off, heading toward her car in the parking lot. "It's a terrible thing that happened, guys. Really sad. But what's done is done. Maybe if someone was looking after him a little better in the first place, he'd still be alive."

Nicks watched her walk to her car, but had nothing to say.

"Well," Fielding said to his partner. "Two more stops."

Two more stops. Two more dead ends. Both parents in those cases had their adopted kids right there with them, providing ample evidence of their innocence.

By 6:45 PM, the agents had wrapped things up. They drove back to the Swampy Inn, picking up some Cajun takeout along the way. When they arrived at the inn, Nicks noticed Special Agent Weirdlee's Grand Cherokee parked in the lot there. He decided not to bother her for the evening.

Their job in the bayous, he figured, was just about done.

~ | ~

-18-

The Gray Witch

Zarah Devillier returned home with Damon to find her two elder sons, Lucien and Korram, both sitting in the living area dutifully awaiting their mother's arrival. Both men had worked hard that day, in compliance with Zarah's spellbound will. There would be no further smart talk coming from either of them, ever again. No more sass. No more needy desires.

Just the way she liked it.

Zarah herself was in a foul mood, having been thwarted in her efforts all day by that meddling witch, Osborne. The old woman trundled up to her small table in the living area and slapped it hard with her open palm. "Gets me my bones over here!" she shouted to Damon, who still carried her belongings. He hurried over to her side and dropped the case that held her gear. He dug into it feverishly to fetch her chicken bones.

"Momma," said Lucien. "We's here for you, Momma."

She leered at him. "Shut up—*boy*. Youz never any good to me, ceptin' fer drivin' me's around. Now youz no good for that, neither."

She snapped her wrinkled fingers and pointed to the staircase. "Get your asses upstairs—the both of ya's," she barked, meaning him and Korram. "Don't be needin' you twos fuckin' around down here."

The two elders, without another word, hurried up to their room on the second floor.

Zarah didn't trust either of them yet as servants of her will. Not having minds of their own for the first time, the newly spellbound had a clumsy way about them. Not good for ceremonies. Damon, on the other hand, had been under her spell for nearly two decades. He was well trained and fully controlled.

He found his mother's chicken bones, stored in their black cloth bag, and put them on the table for her. She stepped around to sit in her chair there.

"Black magick," she spat out. "Black magick's whats we needs. Gets my soul in the right places. Lets me sees with the eyes of the night." She looked at Damon. "Gonna get me's that bitch. That pagan whore. I's gonna gets her good." She grabbed her bag of bones and shook them around in the bag. "I's be guided by the spirits of the dead. My's eyes, theyz be seein' the naked world for what it is."

She tossed the bag onto the table before her.

"Curses to the heretics!" she yelled. "Curses to them all!"

She grabbed the bag once more and untied it. She upended it and shook the bag vigorously as she dumped the chicken bones onto the table.

Her eyes flashed as she examined their scattered lot. "Demons all!" she cried. "Demons of the night! I's calls out to you! Come to me's and show me yourz designs!"

She closed her eyes and shuttered. Then she whispered, "I awaits you, my spirit masters. I waits for you to call."

Damon watched his mother as she sat there, motionless.

She muttered to him, "Fetch me my's candles, boy. Black candles." He obeyed her quickly as she gave him more instruction. "Put dem's in a circle around me. Light 'em and then put out the lights in here. I want a circle of light around me's tonight."

Damon returned with her black candles, five in all. He placed them, evenly spaced, upon the floor all around his mother. He lit each one, and then hurried about to turn off the electric lights in both the living room and the adjoining kitchen. With the place then cloaked in darkness—save for the circle of candlelight encircling Zarah—he returned to stand before her.

"All done, Momma," he mumbled.

"Get out," she demanded of him, her eyes still closed. "Get outside and stay outside."

"Yes, Momma."

Damon hurried off, leaving the house in a rush.

He ran down the steps of the front porch, and then sped desperately through the marshy forest, getting himself as far away from the house as he could. He made it out as far as their little dock by the inlet cove then before he stopped. There, he dropped to his knees and hugged the ground.

Back inside of her home, meanwhile, Zarah sat alone in silence. She took in a deep breath, and then slowly exhaled.

The waiting would thus begin.

One hour slipped by, leading into the next. Then another fell away thereafter, and the sun slipped below the horizon in between. All the while, Zarah Devillier sat motionless and, mostly, in quiet meditation, her mind sifting through her own memories and daydreams. From time to time, too, she'd mutter an utterance—"Move away," or "Come here,"—as she guided herself along through the spiritual plane.

"Stab it," she demanded. "Give it a rub." She chuckled at her mischievous ways.

Outside, at the dock in the shadowy forest, Damon waited it out. Being captured by his mother's will, he could feel her presence within his mind. She was, it seemed, in a retarded way—at first talking to him, and then drifting off into some hypnotic, trancelike state that he couldn't comprehend. Frightened of this, he clutched his head with both hands, covering his ears. "Momma!" he cried out, frightened for her. "Momma, stop!"

Damon Devillier, unlike his two elder brothers, had always been gifted in a spiritual way. Due to a sickly mind, though, Zarah had had little choice but to capture his mind while he was still just a child, and so trap it inside of her own, there for safe keeping.

Her youngest, she determined, could never be allowed to be free of her, to live his life as a man.

Curled up on the ground, his hands covering his ears, Damon whimpered and wept helplessly—too afraid to even imagine the horrors presently unfolding in the ethereal realm.

Upstairs in the bedroom they shared, meanwhile, Lucien and Korram shivered. They kept their eyes locked on each other as they sat on their beds, both dreading the supernatural ceremony taking place below them. This was a gathering of dark souls—the long-ago dead returning to the mundane world to trespass against the living.

Death to the heretics!
Death to the guilty!
Justice!

"Momma..." Lucien muttered fearfully.

Downstairs in the living area, the little flames of the black candles flickered about, their light dancing amongst the shadows that surrounded Zarah.

"Come on," she chided the spirits. "Give it to me's."

She contorted her face, and then sniffled and grunted.

"Ahhk!" she squawked then, disgusted, as visions of worms and maggots filled her mind's eye. "Nasty!"

She swatted the table before her. "Stop it," she said, annoyed. "Give it up." She shook her head. "No!"

She heaved in a deep breath, gasping for air. "Stop it!" she demanded.

What will you be in your next life?

The voice she heard was unfamiliar to her.

See what you will be!

The old sorceress bolted up from her chair. She cried out madly, "Stop it! STOP IT!"

Upstairs, Lucien and Korram leapt from their beds. They stood frozen, trapped in a state of fear!

"STOP IT!" Zarah screamed. "Get away from me! GET AWAY FROM ME!"

She ran about madly, hobbling and staggering, her hands pounding the sides of her head. "Get outta my's head! Get out! Get out!" she screamed, terror-stricken and tears streaming from her eyes. "Stop it!"

The old woman raced as best she could into the darkened kitchen. She came to the counter and pounded her fists on its top and then swiped her hands about— grabbing and throwing whatever she found.

Lucien snapped out of his stricken daze. "Momma?"

Korram, likewise unencumbered, glanced about their room. "Someone's got Momma!" he yelled.

Both men made for the bedroom door. Korram stopped by his dresser to snatch his shotgun, set against it.

All the while, their mother's horrible cries filled the air.

"STOP IT!" she wailed. "GET OUT OF MY'S HEAD! YOUZ GET OUT OF MY'S HEAD!"

In the kitchen, she threw open drawers and dove into them with her hands, blindly rifling through their contents. Finally—after weaving back and forth in a desperate search for *something* she could use to defend herself—she found exactly what she was looking for. Snatching up a butcher knife, she began stabbing at the countertop and at the air all around her, creating what she intended to be a spiritual wall.

Lucien and Korram flew down the stairs, and they raced into the kitchen.

"Momma!" Lucien cried out as he rushed to his mother in the darkness. Korram stopped by the doorway to flip on the light switch.

The lights flashed on.

Zarah spun about—but what she saw and heard was not her son! "NO!" she screamed at him. "I'LL KILL YOU! I'LL KILL YOU!"

Lucien stopped, terrified, as his mother charged at him at a full gait—and she plunged her blade into his chest! "FUCK YOU!" she cried, bludgeoning her son repeatedly. He howled and choked in agony!

"Momma!" Korram cried out in horror.

Lucien's body dropped to the floor.

Zarah cast an angry glare at her second son, then. She scowled at him. "You fucking whore!"

Korram stood aghast as his mother charged at him next, butcher knife upraised. He brought up his shotgun and leveled it on her. "Stop!" he yelled.

She came on, still.

He fired.

Back at the dock, Damon leapt to his feet at the sound of the shotgun blast. "Momma?"

He started out in a dash to the house.

Korram looked down at his mother. The short-range blast had riddled her chest with shot. Her dead eyes stared skyward. He approached her slowly.

"Momma," he whispered, examining his mother's bloodied body up close. His face contorted into a tortured expression, and he wept. "*Momma...*"

Damon raced up to the house—just making it to the front porch before a second shotgun blast rang in the air. He stopped suddenly.

"Momma!" he yelled.

He bolted inside.

The living area he came into lay enshrouded in darkness, save for the candles still flickering around the table there. "Momma?" the youngest of Zarah's own called out sheepishly. "Youz all right?"

He approached the kitchen, from where he saw a light was on. From his vantage point, too, he could see a pair of bodies lumped on the floor.

He crept closer.

Arriving at the kitchen doorway, he saw, quite plainly, that his mother was dead. There, too, lay Lucien, killed by stab wounds. And crumpled on the floor nearby them both was a third body, whom he assumed to be his other brother, Korram—though it was hard to tell, owing to the corpse's face having been blown off from a blast under its chin.

Damon stared at the bloody carnage for a little while. A very strange sensation came over him, then, as he stood there. There was no sorrow inside of his soul—no heartache afflicting his body. It was as if...

My God!

He was free!

FREE!

Free to wander the wilderness! Free to torment and torture! Oh, the things he could do now! He could go wherever he pleased! Do whatever he wanted! Take whomever he wished! He was the master, now! He was his OWN MAN!

Free at last!

Justice...

The voice was like a whisper in his mind.

His eyes darted about the room. "Who's there?"

Cleanse yourself.

"What's that?" he asked, glancing here and there.

Rid yourself of evil.

Yes! he realized, nodding eagerly. *Wash myself. That's what I must do!*

In the pitch of darkness, he jogged back out to the dockside. There, he retrieved the can of gasoline the family kept there, on this night freshly filled. Returning home, he splashed the gasoline about the first floor, and then, with its last few pints, dowsed himself in the refreshing liquid. He giggled as the gasoline tingled his dry skin.

Alight a match, he did then.

Close your eyes.

The house of Zarah Devillier burst into flames.

* * * *

Green candle for Mother Earth.

Red candle for fire.

Blue for waters, pure, and yellow one for air.

Each, in its turn, Joanna Weirdlee blew out, until only a fifth, white candle remained, there to illuminate the shadowy confines of her room at the Swampy Inn. She brought her lips close to this candle and, with a quick breath, she extinguished her doorway into the spirit world.

Imbalance, balanced. Justice restored.

Never before had the Salem witch ended the life another human being. On this night, she had ended three. And so their tainted souls would be delivered to the *Ghede* for their judgment, and thereafter be condemned for all eternity.

On this night, too, did pass Weirdlee's own life as a gentle and innocent white witch. From this time on, and until the end of her days, a gray witch she would be.

-19-

Conspiracy Revealed

*In the news this morning, a house fire has
engulfed and destroyed a home in the
Grand Bayou forest, east of Chackbay,
overnight. Police and fire officials at the
scene say four bodies were recovered inside
of the home. Investigators say evidence at
the scene indicates the fire was set
intentionally, and that at least three of the
victims were killed prior to the blaze. Arson
investigators are still sifting through
evidence inside of the home at this time.
Water was flown in via helicopter and
plane to help dowse the flames, which
spread to the surrounding forest in the
isolated area, which straddles the Grand
Bayous, north of Thibodaux.*

Paul Basil swore at the television, tossing an empty
beer can at it as he shot up from his bed. His refuge on this
morning was a motel room in Houma, where he'd stayed
overnight as he plotted his next moves in the coming days.
Zarah was gone—taken from him by the Salem witch, he

269

knew. He hadn't expected to feel the rage that currently swelled up inside of him, though. Yes, for the past few years, he'd known the old woman was likely to leave him— whether by death of old age or by some other means. But to be outmatched by a pagan?

The *Ghede* had taken sides—that much he was now certain of. And they had chosen a heretic, of all things, as their agent on Earth.

Oh, the betrayal! What sinful deed had he committed to make them all turn away from him? Was he not simply doing their bidding by bringing those whose fates had already been written to their rightful destinations?

God, at least, he assured himself then, *will not betray me.*

He took up his cellphone and tapped it on. Scrolling through his recent contacts, he found the person he was looking for.

One more heretic here to deliver to God, he told himself, *and then I move on.*

Off he'd go for a while to another locale—at least until matters righted themselves there in the bayous, and that wicked Salem witch had departed for good.

* * * *

"You see Agent Weirdlee this morning?" Nicks asked Fielding, coming back to the room they shared at the Swampy Inn.

"She ain't in her room?" Fielding replied, putting on his tie in front of the room's dresser mirror.

Nicks stood at the doorway. "Her car's gone."

Fielding stopped and turned. "You ain't thinkin'—?"

"You know that old voodoo woman she talked to last week?"

"Yeah."

"She's dead."

"No shit…"

Nicks put his hands on his hips. "Her house burned down last night. Her sons are dead, too. The police found their bodies all together in there."

Fielding puffed his cheeks and exhaled. He asked Nicks, "They know what happened?"

"Nope. Not yet. An arson squad is there, now, checking things out. They took the bodies over to the morgue to try and confirm their cause of deaths."

"They burned up bad?"

Nicks nodded. "Yeah, pretty much."

Just then, Nicks overheard a car arriving in the small parking lot. He turned around and saw that it was Agent Weirdlee's Grand Cherokee. "Here she is now," he said to Fielding.

Weirdlee hopped out of her vehicle. She had on her thick-rimmed sunglasses and wore a black pinstriped pantsuit. She held a small bag in her hand and, in the same hand, clutched onto a cardboard four-sleeve coffee cup holder, presently holding two coffees and a tea.

She closed the car door as Nicks came up to her. He eyed the bag. "Breakfast?"

She nodded. "Yup. Tired of oatmeal and yogurt."

The two talked as they walked back to the room that Nicks and Fielding shared.

"You hear about your old voodoo woman—the one who lives in the bayous?" Nicks asked her.

She glanced at him, appearing wholly ignorant of the previous night's bloodshed. "What about her?"

"She's dead."

Weirdlee stopped and looked at him seriously. "Dead? What happened?"

Fielding stepped out just then and walked up to them as Nicks answered. "Her house went up in flames last night. The police found her body and the bodies of her three sons—or so we're assuming, pending autopsies."

"Killed in the fire?"

"Probably not," said Nicks. "The old woman's remains showed some indications of a shotgun wound—deer shot, maybe. They recovered a shotgun, too, right where the bodies were."

"All shot?" asked Fielding.

Nicks shook his head. "I dunno. We'll know more later, I guess."

Weirdlee looked off in thought. "A sad life," she muttered under her breath.

Nicks looked at her. "Maybe worse than we thought, if it led to this. You sure she didn't tell you anything we should know about, Agent Weirdlee?"

Weirdlee gave him a straight look. *Back to formal names, it seems.* "I could never prove it in court, Samuel, but I can tell you with confidence that she helped Mr. Basil in all of his dealings, no matter what they were."

"The boy?" he asked.

She gave a nod to her colleagues' room. "Let's go inside and eat."

They went into the room then and huddled around a coffee table in there. Weirdlee continued as she unpacked danishes and doughnuts.

"Zarah Devillier taught Paul Basil everything he knows," she said. She cracked open the plastic lid on her tea. "She taught him all about her religion—or her cult, if you want to call it that. She taught him how to cast spells. She taught him how to trick people and gain their confidence."

"Like the boy?" asked Fielding.

She looked at him. "Like the people watching the boy, more like."

Nicks took Weirdlee by the wrist to get her attention. "Do you know what happened to Julien Hawkins, Agent Weirdlee? Did she tell you?"

"No," she said, taken aback by his advance. "She didn't tell me anything that I haven't already told you."

She pulled her wrist away from him then and selected a danish.

"How'd you get all this info on her?" Fielding asked.

She kept her eyes focused on the danish she'd picked out. "You wouldn't believe me if I told you," she said. She bit into the danish as she finished, "Let's just say I have my sources."

Nicks sat up straight in his chair and sipped his coffee. "Agent Weirdlee, why do I get the feeling you're keeping things from us?"

"Am I?" she replied. "Sam, if I knew what really happened to the boy, I'd be the first one to let you know. I promised you the other day that I would do whatever I could to help you solve this case, and I meant that."

"What about Basil?" Fielding asked. "Did he kill the boy?"

Weirdlee continued eating her danish, and she took a sip of tea before answering his question. "I'm certain he played a role in the boy's disappearance. But I don't know for sure what that was. And I don't know if the boy was killed afterwards or not." She snapped a look at Nicks. "I mean, I haven't found out yet, same as you guys."

Nicks gave her a long look before he went back to eating a doughnut he'd picked out. For whatever reason, he surmised, Weirdlee had continued to behave as if she were helping out the team of himself and Fielding, rather than actually being a part of that team. He believed she truly wanted to assist them in the investigation, but her continued I-have-to-do-it-alone attitude was troubling to him, as was her "I get visions" thing.

Even so, he had to admit, she had a charm about her that he couldn't help but be attracted to. And he *wanted* to trust her, if only because it would mean she'd continue to join them on their investigations.

"That's the guy we're after, then." he said. "Whether he did it all by himself or he just helped out, he knows what happened to that kid—and where to find him, I'm willing to bet."

"Well, they already got an APB out on him for what he did to Agent Weirdlee," said Fielding. "He's got to be hiding out somewhere pretty damned good."

Nicks looked at Weirdlee thoughtfully. Basil had attacked her, and he couldn't shake that violent image from his mind. He only hoped she wasn't lying about how far he got.

Why would she?

He let the matter go, for the time being.

"After we're done here," he said to his colleagues, gesturing to their breakfast, "we'll split up again today." He said to Fielding, "Why don't you take the rest of the names to the south of here." And then to Weirdlee, "You can take the people north and west of here, Agent Weirdlee. I'll take the east. I want to swing by the Grand Bayou, first, to check out the old lady's house. I imagine the cops will be working their way downriver from the lake with their dragging operations, too."

"Draggin' a bayou's gotta be tough, partner," Fielding noted. "Could be a few days, still. Maybe weeks."

Nicks remembered to ask him, then, snapping his fingers. "We get anything back from the lab on that sneaker yet?"

"Naw," Fielding said, shaking his head. "We ain't gonna hear from them boys for a couple-few weeks. New Orleans keeps 'em busy."

"Yeah," Nicks agreed. "I still think that's a plant, though. And if our guy, Basil, is involved, he could have been the one who put it there."

"Or whoever he's working with," Weirdlee added.

Nicks nodded. "That, too."

"I'd like to visit Ms. Hawkins this afternoon, Sam," Weirdlee said. "Keep her company for a little while."

Fielding cut in, "We goin' to that service of hers tonight?"

Nicks answered him. "We're not family, Agent Fielding. I don't think it would be appropriate, given the circumstances, for us to be there." He looked at Weirdlee. "You two seem to be spawning a friendship, though, aye Agent Weirdlee?"

She gave a weak smile. "Sort of, yes. I'd like to see her today, if I can."

Nicks smiled. "Sure. As long as we're caught up with everything by then."

"There's only a few names left, partner," said Fielding. "We should wrap this up by early afternoon, anyway."

"Good enough," Nicks replied.

The three finished their breakfast, and afterwards broke up to begin their day, each taking his or her own vehicle and heading out.

* * * *

"You heard me. I need another two thousand by Monday."

Paul Basil was in no mood to argue.

"I got the cops crawling up my ass, here, and it's all *your* fault!"

The woman on the other end of the phone call was equally steamed. Two thousand dollars—on top of the two grand she'd already forked over to him? And this had been going on for *three years!*

"Listen to me," Basil said to her. "I been doin' God's work here for a long time, and I've got a lot of work left to do. I been betrayed, I been used, and I got the FBI snooping around, thanks to you. I need to take a vacation after this weekend—and *you're* payin' for it."

"But you promised," the woman fumed. "You said—"

"Fuck what I said!" Basil yelled. "I tricked their eyes, just like you wanted, but I didn't take that little boy. That poor momma of his, she's a good Christian woman. She didn't deserve losin' her child like she did. That's the devil's work, is what it is. And you're payin' for it."

"But we *paid* you!" she cried out.

"Not enough!" Basil shouted back. "I told you, I got God's work to do. And I'll be workin' on my own, now, so I got to start things fresh."

"It's too much."

Basil snarled as he gripped his cellphone close to his face. "Then ya'll better get ready for the cops to stop by. 'Cause they'll be comin' around if I don't get my cash."

A long, quiet pause ensued.

Basil waited, a confident smirk coming over his expression.

"All right," the woman said. "But we can't keep doing this. We can't afford—"

"You'll do it," Basil interrupted, "for as long as I'm breathin' air. I've got you in my retirement plan, you hear me? You shoulda known that from the very beginning. You'll never be rid of me."

A distraught sigh came over the phone.

"I wish this'd never happened," the woman said.

"Tool late," Basil replied. He checked his cellphone for the time. It was almost noon. "I got work to do," he said.

"Gotta a long night ahead of me. I'll meet you at the usual spot on Monday morning, ten a.m. You got that?"

A pause.

"Yeah."

Basil smiled. "See you then."

* * * *

Special Agent Fielding finished his part of the list by just after 1:00 PM. He called up Nicks, who was on his final interview after having stopped by the burned-out husk of Zarah Devillier's home in the morning. The two men agreed to meet up at a small eatery just down the road from Kraemer Park on Route 370.

Nicks got there sometime after Fielding. He joined him at a small, metal lattice table set out on an outdoor patio. The day was bright and sunny, and both men ordered lemonade to quench their thirst in the midday heat.

Nicks leaned back in his chair with one leg crossed over the other. He rested an elbow on the table, relaxed. Fielding, not nearly as comfortable, sat forward with both elbows on the table and cradling his drink in his hands.

"I think it's startin' to look like that boy is at the bottom of a bayou after all, partner," the junior agent said. "Even if he *was* abducted, whoever took him has gotta be long gone."

Nicks mulled the possibilities in his mind. "Maybe."

"I mean," Fielding went on, "if he was abducted by someone who wanted to keep him, like you was thinkin' mighta happened, then they couldn'ta kept him around these parts, right? Folks woulda recognized him by now."

"Shit happens, though," Nicks replied. "You never know. There's been people held against their will for years, and all the while they're locked in a basement in the middle of Mayberry."

Fielding raised an eyebrow. "Sure 'nuff, I guess." He took a swig of his lemonade. "But this is a little kid we're talkin' about. What's the point of abductin' him, if all you're gonna do is lock him away somewhere? Weren't you thinkin' whoever woulda somethin' like that mighta cared about him?"

Nicks looked at his partner. "I could have been wrong about that. Kids are abducted for more sordid reasons, too."

Fielding winced as he held onto his glass. "Don't even wanna think about that kinda shit, partner."

Nicks drank from his own lemonade, still pondering things. "I actually thought we had it nailed when we found that adoption certificate for the Simmons kid. Would have been a nice fit, too."

"Yeah, that was still kind of a long shot, though," Fielding said.

Suddenly, a curious thought popped into his head, and he flopped back in his seat. "Although, what the hell? We never did see that boy of hers, ourselves." He leaned forward, toward Nicks. "Just because she showed us a picture of a kid, doesn't mean that's him. Shit, the photo coulda come with the wallet."

Nicks eyed Fielding, hearing what the agent was saying even as his mind remained focused on the Simmons adoption certificate he'd examined the other day.

A wallet, he pondered...

Or a picture frame.

He sat up in his chair and took a healthy swig of his lemonade. "I want you to contact that Hall of Records again this afternoon."

Fielding gave him curious look. "Hall of Records? But they're closed today, partner. It's Saturday."

"Then call the police in the city and have 'em contact whoever needs to be contacted. We don't need to be inside the building. I'm sure we can access their records on the Internet or something."

"All right," Fielding replied. "What's up?"

"I dunno," Nicks mulled. "Maybe we just didn't go back far enough in our search the first time. I want you to go back the three years prior to 2010 this time. From 2007 to 2009."

"*What?*" Fielding said, slapping a hand on the table. "You want me to go through and compare all those names on our list *again*?"

Nicks shook his head slowly. "Nope." He drew up a finger. "Only one."

* * * *

"You shoulda seen my boy when he was a newborn," Regina Hawkins said to Joanna Weirdlee. "His eyes, they was as big as sunshine, seein' the world for the first time like they was."

It was 4:35 PM, and the two women sat next to each other on the little couch inside Regina's home. Weirdlee had finished her interviews earlier that afternoon and then broke for lunch before driving out there. She'd spent the rest of the afternoon with Regina. The two also made plans to drive out to the church together just before Julien's service was due to begin. Regina didn't have many friends, and with her parents gone, too, the service was likely to be a small affair.

"His daddy wasn't there," Regina went on, looking at Weirdlee with a sad expression. "Said he didn't like hospitals." She looked off, morose. "I knows he out drinkin' with his friends, though."

"You brought up your little boy all on your own, didn't you?" Weirdlee asked her.

Regina nodded. "Yes. I didn't have much choice, ya know?"

Weirdlee wrapped her arm around Hawkins and pulled her in, comforting her. "You're a very good woman, Regina. The kindest person I've ever known."

Regina laughed weakly. "I's just a poor country girl," she said. She looked at Weirdlee. "I don't knows too much at all. Maybe I shouldn'ta taken to bein' a momma, after all."

Weirdlee looked deeply into her eyes. She said to her softly, "I think all mommas should be just like you, Regina Hawkins. The world would be a better place."

Regina returned Weirdlee's thoughtful gaze. "Youz a beautiful woman, miss. You gonna have lots of kids, I think." She finished with a giggle.

Weirdlee smiled. "I think you're going to find yourself a good man one day, Regina. And you'll have kids, too, and they'll be sweet and kind and beautiful, just like their momma is today."

Regina rested her head on Weirdlee's shoulder, her sadness returning. "Only thing I ever wanted was my boy," she whispered.

Weirdlee's mind drifted through the course of investigation—all of the many suspects and all of the possibilities. Nicks, she knew, might not ever find the answer. And as long as Basil was alive and eluded capture, too, she herself would most likely never perceive the truth about what happened to little Julien. He—Basil—was the opaque screen through which her eyes and mind could not see beyond.

Just then, her smartphone beeped loudly with a text message alert. She retrieved the phone from her pants pocket and tapped it on to see the message. It was from Nicks, she saw, and she stared at it, shaken by its words.

Call me. Not around Ms. Hawkins.

* * * *

It was earlier that afternoon when Fielding finished his assignment—a much quicker task with only one name to match up. Nicks then made a couple of phone calls before the two men started out, driving south on what Nicks hoped would be their last journey of the investigation.

The senior agent knocked on the door of a well-kept, cottage-style home. After a short wait, a slim, older black woman opened the door. Nicks recognized her right away.

"Yes?" she asked, first eyeing Nicks, and then shifting her glance to Fielding, standing behind him, and then two state police officers also there. A local cop stood next to Nicks, a folded piece of paper in hand. Behind this officer stood a black woman dressed in a white blouse and black slacks.

"Mrs. Potter?" Nicks asked the woman at the door, who looked just like the woman in the portrait on Henry Potter's desk at the school.

She looked at him with a pale expression. "Yes."

"Is your husband at home, Mrs. Potter?" Nicks asked.

She stared back at him—and from the stone expression on her face, Nicks knew that, finally, they had found their mark.

"Yes," she replied. "What's this all about?"

"Can you call him to the door, Mrs. Potter?" Nicks asked.

"I'll go get him," she said, starting out.

Nicks brought up a hand, stopping her. "Just call him to the door, if you could, ma'am."

She stared at him again, and Nicks saw that there was fear in her eyes. Hesitantly then, she turned, and she called inside for her husband to come to the front door.

281

"Sure," he replied from inside.

Henry Potter walked out from their living room and down a short hallway adjacent to a staircase that led up to the second floor of the home before arriving at the front door. As soon as he saw the FBI agents along with the officers there, his expression went pale.

He stared at Nicks, dumbstruck. "Special Agent..."

The local police officer showed his folded piece of paper to the couple. "Mr. and Mrs. Potter, we have a warrant here to search your home."

"*What?*" Potter replied, a contorted, confused expression gripping his face.

"Will you both please step outside?" the officer asked him.

Potter stood there, shaken. He looked at Nicks, and he asked him breathlessly, "What's this all about?"

Nicks waved him out. "If you can just step outside here with your wife, sir, this won't take long."

Potter's wife, panic-stricken, glanced at her husband and the officers. She stammered, "This isn't supposed to happen."

The local officer waved them on, saying to them, "Come along, please."

The husband and wife looked at each other nervously. *This wasn't supposed to happen.*

They stepped outside onto the open front porch.

Nicks gestured for Fielding and the woman with them— a staffer with the Department of Children and Family Services—to join him in entering the home.

Potter glanced back at them. "We're a God-fearing family. We live a happy life here."

The state police officers followed the agents through the doorway. One of them stayed on by the entrance.

Nicks, Fielding, and the DCFS staffer then entered into the hallway area, next to the stairway. Nicks said to them, gesturing, "Agent Fielding, why don't you check the kitchen and any other rooms back there. Ms. Ferris, can you check upstairs, please, with one of the officers here?"

She agreed, and a state police officer led the way upstairs then.

Outside, all the while, Potters rattled on with their desperate pleas for understanding.

This, after all, wasn't supposed to be happening.

Fielding cautiously walked ahead to the right of the staircase and on through an open doorway into the kitchen. Nicks, meanwhile, turned and looked down the hallway to the left of the staircase, towards the living room. He slowly walked ahead.

Making his way down the hall, he could hear a television on in the living room. Arriving at the room's entrance then, he turned and peeked inside. There, sitting cross-legged on a thick, blue carpeted floor in front of a large flat screen television set, he saw a young black boy. The boy was dressed in a t-shirt, jeans, and white socks, and appeared very much at ease as he watched a television show. Nicks eyed him for a moment, considering what to say, before entering the room.

The little boy—appearing no older than seven or eight years old—looked behind him at the sound of the agent's approach. Nicks himself noticed, then, that the boy bore a striking resemblance—albeit three years advanced—to the Hawkins boy.

"Hello there," he said to the boy as he came up to him.

"Hi," the boy replied, appearing puzzled. "Where's my dad?"

"Oh," Nicks said, glancing back, "he's with your mom on the front porch talking to some people."

The boy turned back to his television show.

Nicks crouched beside the boy. "My name's Sam," he said. "What's yours?"

The boy glanced at him. "Joshua," he said, before returning his attention back to the television.

Nicks looked at the television himself. "What are you watching there?"

"Harry Potter," the boy said.

Nicks smiled at the coincidence of names. "He's got the same last name as you."

The boy nodded overtly.

Nicks thought things out in his mind. He didn't want to alarm the boy, and you don't question kids the same way as you do adults.

"You know," he finally said to him, "when I was a little boy, I had a different name than the one I've got now."

The boy looked at him. "You did?"

Nicks gave a nod. "My friends used to call me Danny," he said, stealing his partner's name.

The boy looked back at him, expressionless.

"You ever had another name before?" Nicks asked him then.

The boy stared at him for a moment. "Yeah," he replied sheepishly. "My dad changed it after my first mom and dad died, though. He doesn't want me saying it anymore."

"He doesn't?" Nicks said with interest. "Well, that's okay. If you tell me what it was, I promise you I won't tell him you told me. How's that?"

The boy looked over at the living room's entrance. "I dunno..."

Nicks placed his hand gently on the boy's shoulder. "It's all right, Joshua. I won't tell him, honest."

The boy looked at him nervously, as if he were about to say something wrong. Then he whispered to the special agent...

"Julien."

* * * *

Regina went about getting herself ready to leave for the church, located just a few miles down the main road. It was just after 5:15 PM.

"We gotta gets there before anyone else does," she said, checking herself in front of her bathroom mirror. "Not that many will come by, I expect." She came out of the bathroom to see Weirdlee standing in the little kitchen area. "We's never had many friends, you know."

Weirdlee offered her a comforting smile. "You have one more than you had a week ago."

Regina smiled back at her. "You're so sweet to me."

Weirdlee's smartphone rang. She took the phone from her pocket and, via caller ID, saw that it was Sam Nicks. She tapped it on and said into it, "Hi Sam. Just a minute, please." She looked to Regina. "I'll be right back," she said to her, thinking it better to take the call outside. She went to the front door then and stepped out.

Regina went back to getting ready for the church service. After just a minute had passed, then, Weirdlee came back inside.

"Regina," the agent said, seeming quite shaken, "why don't we wait here. My colleagues are coming by."

Regina stopped adjusting a light shawl on her shoulders to look at Weirdlee. "Why theys comin' here? We need to be at the church before six."

Weirdlee approached her. "They're coming here to see you, Regina. I told them we'd wait here for them."

Regina saw the expression on Weirdlee's face and didn't know what to make of it. "But we's gots to go, miss. I needs to be there for my boy."

"It'll be okay," Weirdlee said. She put her hands on Regina's shoulders then and hugged her gently. Tears welled up in the agent's eyes as she whispered, "They've got a surprise for you." She drew herself back and looked into Regina's eyes. "We won't be late," she said to her with a smile. "I promise."

Twenty minutes passed by. Nicks had called Weirdlee to inform her that the Hawkins boy had been found and that they were on their way north to return him to his mother. At 5:40 PM, their car, along with a state police cruiser, pulled up into the dirt driveway.

"Regina," Weirdlee said as she saw them arrive through the living room window. "Let's go outside."

Regina had been biding her time, sitting on her couch while perusing a photo album of her little boy, which she intended to take along with her for the service. "We's coulda just met them at the church," she said, getting up from the couch. She hurried over to Weirdlee. "We's gonna be late, now."

Weirdlee took her by the hand. She looked into her eyes, and Regina sensed from the agent's expression that something was amiss.

Weirdlee said to her, "We're not going to the church, Regina."

Regina looked back at her curiously. "Whatchu mean?"

Weirdlee coaxed her along, "Let's go," and she led her out through the front door then and on down a couple of steps to get to the weedy front lawn.

Regina looked off to the cars parked in the driveway. "Why the cops here?" she asked, seeing the state cruiser there.

Special Agents Nicks and Fielding had gotten out of their car when they saw Regina leaving her house with Weirdlee. Presently, they stood in front of the vehicle as they greeted the mother.

"Ms. Hawkins," Nicks said to her.

"Yes sir?" Regina replied.

"We found someone who wants to see you, ma'am. He says he misses you very much."

With that, the rear door of the police cruiser opened. First stepped out the DCFS staffer, Ms. Ferris. She was quickly followed by a very nervous and jittery seven-year-old young man.

Julien looked at his mother, and he said to her inquisitively, "Momma?"

Regina threw her hands up to her cheeks and cried out hysterically, "Oh my God and Jesus!"

The little boy ran as fast as he could to reach his mother. Regina dropped to her knees as he raced up and leapt into her arms. Both son and mother wept loudly and openly then as they held onto each other for the first time in over three years.

Weirdlee watched the emotional reunion with a brimming smile. She looked to Nicks, who had started to walk over to them, and she smiled at him.

"My baby!" Hawkins wept. "My baby boy come back to me!"

Nicks, Fielding, and Weirdlee stepped aside to talk.

"He was at the Potter home all along," Nicks said to Weirdlee.

"They had it all planned out for a long time comin'," Fielding added.

"Mr. Potter is a notary public," said Nicks. "At first, when I saw his name on Ms. Simmons' adoption certificate, I thought maybe she could have paid him off to sign it, or maybe he'd do it for her as a favor. But the way she acted with us the whole time, she was never the least bit nervous or guarded. She even dismissed Potter's name being on the certificate, no sweat. Then, when Fielding, here, mentioned how we shouldn't assume she was innocent just because she showed us a picture, I remembered a photo I saw on Potter's desk—of him and his wife and kid. And I figured, what the hell, maybe *that* was a prop."

"I checked state records," Fielding said, "and sure 'nuff, they had a certificate on file for 2009. Totally bogus, though."

"All he needed to do was get a clean copy of a certificate," said Nicks, "and then, with a little bit of forgery and some Photoshopping...*wallah*."

"They home schooled the boy," added Fielding. "That helped keep him out of sight."

So, for the most part, the plot was revealed, and the reasons for it justified in the minds of those who had planned it. Potter and his wife had long desired a child of their own, but with neither one wanting to care for a newborn, they saw adoption as their only natural recourse. An adopted child without any love, however, is just a trophy child to them. So it was that Potter saw in Julien Hawkins a chance to have a child that he knew he already loved. And, after all, wouldn't he be doing God's work, too, by rescuing that child from what would surely be a wretched life in that awful, impoverished broken home?

A chance meeting with voodoo performer Marcel Unate' helped spawn the plot. The two conferred further, and, after payment for Unate's services was arranged, the Voodoo King of the Bayous put his magick spells to work for the Potter family.

It was Unate'—aka Paul Basil—who deceived the families and the staff at the outing that day, blinding them all to the theft of the child by masking Potter's presence among them.

Regina got up to her feet, still clutching her boy close to her. She said to the FBI agents, her voice choked in tears, but loud enough for all the world to hear: "Before youz ever got here, I prayed to God and the Lord Jesus for them to send an angel down to help me find my boy. I gave up on 'em a long time ago, I swear I did, but God forgave me of my sins, and he sent me my angels. You *alls* my angels! I swear you is, and I's never forget you!"

Another cruiser pulled into the driveway then—this time a parish car. Sheriff Mickens leapt out of it and ran over to Regina Hawkins.

"Mrs. Hawkins!" he exclaimed, overjoyed. "Mrs. Hawkins—praise the Lord!" He came up to her and gave her a big, warm bear hug. "Thank God!" he cried out, and she laughed in his embrace.

He let go of her then, and he looked down at little Julien by her side. He smiled at him. "And you must be Julien."

Julien nodded. "Yes, sir."

Mickens put his hand on the boy's head and gave the youngster's short hair a good shake. "Welcome home, boy. Welcome home!"

Julien smiled, and hugged his mom once more.

Mickens said to Regina, "You are blessed, Mrs. Hawkins. You are surely blessed."

"I know I is," she said back to him, beaming. She looked at Weirdlee. "'Cuz I's had my own angel watchin' over me, and she told me I was."

Weirdlee, for her part, was equally overwhelmed. This was the happiest occasion she'd ever been a part of. She smiled at Regina before looking, then, to her colleague, Sam Nicks. What she saw in that man was the most honorable human being she had ever met before or would likely ever meet again.

She would miss him terribly.

As the scene carried on, and joy and happiness filled the air, Weirdlee's gaze drifted off to the southeastern horizon, where, as the sun continued its slow descent across the midsummer sky, a gathering of dark, ominous clouds approached from the faraway Gulf.

A storm, she saw, was coming in.

The air around her suddenly cooled. She overheard, then, a chilling whisper carrying forth along the distant, windswept sky. It was, she knew, none other than the voice of the Baron's bride, come calling to the witch from Salem, and beckoning her to come along.

It was time.

It was time for Joanna Weirdlee to leave.

~ | ~

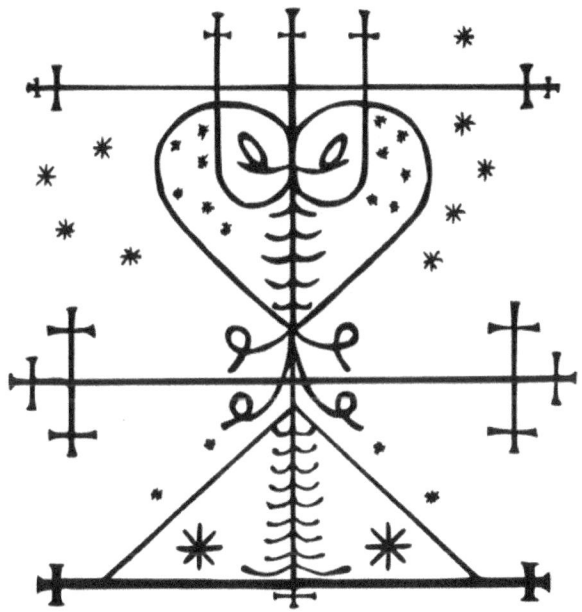

-20-

Death

Darkness ruled over the evening air. Storm clouds, black and billowing, roiled across the tormented sky. Thunder boomed, and lightning crackled and flashed. A drenching downpour soaked the cursed lands, while alligators, hungry and foul, roamed the murky waters.

A nightmare come to life had taken hold in the bayous. Its latest victim—so tormented in her dreams and so compelled to deliver herself into her master's arms—found herself in his grasp at last. And now she, the heretic, would surrender to him fully, and so be sacrificed to God Almighty.

"Come on!" Paul Basil cried out, pulling along a beaten and sobbing Jillian Truscott. "Move your ass!"

Poor Jillian wept desperately. "Please stop!" she begged him, falling to her knees. "*Please!*"

She'd come to him happily enough that day, and he'd turned on her in brutal fashion, inflicting upon her a savage beating that left her battered and weakened, enough so for him to drag her off into the wilderness of the bayous. He'd taken her, as fate would have it, just north of Lake Boeuf—the very same place where just hours earlier the police had scoured the lands, and where, on this night, Basil would now have his way with her.

"God will repay you for your sins!" he declared, shaking her in his grasp as sheets of rain pummeled them. From his belt, then, he unsheathed a serrated blade, and he held it against her bleeding face. "You shall be judged by Him, the Almighty! And I, his chosen one, shall deliver you to your fate!"

Truscott wailed through her tears, "Please don't kill me! *Please!* I want to go home!"

Basil leered at her—there was no mercy in his soul.

"I *am* sending you home, you sinful whore! I am taking you to God!"

He shook her again. "Get up off your knees, heretic! You dog! Or I'll cut your throat where you are!"

Truscott wept on. "Please! God help me!"

Basil released her from his grasp. He snarled and looked down upon her with hatred in his eyes. Her blonde hair, he saw, lay matted and soaked from rain and muck, and her torn clothing was stained with her own blood. She was, to him, a wretched thing to behold.

"So be it," he declared to her. "Die where you are."

Lightning flashed across the sky, lighting up swamp all around them. From its brief illumination, then, Basil spied out of the corner of his eye a dark silhouette cast against the nearby trees. He turned to look upon it, there to see none other than what he perceived to be a holy spirit come to Earth! The figure, cast against shadow as she was, wore a red embroidered corset and long, black slit dress which revealed just enough leg to drive even the spirits themselves wild. Upon her head, she wore a plain black top hat. Black gloves covered her forearms and hands, which she kept extended from her sides, her fingers splayed and palms facing away from the scene of the crime. Her head remained lowered, so that her top hat hid her face from Basil's view.

Even so, the voodoo king recognized her right away.

"Maman Brigitte!" he cried out exultantly. "Maman Brigitte! You have come to me!" He staggered in the muck, steadying himself to behold her. "I knew you would come! I knew you would not betray me!" he cried. He pointed at his victim with his blade. "Look! Look what I have for you! A sinner in the eyes of God!"

The seeming death *loa* raised her head to look directly at Basil, and so it was only then that he beheld the visitor who had truly come to him on that miserable evening.

"*NOOO!*" he wailed in the drenched night air. "Not *you!*"

The witch from Salem was there, dressed as the death *loa* Maman Brigitte herself, complete with white-painted face decorated ceremoniously in rich red and yellow hues, and wide, black-painted sockets surrounding her hazel eyes.

"HERETIC!" Basil screamed aloud. "Pagan whore! I'll kill you! Do you hear me, witch! I'll kill you!"

Run... came a woman's voice to Truscott's ears. *Run away!*

Truscott struggled up from her knees and staggered backwards.

Basil looked back at her. "Don't you fucking move!" he commanded.

Truscott ran.

Basil turned back to Joanna Osborne. He stood there, entirely oblivious to his peril as he hollered in rage.

"I'll kill you! You fucking whore!"

Off he raced then, sprinting headlong at his foe and rival. He ran in a blind fury, staggering across the mottled, marshy ground, littered as it was with pools of swamp water and overwashed streams.

Lightning flashed overhead, and Osborne raised her outstretched arms. She kept her fingers splayed and she turned her palms to face her onrushing enemy, as if welcoming his coming embrace.

Only her cold, cruel gaze betrayed the malice in her heart as she locked her spirit onto his own.

"*Heretic!*" Basil screamed as he ran through the stormy night. "*HERETIC!*"

Then, at last, he came upon her. He leapt into the air, his arms outstretched and ready to grasp onto the witch and take her down for his final kill.

"Die!" he cried triumphantly.

Alas—rather than feel the crush of her body against his own, the voodoo king instead clutched onto nothing but air! He howled, aghast, as he dove headfirst into a marshy pool of black water. He coughed and choked as he quickly came up for air, splashing about to recover. But the cursed man was not alone. In his midst, a trio of beasts—angry for being disturbed—came after him.

"*AAhhhhh!!!*" Basil screamed as the alligators fell upon him in a wild frenzy.

Truscott staggered as she ran, once again falling to her knees. Osborne hurried to join her. The terrified woman, seeing the *loa*-costumed witch upon her, at first drew back in horror. But Osborne quickly calmed her. "It's all right," she said to her, holding her in her embrace. "I'm here to protect you."

Truscott wept in her arms.

Looking off then to witness the death throes of Paul Basil, Osborne kept a hand firmly on Truscott's head, there to prevent the young woman from visiting the butchery herself. She whispered to the weeping Truscott, kissing her rain-soaked head. "Tonight, you are blessed by the spirits of Heaven."

The Salem witch kept her attention on the feasting alligators, until, shortly, Basil succumbed to the ferocity of their jaws. Still, though, as silence took over, she kept watch there expectantly, her eyes darting about the marshy terrain.

There, then, stepping slowly amongst the shadows of the evening, a blackened form appeared. The cloaked apparition, a top hat donned on her head, walked gracefully toward the pool where the alligators still satisfied themselves on Basil's remains. Coming to its edge, the ghostly figure stopped. She stared down at the mutilated corpse of Paul Basil, satisfied by his grisly demise. Osborne watched then as the spirit drew spittle from her mouth and let it drool, syrupy, into the pool.

The death *loa* raised her head then to look at Osborne directly. What the Salem witch beheld was a mostly skeletal face with decomposing flesh that peeled freely from what remained of her neck and chin. Her eye sockets were deep, rotted, and blackened. Most grotesquely, too, maggots wiggled about in her rotting, exposed cheekbones.

This was the same hideous incarnation of Maman Brigitte that Basil had long feared and hated. So it would be, then, that his miserable soul would be reporting to just this likening of the death *loa* as he arrived in the hereafter.

Their deathly work done, the wife of Baron Samedi smiled at her earthly agent as the two arrived at their final understanding of the evening. So the spirit kept her promise, and a thousand tormented spirits, trapped as they'd been in a cold purgatory for over one hundred years, were at once set free, to fly off into the sky and lift themselves up to the Great Beyond, where they would rest in peace forever.

The Curse of the Bayous, its spell released at last, had come to an end.

~ | ~

"She walks with the spirits of Heaven, and she and they are
your protectors."
—*Ezili Dantor*

- Epilogue -

Early springtime in the Berkshire Mountains of Massachusetts brings with it cool mornings and pleasant afternoons. On this particular day—a day many years in the future—a cloudless blue sky brightened the peaceful countryside and a gentle breeze brushed the trees blanketing the rolling hills.

The woman strolled across a steeply sloping meadow, where she'd walked to from her humble cottage home set deep in the woods behind her. Her long brunette hair, which she'd stopped dying red many years before, shared its tresses now with several streaks of aging gray. She wore on this brisk spring day a woven brown cape, its hood drawn back over her shoulders, and, as on most Saturdays, her favorite homespun dress was worn underneath. She matched her outfit smartly, too, with sneakers for this journey she'd taken many times before.

She followed a winding road that took her further down into the little river valley until, at length, she arrived at a railroad crossing where she paused for a moment to look off to the peaceful village just along the way. Her eyes wandered about the town's narrow streets and ways, and visited, too, the river that ran through its heart.

She continued on.

Townsfolk and others along the way stared or glanced at the oddly dressed woman as she walked at her leisure.

Some of them would smile as their eyes met hers, while others, not knowing her, quickly looked away. She came, then, to a gilded bridge which spanned the river, and she started along its way. She kept her gaze mostly ahead of her, while offering, still, a friendly nod to any person passing her by.

Across the bridge, she walked ahead until, some ways along, a rather frail old man who'd been sitting in a chair outside of a café caught sight of her. He hurriedly struggled to get up from his seat. Seeing him, the woman came over to him and helped him to stand. He smiled at her, and in his eyes was an expression of great warmth and love. He took her hand gently into both of his own then and said good day to her. She smiled at him, and she wished him the same.

"Thank you, young lady," he said to her—though in truth her youthful years were long behind her.

She grinned at the compliment, and she kissed his wrinkled brow, whispering to him sincerely, "Bless you, Albert," before continuing on her way.

Others who knew the woman smiled at her and waved as they passed by her, wishing her a very pleasant day. Every so often, too, a mavcar horn would beep at her, and she'd turn and return some driver's fine greeting.

Yes, this woman had brightened the lives of many a soul. And so it was, too, that for each good deed she'd rendered to others, they in turn had revisited her kindness thrice in kind. Never in all of her years, in fact, did this woman ever find herself alone. For just as she had always found a place in her heart for others, so did they, in turn, find a place in theirs for her.

Arriving at a pharmacy, the woman went inside and tended to her business there. She departed soon afterward, and then strolled back down the same street she'd come down before, though this time along its northern walk.

She had gotten about halfway down when, as she approached the bridge once more, a small clutch of children spotted her walking along. The kids all screamed and hollered, and they raced as fast as their little legs could carry them—running directly to the woman, and swarming around her with their needy hugs.

She lowered herself to a knee and took one of them into her arms. "How are you all today?" she asked them.

And they all said very well.

"Arthur pulled my ponytail," complained one little girl. "Can you turn him into a toad?"

"I did not!" Arthur cried out, terrified at the notion!

"Oh," the woman replied, feigning much concern, "I wouldn't do that to him. That would be so mean." She looked at the boy with a phony scowl. "You'll behave, now, won't you, Arthur?"

Arthur lowered his eyes. "Yes, ma'am."

"Show us some magic!" said another little girl, hopping in excitement.

The woman grinned and winked at her, whispering, "Better not here."

"*Pleeease?*" the little girl asked, a pouting expression pressed on her face.

The woman smiled. She could never refuse a pouting child.

She brought her hand up close to the girl's nose, and she snapped her fingers. Off then sprang a butterfly from her palm—and it fluttered away!

The woman feigned amazement as the children all gasped and cheered.

"Come along, now," the woman said to them. She stood up and took the hands of two little children into each of her own. "Let's go to the bridge of flowers and visit the daffodils, shall we?"

The children all agreed, and they happily crowded around the woman and pranced along their way.

Joanna Osborne, the Good Witch of the Berkshires, was truly blessed, indeed.
And truly loved by all.

~ | ~

~ PEACE ~

~ ~

We see you've come to learn...

to learn our ways...the ways of magick
You long to cast our eerie spells
You see the Earth is filled...
it's filled with magick
A place where supernatural dwells

We see you dream to learn,
to learn our ways...the ways of magick
The lore of transformational spells
You long to see beyond...beyond the world's horizons
Behold the secrets that our wisdom tells

But if, alas, you ever learned such a thing
What of all would be the Craft that you'd bring?
Would love be conjured forth by Holy design?
Or would you be, instead, the curse of our time?

We cannot see your soul...we cannot foretell
The spirit world awaits, you know it so well
The Gift they offered you, you cast it aside
You chose a different way, your own place in time

We see you've learned,
you've learned our ways...the ways of magick
Thank God you came along when you did
A life alone, and too, a history so tragic
Lo even so, you brought their fears to an end

She roams the world,
she works her ways...the ways of magick
Her incantations, whispered chants we recall
Our hearts without despair,
where once there was sadness
The Good Witch walks the Earth, she blesses us all

~ ~

If you enjoyed *Cold Case: FBI – The Curse of the Bayous*, please consider reviewing it online.
Reviews play an important role in the placement of books at online retailers.

****

Definitions & Lyrics

Hedge witch: A non-Wiccan witch with traditions closely related to shamanism. Practitioners focus on herbalism, healing, and being close to nature.

White witch: A witch, whether hedge or Wiccan, who lives as one with nature, both spiritually and in the mundane world. The one law of the white witch is simple: harm none.

Gray witch: "*The gray witch, when faced with a dilemma that requires immediate action, doesn't waste time in nail-biting indecision; she sucks it up, acts decisively and swiftly, doing what she needs to do, getting done what needs to be done--righting a wrong, breaking a curse, or casting one if it's needed; creating balance where there is imbalance, and justice where it's called for.*"
- Amythyst Raine, The Gray Witch's Grimoire

Houngan: A high priest in the Haitian vodou religion.

Mambo: A high priestess in the Haitian vodou religion.

The Invisibles: Spirits acting as the intermediaries between the Haitian Vodou god, Bondye, and mortal human beings. Also called *loa*.

Loa (Lwa or L'wha): Voodoo and Vodou spirits, also called the *Invisibles* or *Mystères*.

The "nations" (families) of *loa:*

- Ghede loa
- Kongo loa
- Nago loa
- Petro loa
- Rada loa

Individual *Loa:*

· Adjassou-Linguetor	· Ghede Doubye
· Adjinakou	· Gran Maître
· Adya Houn'tò	· Grand Bois
· Agaou	· Guinee
· Agassou	· Jean Zombi
· Agwé	· Joseph Danger
· Anaisa Pye	· Joumalonge
· Anmino	· Kalfu
· Ayida-Weddo	· Kapitan Zombi
· Ayizan	· Klemezin Klemay
· Azaka-Tonnerre	· Legba
· Bacalou	· Lemba
· Badessy	· L'inglesou
· Baron Samedi	· La Sirène
· Baron Kriminel	· Limba
· Belie Belcan	· Loco
· Boli Shah	· Lovana
· Bossou Ashadeh	· Mademoiselle Charlotte
· Boum'ba Maza	· Mait' Carrefour

- Brize
- Bugid Y Aiba
- Captain Debas
- Clermeil
- Congo
- Damballa
- Dan Petro
- Dan Wédo
- Demeplait
- Deryale
- Diable Tonnere
- Diejuste
- Dinclinsin
- Erzulie
- Filomez
- Ghede
- Ghede Linto
- Ghede Loraj
- Ghede Nibo

- Maîtresse Délai
- Maîtresse Hounon'gon
- Maman Brigitte
- Marassa
- Marassa Jumeaux
- Marinette (Vodou)
- Maroule
- Mombu
- Manze Marie
- Mounanchou
- Nago Shango
- Ogoun
- Papa Legba
- Pie
- Silibo
- Simbi
- Sobo
- Sousson-Pannan
- Senegal
- Ti Kita
- Ti Jean Quinto
- Ti Malice
- Ti Jean Petro
- Wawe.

~ ~

Lyrics

PAUL BASIL'S DESIRE
Witch's wonder! Pagan's soul!
Make her mine—where spirits go!
Ooo-Ma-Ma—Oh, Halo-Da!
Ah No-Mano, Ani-La!
I don't see no witch's brew,
stoppin' me from takin' you!
Here I stand, and here I fly,
Oh sister caster, dreamin' mine!
Oh, La-La, La-Dano-La!
I am yours, and you are mine!

SHAME ON YOU
Ibo Lelc! Hear me's calling!
Hear my's voice upon the wind!
See the souls, and see the spirits!
Help me guides them, from within!

Ibo Lele, show the way!
From your magick, make them pay!

Shame on you, you devil's child!
Shame on you, your soul defiled!
We's will catch you, pull you in!
Bring your spirit up to Him!

Shame on you! Shame on you!
We's will bring you up to Him!

ZARAH'S CRY
Heretics! Heretics young and old!
Here we comes to git yours souls!

JUSTICE DONE
Peace be with the night and morning
On the 'morrow, sunlight bring.
Guard the weak and guide the helpless
Lend the weary strength within.

Water, Earth, and evening Sky
Shield my soul from Evil's Eye.
For on the 'morrow's setting sun
My voice shall carry, Justice done.

FORGIVE ME
Here I walk my pathless journey
With my heart and soul I give.
Bless my words and incantations
Hear me, spirits, and forgive.

THE WAYS OF MAGICK (THE GOOD WITCH)
We see you've come to learn...
    to learn our ways...the ways of magick
You long to cast our eerie spells
You see the Earth is filled...
    it's filled with magick
A place where supernatural dwells

We see you dream to learn,
    to learn our ways...the ways of magick
The lore of transformational spells
You long to see beyond...beyond the world's horizons
Behold the secrets that our wisdom tells

But if, alas, you ever learned such a thing

What of all would be the Craft that you'd bring?
Would love be conjured forth by Holy design?
Or would you be, instead, the curse of our time?

We cannot see your soul...we cannot foretell
The spirit world awaits, you know it so well
The Gift they offered you, you cast it aside
You chose a different way, your own place in time

We see you've learned,
*   you've learned our ways...the ways of magick*
Thank God you came along when you did
A life alone, and too, a history so tragic
Lo even so, you brought their fears to an end

She roams the world,
*   she works her ways...the ways of magick*
Her incantations, whispered chants we recall
Our hearts without despair,
*   where once there was sadness*
The Good Witch walks the Earth, she blesses us all

~ | ~

www.ingramcontent.com/pod-product-compliance
Lightning Source LLC
Chambersburg PA
CBHW070220260626
47160CB00002B/617